I0710495

THE GUILD CODEX: WARPED / FIVE

MAGE ASSASSINS
& OTHER MISFITS

ANNETTE MARIE
ROB JACOBSEN

Mage Assassins & Other Misfits
The Guild Codex: Warped / Book Five
By Annette Marie & Rob Jacobsen

Dark Owl Fantasy Inc.
PO Box 88106, Rabbit Hill Post Office
Edmonton, AB, Canada T6R 0M5
www.darkowlfantasy.com

Cover Copyright © 2024 by Annette Ahner

Editing by Elizabeth Darkley
arrowheadediting.wordpress.com

ISBN 978-1-988153-73-5

BOOKS IN THE GUILD CODEX

WARPED

Warping Minds & Other Misdemeanors
Hellbound Guilds & Other Misdirections
Rogue Ghosts & Other Miscreants
Stolen Sorcery & Other Misadventures
Mage Assassins & Other Misfits
Conquering Reality & Other Misconduct

SPELLBOUND

Three Mages and a Margarita
Dark Arts and a Daiquiri
Two Witches and a Whiskey
Demon Magic and a Martini
The Alchemist and an Amaretto
Druid Vices and a Vodka
Lost Talismans and a Tequila
Damned Souls and a Sangria

DEMONIZED

Taming Demons for Beginners
Slaying Monsters for the Feeble
Hunting Fiends for the Ill-Equipped
Delivering Evil for Experts

UNVEILED

The One and Only Crystal Druid
The Long-Forgotten Winter King
The Twice-Scorned Lady of Shadow
The Unbreakable Bladesong Druid

MORE BOOKS BY ANNETTE MARIE

STEEL & STONE UNIVERSE

Steel & Stone Series
Chase the Dark
Bind the Soul
Yield the Night
Reap the Shadows
Unleash the Storm
Steel & Stone

Spell Weaver Trilogy
The Night Realm
The Shadow Weave
The Blood Curse

OTHER WORKS

Red Winter Trilogy
Red Winter
Dark Tempest
Immortal Fire

THE GUILD CODEX

CLASSES OF MAGIC

Spiritalis

Psychica

Arcana

Demonica

Elementaria

MYTHIC

A person with magical ability

MPD / MAGIPOL

The organization that regulates mythics and their activities

ROGUE

A mythic living in violation of MPD laws

MAGE ASSASSINS
& OTHER MISFITS

I

THERE ARE COUNTLESS WAYS to kill a man with a blade, but only one is an instant death.

I pulled my dagger from the back of the man's neck. Blood trickled from the wound as he slumped forward onto his desk, no writhing, moans, or spurting gore. It was clean and silent.

I stepped back, my pulse drumming steadily in my ears. I could count the minutes by the beat of my heart, as accurate as my wristwatch. Time was everything tonight and the only factor left that could sabotage me. I'd accounted for everything else, but time … time might ruin me.

Seconds slipping past, I turned to the locked filing cabinets along the wall of my target's spacious office.

MY KNIFE SCRAPED against the C1 vertebrae as I slid it into the target's spinal column just below the base of his skull. My arm was locked around his throat, and as he went limp, I lowered him silently to the floor of his hotel bathroom.

Blood had smeared on the sleeve of my leather jacket, but it didn't matter. Everything I wore tonight would be burned to ash, along with the car I'd stolen for transportation. My body was covered from head to toe—gloves on my hands, a mask over my face. I would leave no biological evidence. The potion I'd taken would hide my psychic trail, and the light I was bending around myself obscured my presence. I would leave no fingerprints, fibers, or witnesses.

Moving silently out of the bathroom, I glanced at the floor-to-ceiling windows of the suite's sitting room. In the distance, the illuminated Statue of Liberty guarded the water like a lonely sentry.

The night was advancing, my time slipping away. I wasn't finished yet.

MY THIRD TARGET was asleep in his bed, on his back, with snores rumbling from his open mouth.

I covered his mouth with my gloved hand and slit his throat.

I FOLDED the thick bundle of papers in half and slid them into the black leather pouch buckled to my right thigh. Closing the filing drawer, I turned.

My fourth target was slouched in a wingback chair in front of a fireplace, coals glowing behind the grate and a half-empty glass of brandy on the table. He could've been sleeping if not for the pallor of his wrinkled skin and the stench of released bowels.

I ghosted through the opulent penthouse to the front door. A quick glance at my watch warned that I'd spent too long searching his office. I would have to rush now.

Urgency flitted through me before I calmed my thoughts. I couldn't be hasty. Hastiness led to mistakes.

I bent the light around me and opened the penthouse door. Fatigue washed over my muscles and weariness dulled the sharp edges of my focus. I steeled myself against them. I had no time to rest.

A WOMAN SLEPT beside my fifth target. She was half his age, and she definitely wasn't his wife.

She hadn't stirred yet, but I needed her to stay asleep. I slipped a tiny vial from my pocket, pulled the cork, and dribbled it over her sleep-parted lips. Her tongue darted out, catching the liquid out of reflex. Most sleeping potions were a telltale shade of yellow, but not this one.

Pocketing the vial, I circled the king bed to my target's side. He'd shoved the covers half off in sleep, his naked abdomen fuzzed with frail white hair. He faced the edge of the bed, and the back of his neck wasn't easily accessible to my blade.

In the scant seconds during which I considered my options, his eyes opened.

I clamped my hand over his forehead, holding him still. The long dagger that had been sheathed at my hip was already in my other hand. Terror had only just dilated his right pupil when the blade plunged through it.

His body spasmed, then stilled. I pulled the dagger out. Not a preferred technique. The frontal lobe of the brain could take a surprising amount of damage without it being fatal. You had to strike deep.

I stepped back, blood dripping off the dagger. Sloppy. Any moment where I wasn't in control was one moment too many. I needed to finish this before my stamina ran out.

One more target.

***

INVISIBILITY made everything almost too easy. Existing outside the awareness of other people held a certain intoxicating power. They couldn't see me, stop me, or beg me for mercy. They simply died, unaware of my blade, my hand, my face, or my intent.

Too easy. Becoming invisible, however, the act of it—that was never easy.

I drew in deep, rejuvenating breaths as I released my control over the dim light in the hotel room. It was a far less expensive or expansive space than the other five locations I'd visited tonight. A single room with a king bed, a TV, and a small dinette table with two chairs.

My sixth victim was in his bed. Another back sleeper. Another slit throat. The macabre stain across the white pillows and white duvet drew the eye, out of place in the quiet, clean room.

Standing at the small table, I flipped the lid of the briefcase open, its broken lock rattling. Stacks of folders formed two neat piles, and the steady drumbeat of my heart picked up its tempo in anticipation. I opened the first folder. On the topmost page was a faded drawing of a levitating man surrounded by elemental symbols, a sun emblem on his forehead.

My lips quirked down as I lifted the page. This wasn't what I'd expected.

I checked my watch. It was late. I had no time left. I almost set the paper down and closed the folder—I was taking it all with me, so I had no need to sift through the documents here— but then I saw the page beneath.

It was a photo of an artifact. My gaze darted across it, jumping from the concentric circles to the minuscule lines etched into its metal surface.

Still holding the first page, I reached for the second.

The briefcase jerked out from under my hand. It flew into the air, the lid snapping closed with a *thunk* that shattered the silence, and soared across the room.

Its handle smacked into the palm of the woman standing in the short hallway leading from the hotel suite's entrance. She clutched the briefcase, but she wasn't looking at it. She wasn't looking at the dead man in the bed either.

She was staring at me. Because I wasn't hidden. I had released my magic to conserve my near-depleted stamina. Every inch of my skin was covered except for the two holes in my mask for my eyes. But it didn't matter how I disguised myself. She would know me anywhere.

"Darius."

Aurelia.

I didn't speak her name. I didn't utter a sound, even though the hoarse, agonized rasp in her voice cut through me like my own blade. Why was she here? How?

But I knew the answer. Time. I had taken too long. At least two of my victims had been discovered, and Aurelia had guessed the connection between them. She'd figured out who was being targeted and had rushed to intercept the killer.

Judging by the fact that no other agents were gathered in the hall behind her, she had also guessed who the killer was. She knew what I did for a living. She knew my methods.

My hand tightened, creasing the paper I held. Then I bent the light around me and vanished.

"*Darius!*" This time she howled my name. It was neither a shout nor a scream, but a soul-wrenching symphony of anguish, betrayal, fury, and despair.

She flung out her hand and the coffee maker on the built-in sideboard hurtled through the air toward the spot where I'd vanished, but I'd already moved.

"Why?" she raged. "Why did you do this?"

A chair lifted from the floor and whipped across the room. I ducked, barely evading it, my muscles trembling as the renewed use of my power drained the last of my strength.

"The *Supreme Judiciary Council*," she choked. "Why are you killing them? Why—"

Grabbing the briefcase, I tore it from her grasp and hid it with my magic as I sped past her.

An invisible force yanked me backward.

I wasn't ready for it. What telekinetic could move an invisible target? Only one as skilled as Aurelia, of course.

I slammed down on my back. My power wavered, revealing me, and she pounced. Her weight shoved the air out of my lungs and her telekinetic force pinned my arms.

Her face was twisted, her eyes glistening but no tears marking her cheeks. Her long blond hair was falling out of its messy ponytail, her blouse was wrinkled, and no makeup smoothed her skin.

"Was it for money?"

Her hoarse question might as well have gutted me. Hidden by my mask, my face contorted.

"You," she gasped, fighting hard for composure. "You always talk about responsibility. You always talk about unchecked power and how destructive it is. And you let someone *buy you?*"

No.

"Or do you just love the hunt too much?" Her jaw quivered and her chest heaved. "How could you choose killing over me?"

I hadn't.

"*Answer me!*" She grabbed the front of my leather jacket and dug her knuckles into my sternum. "You convinced me you weren't like them."

I wasn't.

Tears spilled down her cheeks. "I *believed* you."

I gritted my teeth behind my mask, holding back the words I wanted to say. The words I could never say.

She reached for my mask to pull it off and reveal my face. But she'd lost her focus. Her power was no longer pinning my arms.

I grabbed her wrists and threw her off me. As I rolled onto my feet, my gaze caught on the briefcase—but she was already jumping up. She was fresh and furious, and I was exhausted. I couldn't chance it.

Bending the light around me, I fled. She screamed my name as I went, my betrayal chasing me out into the night, where the false dawn tinged the eastern horizon with a faint blue glow.

Only when I reached my stolen car, my breaths harsh and muscles burning with weakness, did I realize I still clutched the single page from the briefcase in my hand. I smoothed the creases, glanced at its indecipherable drawing, then climbed into the car. My work wasn't done yet. I needed to destroy the evidence.

Aurelia knew. And the mythic world would suspect.

But no one could ever prove that the Mage Assassin had killed this night.

2

THERE'S A DENZEL WASHINGTON MOVIE called *Man on Fire*.

I was that man—not because I was Dakota Fanning's hyperviolent bodyguard, but because I'd made the indefensibly idiotic decision to visit Florence, Arizona … in August. The thermometer currently read somewhere between "heart of an active volcano" and "the actual goddamn sun." It was so hot that my sweat evaporated the instant it left my pores.

Thankfully, I was hunkered down in the shade at a café, which meant the temperature was closer to "surface of a fired-up BBQ." I could handle that for now.

Sitting across from me at our small table was Miriam Baker, an affable woman in her sixties with sun-bleached hair and a perfect tan. These days, she worked part-time managing the mini-golf and arcade establishment adjoining the café, but before that, she'd been a middle school teacher.

And she was the reason I'd flown over a thousand miles to bake in the unrelenting desert heat.

"It's so strange to hear you call him that," she said with a shake of her head.

I shrugged. "It's his name."

"We always used to call him Benjamin. Or even Benny."

"Benny Kade." I snorted. "It makes him sound like a late-night talk show host from the seventies."

Miriam's amusement only lasted a second before her mouth flattened. "What kind of investigator are you, Mr. Morris? I don't understand why anyone would come all the way down here from Canada just to talk to me about a former student from thirty years ago."

On the surface, that was a perfectly reasonable question. She didn't know that her former student had grown up to be a terrifying, bloodthirsty assassin for a corrupt shadow organization with its influence running deep in the globe's secret magic community. And I wasn't going to fill her in on that little tidbit.

"I'm a private investigator," I fibbed.

She pursed her lips, unconvinced. "I tried looking you up online. I couldn't find anything."

"Emphasis on *private*."

"Benjamin is involved in your investigation?"

He *was* the investigation. After Kade had murdered Söze and disappeared on a black helicopter, he'd become our precinct's enemy *numero uno*. Captain Blythe—once she'd recovered from his attempt on her life—had given me carte blanche to hunt the bastard down.

My investigation hadn't exactly been fruitful. MPD records on Kade were limited, and his personal history outside our agency was even harder to uncover. All I'd managed to discover was that he'd grown up in the Florence area and attended a mundane middle school called West Hills, where Miriam had worked.

"I can't divulge details, Ms. Baker." I tapped my pen lightly on the pad of paper in front of me. "But I would like to ask you a few questions about him."

Her eyes narrowed. "He did something, didn't he? Something bad."

"What makes you say that?"

She glanced over her shoulder, as though the coterie of white-haired snowbirds populating the café were all potential spies. To be fair, I shared her paranoia. To keep any eavesdropping geriatrics from sitting at the spot next to us, I'd given it a warped makeover: a smear of jelly donut innards across the table with a few additional droplets on one of the chairs.

It was a simple warp—one I would've taken for granted in my younger days. But ever since experiencing the magical vacuum in my mind after reality warping had zapped all my psychic powers, I was perpetually thankful for the magic I had.

"Are you recording this?" Miriam asked in a hushed tone.

I quirked an eyebrow. "Should I be?"

"I'd rather you didn't. In fact, I'd rather this be off the record altogether."

"That's fine." Leaning forward slightly, I lowered my voice. "You seem worried."

Tension suffused her shoulders. "Talking about him makes me … uncomfortable."

"Why's that?"

"Benjamin was always a troublemaker." She waved her hand as though swiping away her statement. "No, not a troublemaker. I've dealt with plenty of kids who made trouble—perpetually late, disruptive, didn't do their homework—but Benjamin … he was different."

I waited as she searched for the right words, using the quiet moment to jot a few notes on my pad.

"He was cruel," she finally said. "Kids can be meanspirited. Every teacher knows a bully when they see one, but a bully's behavior is easy to understand once you boil it down. They take the pain they feel and use it as a weapon against others."

She paused as a server showed up with a coffee for each of us. My guess was that the staff poured it cold and let it boil in the sun as they walked it over to our table. Why had I ordered a hot drink on a day scalding enough to cook prime rib to medium-well on the sidewalk? A cup of liquid nitrogen would've been a better choice.

I thanked the server before turning back to Miriam. "So, would you call Kade a bully?"

"No." She poured cream into her coffee. "He didn't torture other kids to deal with his pain. He did it because he reveled in it."

"'Torture' is a strong word," I observed.

She met my eyes over the rim of her coffee mug. "It's an accurate word for Benjamin."

I thought back to the sickening glee on Kade's face as he'd explained to Lienna and me all the ways in which he would slowly, painfully kill us. It seemed that wasn't a trait he'd developed as an adult.

"Can you give me an example of him torturing other students?" I asked.

She huffed a sigh. "That's the problem. I never caught him in the act. He was slippery."

"Slippery?" I echoed. "How so?"

"When he was in seventh grade, our class had a pet turtle named Donatello."

I couldn't help but smirk. "Classic."

"The kids really loved him. They all took turns feeding him, cleaning the aquarium, that sort of thing. One day after lunch, one of the students went to check on Donatello."

I grimaced, already having a pretty good idea where this anecdote was headed.

"The poor kid—he screamed and screamed," she continued. "It took me a minute to calm him down, and by that time, a bunch of students had gathered around the aquarium. Let's just say, Donatello did not go out pleasantly. It was gruesome. The kids were absolutely distraught."

"What about Kade?"

"I remember his face." She let out a slow breath. "He wasn't looking at the turtle's remains. He was watching the other kids … enjoying their reactions."

She paused to gather herself. "I pulled Benjamin aside and asked him why he'd hurt Donatello. He looked me straight in the eyes and told me no one saw what happened. Anyone could have killed the turtle."

"Could it have been someone else?" I asked. "Another student? Or a staff member?"

"Not a chance," she answered quickly. "I know it was him. I tried getting the principal involved, but he said there was no proof."

Had the principal been protecting murderous little Benny or just super committed to upholding due process in his elementary school?

"I could tell you a dozen more stories about Benjamin," Miriam said. "He was the most frightening student I have ever taught. Manipulative, arrogant, remorseless, aggressive. He was a compulsive liar. A few of the boys in the class looked up to him, but most students were terrified of him."

A manipulative, arrogant, violent liar who lacked empathy and delighted in murdering small animals? According to my armchair psychological assessment, that ticked off all the boxes on the psychopath checklist. It was chilling to realize Kade had *always* been this way. Evil was in his DNA.

"Was he ever punished?" I asked. "Any suspensions or anything like that? I know he transferred out of your school during seventh grade. Was he expelled?"

"Not that I know of. He had his fair share of detentions, but like I said, he was slippery." She leaned back in her chair and sipped her coffee. "In the middle of the second semester, I was doing parent-teacher interviews, and for the first time, Benjamin's father attended."

I perked up. Nowhere in all my searching had I found a single reference to Kade's parents. As far as MPD records were concerned, the bald-headed shitstain was decanted from a cosmic vessel of unfiltered malevolence.

"What happened?" I asked, somewhat too eagerly.

"I'd met his mother before." She tapped her fingers against her mug. "I can't remember her name now. She was a timid woman. Whenever I'd bring up Benjamin's behavioral problems, she'd promise to talk to him, but nothing ever changed. His father, on the other hand ..."

"Do you remember *his* name?"

"Peter," Miriam answered. "I don't think they were married. Or, if they were, he wasn't around very much. He was a severe man. The kind of person I always imagined—always *worried*—Benjamin would grow up to be."

I jotted the name down on my pad of paper. I would most definitely be doing a deep dive on "Peter Kade" as soon as I got back to Vancouver.

"I told him about Benjamin's issues, even what happened to Donatello, but he was very dismissive. He had a 'boys will be boys' attitude about the whole thing."

I scrunched up my nose. Gross.

"But his demeanor completely changed when I brought up Benjamin's slipperiness."

"Changed how?" I asked, drawing a circle around the word "slippery," which I'd written on my pad the first time she'd used it.

"He got very serious," Miriam said. "I told him that his son had a sixth sense that helped him get away with all sorts of bad behavior. He seemed to always know when other people were around or not. It was unsettling, to be frank."

That lined up with my experience battling Kade. Even when I was invisi-warping or Darius was hiding himself with his lumina magic, Kade had known where we were. It hinted at a psychic ability, but according to all the official MPD files, Kade was a standard sorcerer and nothing more.

I tapped my pen against my notepad. "Is there anything else you remember? Another example of his slipperiness?"

She squinted in thought, then nodded slowly. "During the lunch break one afternoon, I was tidying my classroom on the second floor, and I happened to glance out the window. I saw Benjamin near the bike racks. He was crouching beside a pink bicycle. It wasn't his. He took the bus to school.

"All of a sudden, he straightened and walked away. It was very abrupt, the way he jumped up. A few seconds later, a teacher rounded the corner. Nothing came of it that day, but the day after, someone punctured all the bikes' tires. No one saw who did it."

"A real mystery," I remarked dryly.

"I had no doubt it was Benjamin's work. What stood out to me was the way Benjamin abandoned his first attempt. He couldn't have seen that teacher coming, and she was far enough away that I don't think he could have heard her either. But he still seemed to know she was about to come around the corner."

"Weird," I mumbled. "When you were talking to Kade's father, what did he say after you mentioned Kade's sixth sense?"

"He told me he could tell I was scared, but that I didn't have to worry. Benjamin would no longer be attending our school." She paused, frowning at her half-empty coffee mug. "I think he meant to sound reassuring, but it came across more like a threat."

I arched an eyebrow. Assuming the apple didn't fall far from the tree, I suspected Peter Kade had indeed been making a threat. "Did you ever see Kade again after that?"

"No." Miriam looked up, unease deepening the wrinkles around her eyes. "And to be honest with you, Mr. Morris, I hope I never do."

LESS THAN AN HOUR LATER, I stepped into the deliciously cool atmosphere of my hotel's air-conditioned lobby. It was like receiving a long-awaited hug from a benevolent frost giant. Bad for the environment, good for the Canadian boy who'd lost a significant fraction of his body weight to sweat on the walk back from the café.

I had my head down, eyes on my phone, swiping back and forth between my contact list and a page showing flights to LA from Phoenix, which had the nearest airport to Florence.

It'd been five months since Lienna had flown home to help her family while her dad underwent cancer treatments. Since I was already this far south and I'd accrued a hefty number of vacation days, maybe I could extend my American work-cation and pay her a visit.

My finger hovered over her name. One little tap and I could call her, propose my travel plans, and book a flight.

But …

I groaned internally. *I* wanted to call her. I just didn't know if *she* wanted me to call her.

Before leaving, Lienna had asked me about Gillian, promised to tell me about her own childhood, fallen asleep cuddling with me on the sofa … then taken off to the airport without saying goodbye. Since then, our communication had been normal but kind of distant.

Undoubtedly, some of that distance was due to Lienna's stress levels while living at home with her family, dealing with Papa Shen's illness, and trying not to ask questions about my investigations that I couldn't answer via phone call or text message. But I also wondered how much of the distance was because of the awkwardly unacknowledged cuddle session followed by her painfully abrupt departure.

But that's all it was, right? Once the miles between us were reduced to zero and I was face to face with her again, things would go back to normal—or some semblance of it, at least.

I stared down at my phone, practically tearing myself in half with indecision, then glanced up to make sure my weird, hesitant hovering wasn't inconveniencing any hotel-goers sharing the lobby with me. And that's when I saw a well-dressed man with salt-and-pepper hair reading a newspaper in one of the cushy chairs across from the welcome desk.

My reunion with Lienna would have to wait.

Pocketing my phone, I crossed the lobby and dropped into the chair opposite him. "Fancy seeing you here, Darius."

His gray eyes analyzed me from over the top of the newspaper. "How was your interview?"

"Interesting. How long have you been in Florence?"

"I landed in Phoenix this morning and came straight here."

"What brings you to the land of sand and cacti?" As I asked the question, I took in his standard vest-and-dress-shirt getup. "And why in the name of Seth are you wearing long sleeves in the desert? It's, like, a bazillion degrees out."

"Linen is a very breathable fabric," he informed me with a hint of amusement. Folding up the newspaper, he set it on the glossy end table. "We have a meeting."

Of course we did. There was less than a zero percent chance that Darius had flown all the way to Phoenix and then driven to Florence for an impromptu social call.

"Which of your old friends is it this time?" I asked.

"Tino. He's the last one."

Over the past five months, Darius and I had met up with—or in some cases, unexpectedly dropped in on—four of his former acquaintances and allies from Ye Olden Times, AKA when I was still in diapers. Or, more relevantly, when Darius had been an MPD-contracted assassin undertaking assignments that were not only above my pay grade but above Blythe's too. Or, in straightforward numbers, about twenty years ago.

Each of these former accomplices held a piece of the very dangerous puzzle we needed to complete. It was like one of those video games where, in order to acquire an enchanted sword, you needed to beat a handful of minibosses. Except instead of battling three-headed dragons and undead goblins, we were tracking down mythics who didn't want to be tracked down and asking them to hand over valuable—and potentially deadly—information.

"Tino is an archivist from El Paso," Darius continued. "He's rather skittish, so we'll need to keep things light and easy. Deception, surprises, or power plays will send him running."

"We're going to Texas?" I asked with a frown, already sorting through possible excuses to give my captain for yet another impromptu change in my travel plans and wondering if we could hit up a brisket joint along the way.

"He's coming to us," Darius clarified. "A direct train from El Paso to Maricopa. He'll be arriving in"—he glanced at his watch—"just over an hour."

So, ixnay on the isket-bray.

"A train?"

"Indeed." Dry amusement touched Darius's expression. "Tino doesn't trust air travel. But he's bringing what we need, and that's all that matters. Assuming he shows up," he added as an afterthought, as though it would only be mildly inconvenient if a skittish archivist carrying the ultrasecret documents we needed disappeared somewhere in the desert.

I took another look at Darius's attire, then glanced down at my own ensemble of board shorts, a plain white t-shirt, and flip-flops. "Where are we meeting this guy? Because if it's another one of those members-only cigar joints, I didn't pack my formal wear."

"There will be no cigars to tempt you this time," Darius said, rising to his feet. "We're meeting Tino at the train station for a quick handoff. It should be very straightforward. Tino won't want to linger."

Sounded like a charming guy, this Tino.

As we headed toward the elevator so I could collect my belongings from my room and check out, I wondered if it would indeed be the quick handoff Darius had promised. This wouldn't be the first time the ex-assassin had—perhaps unintentionally—glossed over the potential for hair-raising complications.

Like the cigar incident.

Our previous meet-up had been with a Croatian ex-pat named Josip, who ran a string of elitist clubs in Quebec City. Darius had been light on details, but from what I'd gathered, twenty years ago, Josip had been a master networker of sorts. You know in spy movies when someone says, "I know a guy who knows a guy"?

Well, my understanding was that the Croatian was the guy who knew the other guy.

I'd already been in Montreal on a fruitless hunt for one of Kade's former work comrades, putting my high school French to work, which, not to put too fine a point on it, was *très mal*. Darius co-opted my Blythe-sanctioned work trip so we could drop in on Josip, who was "a difficult man to contact," according to Darius. Or, as I'd come to realize, he was a man who might immediately make himself unavailable if he knew we were coming. While we could have utilized our respective invisibility skills to sneak inside the Croatian's smoky establishment, we needed to blend in once we were past security. So, under Darius's guidance, I dropped an appalling percentage of my monthly salary on a tailored suit in downtown Montreal before we drove east to Quebec City.

Yes, I could have technically warped a suit for myself, but maintaining a halluci-bomb with all the details of a fine, hand-tailored masterpiece would have been too taxing—and I didn't know the difference between a shawl lapel and a welted pocket. So, I opted to pay the price in dollars instead of brain cells.

Our plan was going swimmingly right up until, in an ill-advised attempt to look like I belonged among the club's seven-figure patrons, I lit up a Cuban cigar and promptly hacked my lungs out like an aging coal miner in the middle of a toxic tire fire.

Luckily, Josip escorted us into his office before his clientele could get too curious about the wheezing, college-aged guy in their midst. He was apparently only mildly miffed at our unannounced arrival, because he offered us each a glass of whiskey old enough to call Darius "kiddo," handed over his share of the documents, and wished us good luck.

I came away from that little adventure with another piece of the puzzle we were assembling, a new Italian suit, and a stinging distaste for tobacco.

"I'm not expecting any problems this time," Darius told me, interrupting my unpleasant reminiscing.

I shot him a startled look.

He didn't quite smirk. "Your expression was remarkably similar to the one you made when you took that first lungful of cigar smoke."

Ugh.

"But we should be prepared regardless," he continued. "I have a map of the train station you can review on the drive."

"Is there time for me to get a drink from the poolside bar before we take off to Maricopa?" I asked as I unlocked my door.

"Probably."

I started to grin.

"But I don't want to chance it," he finished implacably. "Tino won't wait around if we're late."

Sighing, I strode over to my backpack and started shoving my belongings into it.

Just as I was unplugging my laptop cord to stow it away, Darius's phone rang. He slid the device from his pocket and glanced at it.

"It's Tino." He tapped the screen. "This is Darius."

"Darry, where are you?" the voice on the other end asked, the phone speaker amplifying his frantic whisper.

I raised an eyebrow. Darry?

"Florence," Darius answered, ignoring my look. "I'm about to head to Maricopa. Is everything okay?"

"It was—I mean, so far. Maybe." Chaotic rustling cut through the end of his disjointed reply. "But I think … *shit.*"

"What's going on, Tino?"

"I don't—damn it! I think someone's following me!"

Darius's eyes narrowed. "How certain are you?"

"Eighty-five percent—no, ninety percent. There are two men and … and a woman. Scary types." Tino's hushed tone was pitching up toward full-blown panic. "What should I do?"

"Consilium?" I mouthed soundlessly. We couldn't be sure, but considering that those assholes had murdered Georgia Johannsen and Anson Goodman—two of Darius's other old-school allies—it was the logical assumption.

Darius nodded. "Where are you right now?"

"We just left Tucson. I was in the dining car when they boarded. I noticed them staring at me, so I went back to my cabin. They followed me, and now they're waiting in the corridor."

"Lock the door," Darius instructed him. "Do you have the package with you?"

"Yes, yes. In my hands."

"Are either of the men bald?" I chimed in. "Big shoulders? Evil glare?"

"Who the hell is that?" Tino squawked.

"An ally," Darius assured him. "Is there a bald man?"

"Uh, let me check." There was a short pause before the archivist said, "No, they both have hair. One blond, one brown."

Whoever this trio of Consilium goons was, Kade wasn't among them. That was a small relief.

"Are you armed?" Darius asked.

"Come on, Darry, you know I never leave home without my pistol. But I don't know how much good it'll do me. They're camped outside my door. I doubt they'll just let me walk off the train in an hour."

That'd be generous; they probably wouldn't wait for the train to stop. Tino's time was ticking.

"Stay in your compartment, Tino," Darius said calmly. "We'll intercept them before they make a move."

We would? Unless I'd fundamentally misunderstood some pretty basic concepts like "on a moving train" and "speeding across the desert like a jet-powered cartoon roadrunner with the added inertia of a few thousand tons," I wasn't grasping how we would intercept anything.

Pondering this conundrum, I missed the last of Darius's assurances for Tino and only tuned back in when the GM pocketed his phone.

"Uh, so …" I squinted at him. "You have a plan, right?"

"I do."

"And it *doesn't* involve boarding a moving train, does it?"

Darius arched an eyebrow. "First time, Agent Morris?"

I swore under my breath. I would never believe another "it should be very straightforward" statement from this man. Ex-assassins really sucked at risk assessment.

3

"NINETY MILES AN HOUR," I grumbled.

Darius had his eyes glued to the highway, pushing his rental sedan well past the posted speed limit as we left Florence in our dust.

"I just looked it up," I said, waving my phone. "This particular passenger train can hit speeds of up to ninety miles an hour. That's one hundred and forty five kilometers an hour in maple-syrup speak."

Darius didn't reply as he changed lanes to pass a semitrailer hauling a precariously large load of steel beams. Fortunately, a Tuesday afternoon wasn't prime time for traffic on this two-lane highway, allowing him to keep a heavy foot on the accelerator.

"Do you know what happens to the human body when it lands on something going ninety miles an hour?" I asked.

Darius didn't even glance at me.

"Because I don't!" I informed him emphatically. "But every ounce of common sense my favorite foster mom swore I had is telling me it isn't anything good."

"Have you located an overpass yet?" he inquired, as though I'd merely been commenting on the abundance of brown grass and blue sky surrounding us.

"Yes, obviously, or I wouldn't be resurrecting my high school algebra with train speed calculations."

He finally took his eyes off the road to give me a pointed look. "We don't need a precise calculation, Kit. We just need to slow the train down."

"How the hell are we going to do that?" I flipped open a new tab on my phone's browser to see if the internet had any advice on how to reduce the velocity of a literal speeding locomotive. "Unless you were recently bitten by a radioactive spider and are going to do some web-slinging shit."

Darius, as he had a habit of doing, did not respond to my pop-culture jocosity.

I found an online forum of delightfully detailed train enthusiasts nerding out over every conceivable aspect of railway life. I cross-referenced what I gleaned from their posts with the map I'd pulled up of our route along the interstate.

"There's an overpass a mile away," I told Darius. "If you're dead set on us James Bond-ing ourselves onto Tino's train, that's the best spot to do it. Passenger trains have to slow down near residential areas, and that overpass is right next to a school. I don't know if that technically qualifies as a residential zone, but there's also a town three miles away, and the train might already be slowing down for it by the overpass. If not ..."

Darius glanced at me. "If not?"

"I can give them a little extra motivation to hit the brakes." I rolled my eyes up in thought. "Maybe a herd of cows crossing the tracks?"

"I believe cattle on the tracks is the reason many trains are fitted with cowcatchers."

A wild image of enormous baseball mitts corralling flying bovine launched from beef-loaded trebuchets popped into my head before I realized he meant those grates on the front of train engines for shunting obstacles off the tracks.

"Right." I racked my brain for something that would *actually* force a conductor to decelerate. "How about a school bus full of innocent children?"

"That should do the trick."

A few minutes later, we reached the overpass. Darius pulled the rental car onto the shoulder, and we both got out. A single lonely pickup truck roared past before we crossed to the opposite side of the overpass. A cement barrier prevented sleepy drivers from plummeting fifteen feet onto the railway below and seemed distinctly designed to prevent idiotic mythics from, oh, say, jumping over the edge with the intention of landing on top of a speeding train.

Said train was chugging along the tracks toward us, several football fields away. It was difficult to tell how many miles per hour less than its maximum human-obliterating ninety it was traveling, but I didn't really care. I was all for slowing it down as much as possible.

I concentrated, whipping up a school bus halluci-bomb that would extend far enough to reach the train conductor—or so I hoped. I didn't normally work at this sort of range. My imaginary big yellow tube on wheels approached the railway from an access road running parallel to the tracks, then hung a left to turn onto said tracks.

The train blasted its horn. Halluci-bomb success confirmed. I made the bus, now fully across the locomotive's path, jolt to a halt and rock back and forth as though it was stuck on the tracks.

Was that realistic? I didn't have the faintest idea. Would your average conductor be contemplating the realism of the bus full of innocent kids he was about to plow through? Hopefully not.

Another blast of the horn accompanied the train's brakes screeching like a demon's claws down the world's biggest chalkboard.

"It's working," I observed unnecessarily.

"So it is," Darius agreed, also unnecessarily. Maybe he wasn't quite as cool with this plan as he seemed. Maybe he even felt like I did—as though every molecule of his body was suddenly, violently allergic to trains and getting one inch closer to a train of any kind would result in instant petrification.

If the former assassin *was* afraid, he didn't show it as he swung his leg over the cement barrier. I copied his action, straddling the waist-high wall and doing my absolute best not to look down. Instead, I focused on my warp and the reassuring screech of brakes growing louder by the second.

Out of mercy for the poor, likely traumatized conductor, I didn't wait until the last possible moment to make the school bus reverse course. It backed off the rail line with a solid five seconds to spare before it would've been turned into a cloud of yellow shrapnel.

The train was almost below us and, from my perspective, still moving pretty damn fast. Being a choo-choo of the passenger variety, it had far fewer cars than your standard two-mile-long freight train, meaning Darius and I didn't have a whole lot of time to make our jump.

"Don't fall off," Darius suggested helpfully as he swung his other leg over the edge. Without another word, he jumped.

Holy shit, we were really doing this.

I looked down at the shiny roofs of the train cars speeding beneath the overpass. Darius had vanished—hopefully, he was safely hanging on somewhere and not bouncing around like a rag doll under the train's wheels.

I yanked my other leg over the cement barrier, and before the survival-centric part of my brain could convince me otherwise, I let go.

For some reason, I thought I'd have more time to adjust my body as I fell toward the train, but in reality, it was only six-ish feet below me, so I hit the roof almost immediately. My shoes hit the steel roof, friction yanked my feet out from under me, and I face-planted.

Inertia and a buffeting wind tried to rip me off the train car roof, and I slid a terrifying five feet before getting a painfully solid grip on a vent-type thing sticking up a few inches from the slick steel.

I clutched my handhold, heart beating so fast I was dizzy. A few deep breaths later, I dared to raise my head enough to see that I was sprawled on the front end of the second-to-last car.

"I can't believe that actually worked," I muttered, my voice whipped away by the wind.

I shimmied myself to the edge of the car, threw up an invisi-warp, and dropped onto the gangway connection. My leg buzzed as soon as my feet hit the steel, and it took me a moment to realize it wasn't the incessant vibrations of the train but my phone ringing in my pocket. I pulled it out to see a familiar name on the screen: Darius.

"You survived," I answered.

"As did you."

Another voice—distinctly nervous, almost to the point of squeaking—chimed in. "I'm also alive, thank you very much."

"Tino's on the line," Darius informed me.

I peered through a small window into the train car. "How ya holding up, Tino?"

"They're right outside," the archivist whispered. "All three of them! I think they're waiting for me to leave."

"Where are you, Kit?" Darius asked.

The car in front of me featured two rows of restaurant-style booths half-populated by hungry passengers.

"I'm right behind the dining car."

"I'm in the car in front of that one," Tino said.

"And I'm a couple cars farther ahead," Darius added. "Kit, I'll meet you in Tino's car and we'll come at them from both sides at once."

"The usual?" I suggested, layering my warp to hide the sight and sound of me opening the dining car door from the commuters inside.

"That seems best," he agreed. "Let's keep this quiet and bloodless. I'd prefer not to draw any attention."

Lucky for the two of us, we were both very good at moving around unseen.

"Got it," I told him as I closed the door and slipped through the dining car, taking care not to bump, brush, or otherwise disturb any of the travelers, who were all oblivious to my presence. I kept my phone to my ear, the call still active, but no one spoke. The only sound was Tino's nervous breathing.

I stepped onto the gangway connection joining the dining car to Tino's car. Through the window, I could see a man with an artificially platinum crewcut hovering near a closed cabin door. At the far end of the car, a handsome guy with wavy brown hair leaned casually near the door, ostensibly reading something on his phone. And the third Consilium goon, a woman with auburn bangs, square glasses, and a scowl that made her look like an evil version of Velma from Scooby Doo loitered near the door I was in the process of sneaking through.

"Are you ready, Darius?" I whispered into my phone, carefully closing the door behind me.

If Darius was already in position at the other end of the car, I couldn't see him—which was the whole point. He could use his lumina magic to bend light and make himself *actually* invisible, as opposed to my hallucinatory disappearing act.

"On your signal," came Darius's hushed voice.

"Whose signal?" Tino asked. "Should I run now?"

"Stay put," Darius told him. "Don't move until we reach you. I'm ending the call."

I pocketed my phone and focused on the minds of the three goons. Time for a Blackout Flash.

First, I hit the Consilium threesome with a super-quick Blackout warp, just long enough to disorient them but not so long for the inevitable screaming to start. Darius followed that up with a targeted blinding flash of light. It was a one-two combo that utilized the nastier bits of our psycho warping and lumina magic powers without burning up our stamina—and it left the three unprepared mythics reeling.

I sprang forward and clamped Evil Velma in a chokehold, dragging her to the ground as I dropped an easy—for me, not her—Funhouse fractal over her brain so she'd be too disoriented to fight back effectively. In my peripheral vision, I saw the handsome dude's head bounce off the wall. He slumped to the ground. Darius flickered in and out of sight as he shifted the light around himself.

Unfortunately, there were only two of us and three of them, meaning the platinum-haired goon—who had recovered from the Blackout Flash—was left wholly unsupervised. Apparently, saving his pals from invisible assailants was lower on the priority list than acquiring Tino's documents; he obliterated the archivist's door with a roundhouse kick full of so much rage that I figured his next step would be to rip Tino's head clean off his body before stealing the documents.

But he didn't get the chance.

With a frightened bellow, Tino charged out of his cabin, clinging to an old duffel bag like it was his security blanket. His appearance matched his voice almost too perfectly: short, slight, with small panicky eyes and a greasy bowl cut plastered to his skull.

He shouldered past the surprised blond goon and sprinted for the nearest escape—my end of the car. But he couldn't see me, only Evil Velma, who was half sprawled on the floor as I choked her. He jumped over her legs, hitting me square in the face with his duffel bag as he went.

I fell backward, chokehold and Funhouse warp broken. Tino flew out the door, and the blond goon charged after him. Evil Velma rolled to her feet, but when I jumped up to stop her, a solid weight collided with my back.

Invisible Darius had run into invisible me with enough force to knock me into the wall—and judging by the loud thump across from me, he'd collided with the opposite wall. I felt like a pinball in a comedy of errors machine.

Evil Velma reached the door but didn't run through it. She spun back around as her hands lit up with fireballs.

Oh, goody. A pyromage.

She clapped her hands together and a six-foot-tall pillar of flame filled the corridor before shooting forward. For a breathless second, all I could think was that I wished Lienna were here. Not only did her presence make just about everything better, but her abjuration sorcery was also uniquely handy at solving problems like, say, giant goddamn fireballs.

Darius grabbed the back of my shirt and hauled me into Tino's abandoned cabin. The inferno roared past the open doorway toward the opposite end of the car, heat blasting us as it went.

Darius released his lumina magic, appearing a step behind me in the cramped quarters. "This is getting out of hand."

I dropped my invisi-warp. "Understatement of the month, *Darry.*"

Re-invisifying myself, I poked my head out into the scorched corridor. The pyromage had gone through the exit, and I could see her just outside the dining car on the gangway connection. She was facing our way, a fireball glowing in her hand, ready to lob it through the open doorway at the first glimpse of an enemy.

This was less than ideal for multiple reasons.

For starters, neither my psycho warping nor Darius's light magic had any anti-inferno properties whatsoever. And second, this conflagrating crackpot was wielding her magic in full view of any unfortunate human passenger or staff member nearby.

"Any brilliant ideas?" I asked, sparing an extra bit of brainpower to opt Darius's mind out of my invisi-bomb. We didn't need another friendly fire collision to further complicate this decidedly un-straightforward mission.

"Distract her," Darius said. "I'll take her out."

"Shall do."

I hastened out of the cabin and into the corridor, stepping backward so Darius could go ahead of me. He vanished as I targeted Evil Velma's mind and considered which of the many distractions in my arsenal to smack her brain with. Since she was a fire-type Pokémon, I landed on my underutilized Fwoosh warp.

I concentrated on the roar of flames and their blistering heat, then applied all that imagination juice to the grapefruit-sized fireball in the pyromage's palm. It *fwooshed* into a cataclysmic combustion that exploded upward. She screamed and recoiled, so startled she didn't realize it was fake fire.

The open door clattered against the wall as an unseen Darius zipped onto the gangway connection. The pyromage slammed into the exterior of the dining car as he made contact, and a moment later, she collapsed unconscious.

Reappearing, Darius tossed a tiny potion vial off the train to shatter somewhere on the rocky ground bordering the tracks. He pulled the limp woman up with easy strength, and I held the door for him as he unceremoniously tossed her back into the car. The formerly handsome goon Darius had taken down was still lying at the other end, now thoroughly singed by his comrade's fire.

One goon left.

I was right behind Darius on the gangway connection, and as he blinked out of view, I added a fake door to my halluci-bomb before he opened it. I hurried in behind him.

For a second, I thought I'd stepped through a portal into a polar hellscape that looked like the sequel to *Frozen* as directed by Quentin Tarantino. It was, however, the dining car, but with snowy shards and icicles protruding from the walls and ceiling, frost covering every window, and all the poor humans who'd been enjoying a nice meal cowering under their tables.

The final goon was flailing in the middle of the aisle. Ice flew from his hands as he yelled incoherently. He looked like he was caught in my favorite Swarm warp, except all I was doing was keeping myself invisified.

The source of his distress was probably the fluorescent orange potion splattered all over his left arm. At the far end of the car, Tino was sheltering behind a table, his beady eyes fixed on the kryomage. He was holding what looked like a pistol-sized Super Soaker, its reservoir loaded with sloshing orange potion.

Huh. He hadn't been kidding about being armed.

Wasting no time, I hit the goon with a full Blackout Warp. He calmed down a little with his senses erased, which was a new one for me. What the hell was in that neon potion?

Darius popped back into view, produced another tiny vial, and dumped it on the man, who fell limp. The first time I saw him down a guy with one of those, I'd thought Darius had killed him with a super-assassin poison. But it turned out it was actually a super-assassin sleeping potion—an obscure, probably highly secret formula that left no trace on its victims.

As silence fell over the dining car, terrified humans cautiously poked their heads out from under their tables, eyes wide.

Since Darius was fully visible, I went ahead and dropped all my warps.

"Well," I drawled. "I guess we're getting a big, fat zero out of ten on the 'not drawing attention' section of our report card."

Darius nodded, his gray eyes traveling across the wintry mess. "Do you know the Dissimulation Department's emergency number?"

I sighed. "Yeah."

"Call them."

My eyebrows rose. Didn't he know how much paperwork a DD call created? I'd be buried alive. "And you can't because …?"

Darius arched his brows to match mine. "Because I was never here."

Then he vanished.

DARIUS ABANDONED ME.

It was better that no one from the MPD see us together, let alone write up a whole bunch of reports with both our names on them. I knew that. I understood that.

But I still didn't like being abandoned.

"So … what's an agent from Vancouver doing in Arizona?" the man in front of me asked with a professional lack of curiosity.

Agent Johnson, as he'd introduced himself, was the lead dude on a team of four Dissimulation Department agents. His three subordinates were currently aboard the stationary train behind us, corralling all the humans who'd witnessed the magipocalypse in the dining car so they could zap their memories into oblivion—not unlike *Men in Black*.

The DD agents' potions couldn't rewrite civilian memories the way Will Smith and Tommy Lee Jones's neuralyzers could, but they fuzzed each unfortunate bystander's recollection of today's events enough to keep the sacred secrecy of magic intact.

"I was visiting friends," I told Agent Johnson. "Some guys in my fantasy hockey league. The season starts in a couple months, and we need to re-jig the rules. Last year, my buddy Travis got McDavid *and* Kucherov in the draft, so he kind of ran away with the whole season. Couldn't let that happen again."

Johnson made a note on his clipboard before asking in a deliberately *not*-skeptical tone, "You took a train to Maricopa to visit your fantasy hockey league?"

"No, I took a train to visit them in El Paso," I corrected, "and I'm on my way back to Phoenix to fly home. I'd never been on a train before, so I thought why not have some fun while I'm here, right? Though based on this experience, I'm not sure I'll be a return customer."

"So you just *happened* to be aboard at the right time to stop a coordinated mythic attack?"

And there was the skepticism.

"Lucky, eh?" I said, upping my Canadian accent. Canadians were simple, honest, puck-loving folk. We'd never, *ever* illegally board a train, death-battle the minions of a secret, corrupt cabal, then lie about it to the authorities.

Agent Johnson sighed. "Well, I'm glad you were there to intervene."

"Just doing my duty."

"And you don't know why they attacked human civilians in the dining car?"

"Nope."

"It's a shame they escaped while you were seeing to the civilians." Agent Johnson handed my ID and badge back. "I may need to follow up with additional questions, and you'll need to complete forms DD19—"

"I know," I cut in before he could depress me with the full list. "Just email them to me, and I'll fill them out as soon as I'm back at my precinct."

He agreed, and a moment later, he was boarding the train to check on the memory-zapping. The first few passengers from the dining car were disembarking onto the platform, their expressions vague and confused, like docile zombies. Tomorrow, they'd all wake up with a nasty hangover and a weird sense that yesterday hadn't exactly gone to plan.

Brain erasure was just one of the Dissimulation Department's jobs. They were also the guys who took down websites and videos that hit too close to the truth, discredited and silenced loudmouthed whistle-blowers, and fueled the conspiracy-theory fires that had most of the public convinced magic was an idiotic joke.

The only time they actually showed up on-site was for big public-exposure oopsies. You know, like a kryomage turning an Arizona passenger train into the literal Polar Express.

For the most part, local agents managed minor incidents. It was part of our basic training, which was why I knew all the fun details of the potions those poor witnesses had been force-fed.

As I watched another passenger zombie-walk off the train, my gaze snagged on the nearby train car—the one where I'd *fwooshed* the pyromage into hysterics. Black scorch marks marred the exterior of the car all the way to its roof.

Weird.

Had she panicked and fired off a real *fwoosh* when I'd warped the fake *fwoosh*?

My phone buzzed, snapping me out of my musings. I pulled it out to find a text from Darius.

```
Our friend is on his way home, and the
trash has been relocated. Come see me once
you're back.
```

Typical assassin, not putting anything in writing unless it would self-destruct after being read.

Using my Darius decoder ring, I surmised that "the trash" was the three Consilium goons. We'd hauled them to the back of the train before reaching Maricopa, and when I'd gone to intercept Agent Johnson on the platform, Darius and Tino had dragged them away. The plan had been to dump them in some inconspicuous bed of cacti where they could sleep off Darius's potion.

They'd inevitably run back to their Consilium handlers, picking out succulent spines and reporting their failure, but it was better than letting the DD interrogate them. Who knew what they'd reveal?

We could have killed them, of course, but casual murder didn't sit well with me. We were supposed to be the good guys.

Plus, as Darius had mentioned, dead bodies tended to attract a lot of unwanted attention.

The "friend" from Darius's message had to be Tino. And if Tino was on his way home, that meant Darius had the documents we'd come for. The last set.

I pocketed my phone and strode across the platform, ready to put my Arizona adventure behind me. It was time to focus on the big picture: bringing down the Consilium.

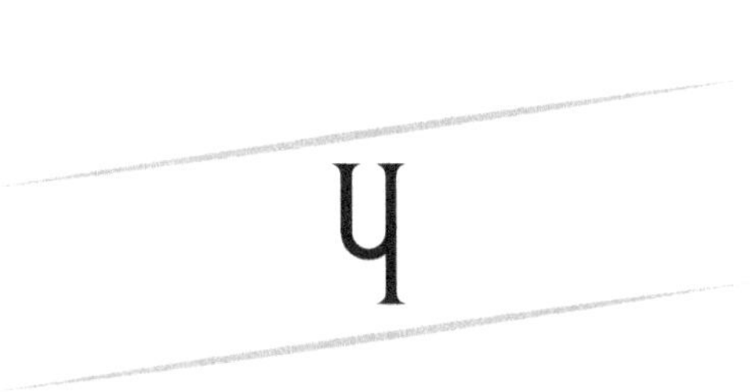

DESPITE MY GUNG-HO ATTITUDE after leaving Maricopa, I didn't make it to the Crow and Hammer until lunchtime the following day. My red-eye flight out of Phoenix and the desperate need for a midmorning nap had postponed my Consilium-abolishing aspirations.

I was still yawning as I walked into the guild. It turned out that leaping off an overpass onto a moving train, battling three Consilium pseudo-assassins—calling them *real* assassins would insult the former title of my co-conspirator—and dodging my way through an interview with a DD agent had drained my batteries more than I'd expected.

The Crow and Hammer's main floor pub was as dimly lit and shabbily cozy as always, the wood-paneled walls and heavy beams across the ceiling leaning hard into the old Irish pub mood. Fifteen or so members were grouped at the tables, and a low hum of conversation filled the air. The chill vibe was pleasant, and a knot of tension unraveled from between my shoulder blades.

A familiar redhead was perched behind the bar, but I'd only taken a few steps toward her when voices rang out.

"It's Kit!"

"Hey, Morris, over here."

"Kiiiit!"

I swerved off course, heading toward the largest group in the pub, who were clustered around two tables that had been pushed together.

"Nice timing, Kit," Zora declared, slapping me on the back as I stopped beside her. Despite being a five-foot-nothing sorceress, she delivered her playful smack with the force of an MMA fighter. "We need your expertise."

I arched my eyebrows. "Are you debating whether or not Deckard was a replicant? I think we all know he was."

Blank stares and snorts sounded from the rest of the group, which included a stocky telekinetic, several other Arcana mythics, and a hydromage—all bounty hunting combat specialists.

"Okay, so, *hypothetically*," Zora began, "if a small bounty team had just taken down a pair of vampires, and while they were cleaning up the mess, someone's dog happened to snatch a dismembered hand before we—I mean, the hypothetical team noticed, would it be legal or illegal under MPD law to use magic to get the hand back?"

I gave her a squinty look. "Where is this hypothetical scenario taking place?"

"In an alley beside a park. But it's late at night."

After a moment's thought, I said, "I guess it would depend on the magic used."

"Telekinesis," Drew stated. Coincidentally, he happened to be a telekinetic.

I shrugged. "As long as no one saw. That's all that really matters."

The group exchanged looks.

"Right." Zora nodded. "But what if, hypothetically of course, the telekinetic didn't realize the dog's owner was … uh … basically right there?"

I groaned. "Seriously?"

"It was dark! He blended in!" Drew protested. "Hypothetically."

"So, *hypothetically*," I said, "some poor shmuck going for a late-night puppy stroll not only got to see a gory severed hand in his precious pooch's mouth, but said hand then flew off into the night of its own volition right before his eyes?"

Silence answered me.

"It wasn't an off-leash park," the hydromage, Laetitia, tossed out. "The dog owner broke the law first."

"That definitely justifies the years of horrific nightmares he's bound to suffer." I rolled my eyes in an excellent Lienna impression. "What did he do after the hand floated away?"

"He just sort of stood there for a minute," Drew muttered. "Then he put the leash on his dog and turned around to walk in the other direction."

Probably questioning his sanity and/or whether someone had spiked his water supply.

"Assuming you included all relevant details in your report," I told them, "it'd be a minor guild fine for reckless magic use. But if the traumatized dog owner shows up on *The National* to warn the world about an autonomous-zombie-limb invasion, you might have the DD come knocking."

"Shhh," someone hissed at me. "Saying the name three times makes them appear, you know."

"The DD?" I repeated.

Everyone at the table shushed me. I indulged in another eye roll since Lienna wasn't here to do it. Mythics could be so superstitious—though I couldn't really blame them. The DD had the power to levy some of the biggest, meanest fines the MPD could muster against misbehaving guilds. Plus, the literal mountain of paperwork that followed their agents everywhere.

Which reminded me of the very non-hypothetical DD paperwork waiting for me at the precinct. I suppressed a cringe.

I chatted with the group for another minute, then extracted myself and headed for the bar.

Tori watched me with an uncharacteristically saccharine smile. I cautiously leaned on the bar in front of her.

"Kit," she said sweetly.

Uh-oh. "Yes, Tori?"

"Are you free next Saturday evening?"

"Nope."

Her eyes narrowed.

"I'm working a lot of overtime," I said truthfully.

She huffed and tossed a white towel onto the counter behind her. "Twiggy has gotten himself addicted to noir detective films."

I grinned before I could stop myself. Twiggy was her roommate, who happened to be a woodland faery with an obsessive love for the motion picture arts. My kind of fae.

"He keeps skulking around the house, narrating everything I do in that dumb noir drawl, and"—she glared at me like this was somehow my fault—"he keeps trying to imitate smoking. My apartment stinks."

I couldn't help it. A fit of laughter bent me over the bar. It took me a moment to pull myself together. I cleared my throat. "What does this have to do with me being free on Saturday night?"

She sighed. "I was hoping you could do a movie night with him and get him hooked on something new. Something *without* chain-smoking detectives."

Finally, someone who appreciated my pop-culture worldliness.

"What are you thinking?" I asked with a smirk. "Slasher flicks? Mobster movies? Boxing films?"

I could only imagine the utter chaos that would ensue if Twiggy started emulating any of those genres. Based on the contemptuous glare Tori leveled at me, she was imagining the same.

"I was hoping for something without violence, swearing, or excessive drinking," she growled.

"Why can't you get him started on a new film genre?"

"I'm running out of ideas, to be honest." She pointed her thumb over her shoulder at the shelves of liquor. "The usual?"

"Nah, just a Coke. Is Darius in?"

"Not yet." She pulled out a glass, dumped in some ice, and filled it with fizzy liquid to the brim. "I think he's back in town, though. Do you want me to ask Clara?"

"No need." I'd already texted him that I was on my way to his guild. I also knew the slick silver fox had beaten me back to the land of poutine and polar bears by a solid ten hours, despite his "recover the abandoned rental car on a random overpass in the desert" side trip.

"Your aura is troubled, Agent Morris."

The crooned words sounded in my ear, and I turned to find Rose, a diviner, standing beside me and leaning close to peer into my face. I didn't know if it was intentional, but with her short white hair, colorful shawl, and turquoise-framed glasses, she personified every single aspect of the stereotypical "elderly fortune teller."

"Sorry, what?" I muttered.

"You're troubled." She fanned out a deck of worn tarot cards. "Would you like guidance? I sense much turmoil on the horizon for you."

I sighed. I didn't need a diviner—especially one as pushy as Rose—to tell me that making an enemy of the Consilium, chasing down Kade, and hiding my partnership with Darius from Blythe would spell turmoil for future Kit.

I shot a look at Tori, silently pleading for an escape.

She raised an eyebrow and mouthed, "Saturday?"

I scowled back at her.

Rose leaned closer, her eyes glittering. "I can feel it. Your future will be magnificent—or catastrophic. I *must* divine for you."

"Oh, that sounds ominous, Kit," Tori said, her grin taking on an evil edge. "Rose, you'd better do a reading for him right now."

"Yes," the diviner agreed fervently. She began shuffling her cards. "Agent Morris, begin by clearing your mind—"

The bell above the guild's door jingled, and I looked desperately over my shoulder.

"Darius!" I exclaimed with way too much enthusiasm. "Sorry, Rose. Work to do."

Her face fell. "But your future—"

"I'll manage, thanks." I turned to Tori. "By the way, I'm busy every weekend for the next three months."

Her mouth fell open. "What? Why?"

I gave her a "you could've helped me, but you didn't, and that's what you get" look, to which she responded with a "your next drink may contain arsenic" look, and then I zoomed away from the bar to join Darius by the stairs.

"It's so weird," I commented as we started up the steps, the guild master in the lead.

"What is?" he asked over his shoulder.

"Most people in this guild actually like me." I tilted my head in thought. "They all seem to like each other, too."

It shouldn't have been that strange of a phenomenon, really. But my experiences with KCQ, my first guild, had involved a lot less good-natured banter and a lot more checking your back for unexpected knives. My precinct wasn't exactly populated by Judases and Brutuses, but there wasn't a ton of camaraderie either. Agents worked with their partners or small teams, but otherwise, we did our own thing.

"I'm sure Tori has a list of guildmates she'd be happy to never see again," Darius remarked.

"Not a list," I mused. "A dartboard. With photos of their faces."

"A definite possibility."

We passed the second-floor landing, which led to a communal work room, and continued up to the guild's third level. When we reached the top, I took two quick steps to fall in beside Darius.

"Seriously," I said as we walked down the hall. "Do you have some secret trick for the friendly 'extended family' vibe here? Is there a *Seven Habits of Highly Affable Guilds* how-to book?"

He shrugged as we rounded a corner and stopped at a closed door. "Not all members are close, but we're all committed to the guild as a whole. It's difficult to unite individuals to other individuals, but it's easy to unite them under a shared ideal." He unlocked the door with a key from his pocket, and as he pushed it open, he added, "That concept also works for our enemies, unfortunately."

The space we entered had previously served as a rarely used boardroom. It was now our center of operations—or, at least, our depository of information. Piles of papers and stacks of bulging folders that would have made Blythe envious covered the long table, chaotically marked with colorful sticky notes. The only thing missing was a giant corkboard covered in newspaper clippings, blurred photographs, and red string.

I'd spent so many hours in this room over the past five months that I knew exactly which documents had come from Tino. They were the only ones I didn't immediately recognize. Zipping straight to the end of the table, I dropped into a chair and leaned over the new stack. The top sheet featured a grainy photocopy of an Arcana circle and lots of tiny handwritten Latin. I quickly flipped through the stack, finding more poor-quality copies and a few sheets of aged, yellowed paper.

"You might find the other pile more helpful," Darius said as he settled in the chair beside mine. "I only asked Tino to store the documents for me, but he can't resist anything older than fifty years and in need of translation."

I turned to the second stack, which had seemed less interesting at first glance—a stapled bundle of lined pages full of boxy printing. I skimmed the first page, eyebrows rising, then flipped rapidly through it.

"Wow, Tino is one thorough dude."

"One of his many admirable traits," Darius replied, and damned if I couldn't tell whether he was being sarcastic or not. "He translated each document and noted his interpretation of the purpose for each, where applicable."

I nodded distractedly as I skimmed Tino's notes about that top page with the Arcana circle—which was actually a *very* nasty mass-murder spell outlawed in the 1500s. It surprised me that something so horrific had only been illegal for half a millennium. It should've been illegal since the dawn of humankind.

"So Tino saved us a whole bunch of time figuring out which of this outlawed, illegal, and/or extra evil magic might be of interest to the Consilium," I concluded.

"All of it was of interest to them at one point or another." Darius tapped the stack of old documents. "I found all of these in the hands of various Consilium supporters."

Consilium supporters he'd murdered, but he didn't say it and neither did I.

"What we don't know is how active their interest in any of them is, or whether they have plans to utilize any—or all—of these options." He leaned back in his chair. "Though I doubt they'd use *all* of them."

"Yeah, no kidding. Is this for real?" I waved at the page of Tino's handwriting I was skimming. "An experimental spell to explode the moon?"

Darius's mouth curved up. "My point exactly."

Shaking my head, I started flipping through the original documents, searching for the moon-splosion one, when I stopped on a page that featured an illustration, not a spell.

It was a drawing of a single man that resembled an odd combination of an Egyptian hieroglyph and a medieval medical sketch. His arms were spread wide, and he appeared to be levitating off the ground. Above his left hand hovered four symbols: a flame, a water droplet, what was probably a rock, and a trio of squiggly lines I assumed was either meant to represent wind or perfectly cooked bacon. Over his right hand sat an Arcana circle surrounded by sparkly dots. Beneath his levitating feet were leafy vines and swirly lines, and above his head were three more symbols: a hand, an eye, and a triangular shape I couldn't interpret.

And at the center of the man's forehead, the artist had drawn a sun-shaped emblem.

"What's this one?"

"Ah." Darius shrugged. "That one isn't likely to be useful. The rest of the documentation that went with it was lost."

I frowned at him. "Lost how?"

"I was interrupted and had to leave it behind." He rolled his chair back. "I'd hoped to steal it out of MPD evidence storage, but it disappeared before I had the chance, as evidence relating to the Consilium typically does."

"Damn," I muttered, staring at that odd sun symbol on the illustrated man's forehead.

"You'll want to read Tino's notes from front to back." Darius rose to his feet. "Twenty years ago, the Consilium was very interested in illegal magic and artifacts. That probably hasn't changed."

Nodding, I resettled the stack without disturbing the order of the pages and swiveled to face Darius as he sat down in front of a laptop halfway along the table.

"How did it go with your current batch of stooges?" I asked, using my feet to wheel myself along the table until I was parked beside him. "Mine, by the way, were a bunch of dead ends. Again."

Darius nodded without surprise. "Mine as well, though I'm waiting to hear back from a contact on the artifact broker."

"How many more suspected Consilium lackeys do we still have to probe?"

"Fewer than fifty."

I winced. Fifty was still a lot of frustrating sleuthing. Twenty years ago, Darius and his allies had collected a giant list of suspicious mythics who were possibly involved with the Consilium's activities. Darius had left the list with Josip—the cigar-smoking, Croatian guy-who-knows-a-guy—for safekeeping.

After recovering the list last month, we'd been divvying up the names and digging into the backgrounds of everyone on it, trying to figure who might still be buddy-buddy with the Consilium of the twenty-first century.

"Oh," I said as a thought popped into my head. "We didn't happen to skip over a Peter Kade on the list, did we?"

"Not likely. Who is *Peter* Kade?"

The name "Kade" would've rung about a bazillion bells if it'd been in any of these files. Nonetheless, I pulled the folder over to me—yes, I knew exactly which one without having to look at the label—and skimmed down the master list of names, just to be sure.

While I fruitlessly triple-checked everything, I filled Darius in on what I'd learned from Kade Jr.'s middle school teacher. When the list, as expected, produced exactly zero "Kade" references, I rolled my chair back down the table to Tino's notes, leaving Darius at the laptop, where he dug into yet another two-decades-old name from the list.

As I picked up the fat bundle of translations, I gazed across the overflowing table. It was wild to me that Darius and his allies had gathered this level of intelligence on the down-low—and in the age of dial-up internet, no less. From suspicious financial records within the MPD—provided by a mysterious contact Darius would tell me nothing about—to a list of MPD-sanctioned contract killings—provided by an old assassin buddy of Darius's—to business records of suspected Consilium puppet companies, we had oodles of info.

Unfortunately, half of it was out of date, and we had yet to find a solid lead on the Consilium's current operations or who their top guns in the upper echelon of the MPD were.

Not for the first time, my thoughts slid to Lienna. I wanted her here helping us, and not just because she was insanely good at this kind of academic paper-pushing. And not just because I missed her, either. There was something magical about our two minds working in concert to solve puzzles that I just couldn't replicate with anyone else.

Before I could start thinking about texting her—or how many days it'd been since she'd last texted me—I got to work. Tino's notes were insanely detailed. Maybe a bit too detailed. I really didn't need to know the historical context of all this ancient illegal magic. I just needed to know what it was and how scared I should be.

Darius and I toiled for over an hour before my phone chimed in my pocket. I pulled it out enthusiastically, hoping for a message from Lienna, but instead, Blythe's name glowed on my screen.

"Time's up," I informed Darius as I rolled my chair back. "Captain Blythe wants a report."

With anyone else, I might've quipped about Captain Kill-Joy, but I'd noticed that Darius didn't like me throwing anything resembling disrespect in Blythe's direction. Not that he'd ever commented, but I was getting the hang of interpreting the cagey GM's non-expressions. He didn't even like me calling her Blythe, sans Captain.

I'd tried calling her Aurelia once, mostly to see the reaction I'd get. He'd barely acknowledged the first-name-dropping, but his expression had been cold enough for me to never dip a toe in those waters again.

We conferred briefly on a few more names for me to investigate from the MPD archives, and then I let myself out, feeling the weight of impending doom on my shoulders. It wasn't that Darius and I hadn't made any progress. We had dozens of potential avenues of investigation we could pursue, but none of them were strong enough to stand out.

With every week that passed, I worried that an invisible timer we didn't know existed was ticking down, and when it hit zero, it would be too late.

5

THE PRECINCT was a twenty-minute walk from the Crow and Hammer, and a midafternoon urban hike would give me a chance to clear all the ancient magic facts from my brain and get back into Kade-hunting mode.

I wove through the foot traffic congesting the sidewalks of Powell Street until I reached Gastown, where weaving was no longer an option; it was too damn crowded. The best I could do was tread past the boutique furniture shops and overpriced coffee joints at the lackadaisical pace of all the other pedestrians.

As I bobbed through the crowd, mentally organizing my recently learned tidbits about Kade's past for my inevitable debrief with Blythe, I glimpsed something in the reflection of a parked car that sent a jolt down every nerve in my body.

It was the unmistakable shape of a bald head among the crowd a few yards behind me.

Now, don't get me wrong—there are a lot of bald white dudes in Vancouver. Steering hard into the curve of your receding hairline by the handle of a razor blade is practically a fashion statement in these parts. But something about this particular cue ball sounded alarms in my head.

My gaze swept across all nearby reflective surfaces to catch another glimpse without turning around to look. It couldn't be *him*, though. My brain was just filling in a Kade-like profile because I was thinking about him while I walked.

My heart rate was finally beginning to slow, calmed by an internal stream of logic delivered in Lienna's "don't be silly, Kit" tone, when a pedestrian heading in the opposite direction passed so close she nearly clipped me with her shopping bag. Her dark-tinted sunglasses reflected my own face back at me— and framed over my shoulder was Kade's steely-eyed countenance, barely three strides behind me.

Adrenaline dumped into my bloodstream. Eschewing courtesy, I shoved my way through the milling throng, garnering more than a few glares and grumbles. I really didn't care, not when the psycho who'd threatened to torture Lienna and me to death, and who I'd last seen decapitating Agent Söze in a parking lot, was right on my tail.

No longer pretending I hadn't noticed him, I looked back to find he'd fallen a few more paces behind—but he was moving steadily toward me, pedestrians instinctively clearing a path for his wide shoulders, probably sensing the predator in their midst.

Was he alone?

I scanned the multitudinous heads jam-packed onto the sidewalk, dreading the potential sight of any other Consilium cronies, but none were immediately obvious. That didn't mean they weren't there.

The awkward intersection where Water Street connected diagonally with Cordova was just ahead. I picked up my speed and jaywalked to the other side. If I could cut across Cordova and disappear down one of the subsequent back alleys, I could put some space between me and Kade—and any of his goons. Then I could figure out what the hell to do.

Kade, the man I'd been unsuccessfully scouring the continent for over the past five months, was here. In Vancouver.

I'd thought I was hunting him, and the sudden role reversal was turning my heart rate into "The Flight of the Bumblebee."

I made it to the intersection, but a bevy of traffic combined with a badly timed red light stopped me at the corner. Ineffectually shielded by a clump of afternoon shoppers, I looked across the street to the sidewalk I'd illegally vacated.

Kade stood on the corner, ramrod still, eyes unwaveringly on me. His expression betrayed nothing other than unshakeable focus.

Had he come back to finish me off? Why now? Why approach me on a busy street full of humans? My head spun, my thoughts muddled by the animal part of my brain yelling at me to run for my life.

In theory, I could create a warp—a massive halluci-bomb to mess with the traffic lights or create a chaotic distraction—but out in public, with this many non-mythics surrounding me, I couldn't risk it. Just yesterday I'd been involved in a magic-exposure incident involving a dining car full of train passengers. If I created magical mayhem in front of dozens of unassuming humans on a street corner in broad daylight, I'd be DD toast.

Instead, I stared back at Kade and targeted his mind. He'd always seemed impervious to my warps, but I only needed to distract him for a few seconds so I could slip away.

Keeping it simple, I created a single voice that crept into his mind like a bad memory.

"You think you're hunting me," disembodied Kit whispered, "but the real hunters are behind you."

I hoped Kade would at least give a cursory glance over his shoulder, providing me with a split second to vanish into the crowd, but he didn't move. Even from across the street, I could see his eyes narrow and a sneer crawl onto his lips.

Nice try, Morris, his voice replied clearly inside my head.

I barely had time to register the low pitch of his voice invading my gray matter before the people around me started hustling into the intersection. The traffic lights had changed. Shaking my head as though I could dislodge Kade's voice, I rushed into the throng.

So did Kade, his eyes still on me.

I reached the far sidewalk, took a couple of quick steps along it, then Split-Kit myself. Fake Kit melded with the crowd while invisible me spun a hundred and eighty degrees and sprinted back across Cordova Street just as the light went yellow.

For whatever reason, my warps didn't work well on Kade, but as I'd hoped, it took him a couple seconds to lock onto the real me. That was enough. He started into the street, only to reel back toward the sidewalk as a honking mail truck accelerated through the intersection.

I kept running, retracing my steps down Water Street and doing my best not to shoulder-check any pedestrians into oncoming traffic. I didn't slow down until I found another intersection and hung a hard right.

In the shade of an Irish pub, I caught my breath, half expecting Kade to come barreling around the corner.

But he didn't.

As far as close shaves went, that had been tight enough to make Sweeney Todd wince. What the hell was Kade doing back in Vancouver? My first thought was that he'd returned to complete his previous mission: murdering Darius. But why would he come after me? Compared to the infamous Mage Assassin, I was a literal nobody.

"Damn it," I growled.

The target of my slow, tedious, five-month-long investigation had been within spitting distance, and I'd run away like Cinderella at the stroke of midnight.

I leaned against the brick façade of the pub, pulse thudding in my ears, smells of seafood chowder and heavy stout wafting into my nostrils, and a nagging voice in the back of my head belittling my cowardice.

Taking a long, deep breath, I tried to imagine what Lienna would say if she were here. What would she tell her partner who'd fled the relentless, slippery psychopath who'd almost killed us multiple times before?

Yeah, I'd run, but I also wasn't armed with anything but my warps, which failed to work properly on that bald bastard. Alone, I was outmatched. As I'd learned the hard way during my two failed field exams while trying to earn my agent title, I was at a huge disadvantage against certain psychic powers.

I replayed the sound of Kade's voice. *Nice try, Morris.*

The truly unnerving part was that it made sense. Based on his ability to see through my warps, how he handled Darius's lumina magic, and the stories Miriam Baker had told me about adolescent Benny, I could only draw one obvious conclusion.

Kade was a telepath.

I WAS STARING at a woman in her early twenties. Her wavy, chocolate-brown hair had tasteful golden highlights and hung around her shoulders. She had soft features and a huge, playful smile.

She was just an image on a phone, but I was utterly baffled by her.

"Her name's Kayla," Vinny told me.

Leaning against the wall of his cubicle and trying to hide my bewilderment, I managed a monosyllabic, "Wow."

"It's been a little over a month now," he said, turning the screen back to himself and taking in her photo one more time before pocketing his phone.

"No shit," I muttered.

"What do you think?"

His question caught me off guard. What did I think? I thought it was a weird-ass question to ask your coworker about your new girlfriend based on no more information than a single photo and a first name. What the hell was I supposed to say? She was pretty? She looked fun? The digital representation of her face indicated friendliness?

"Uh, I …" Come on, Kit. You can say anything, literally anything … as long as it's nice. "She seems—"

"Beautiful?" Vinny interrupted. "Too beautiful?"

I frowned. "What?"

"So beautiful that she's got to be out of my league, right?"

"No, man. I wasn't going to—"

With a heavy sigh, Vinny slumped back into his chair, ruffling his neatly pressed suit. "You're right. Of course you're right."

"I'm sorry, but what am I right about?"

"She's out of my league!" he exclaimed with a note of desperation. "There's no way this is going to last."

He ran a hand through his hair. Or, more accurately, his fingers dragged across his mohawk, knocking several heavily gelled strands out of whack. This was a gesture I'd never seen Vinny do, not once since we'd started working together.

And it worried me. I was far more used to his apoplectic frustration with my semi-regular pranks at his expense, but here he was, anxiously ruining his perfect hair and spouting insecure babble … over a girl?

Actually, on second thought, it made perfect sense. Men are stupid.

"Any day now, she'll look at me and realize she could do so much better," Vinny rambled. "On a good day, what am I? A seven out of ten? And Kayla, she's a ten! Maybe you'd say a nine. No lower than an eight-point-five, right? I don't know your type—well, I do. It's Agent Shen, but still—"

"Wait, what?" I interjected. Was I that obvious? Even Vincent Park had picked up on it?

Motor-Mouth McGee kept chugging. "That kind of disparity just isn't sustainable. And it's not just looks. She's on track to become an officer at her guild, and I'm just—"

"Vinny," I said firmly, placing a hand on his shoulder. "Take a breath, dude."

He stared at me for a second, then inhaled deep and slow through his nose.

"Good." I sat on the edge of his desk so I was closer to eye level with him. "You know, part of me agrees with you."

He winced. "You do?"

"On the looks front? Absolutely. As far as I'm concerned, you're about as attractive as the wrong end of an irritable donkey."

An unexpected snort-laugh burst from Vinny.

"But you know what they say. Beauty is in the eye of the beholder." It was my turn to wince. Was I really devolving into cliches? Romantic pep talks were not my strong suit. "Besides, you've got lots to offer besides looks."

"Yeah?"

"Yeah."

There was an uncomfortably long pause. Did he want me to list said offerings? This was not the conversation I'd been expecting when I'd stepped into his cubicle five minutes ago.

Since Vinny still seemed to be waiting expectantly, I gave it a shot. "I mean, you're smart. And you're in great shape."

He shrugged. "That's just part of the job."

"Yeah, because you take down bad guys for a living, Vinny. That's awesome. Not to mention your eye for detail, which I'm sure Kayla will appreciate when she gets a haircut and you notice before she has to prompt you."

The mohawked agent grinned and sat up in his chair. "That actually happened last week."

"And she loved it, didn't she?"

"She did!"

"There ya go." I stood up from my spot on the edge of his desk, desperate for this conversation to change gears. "Speaking of that eye for detail. I'm wondering if you can do some digging for me."

"What kind of digging?"

"You know the MPD's elite Defense, Recon, and Arcane Field Tactics team?"

He nodded. "DRAFT. Yeah, Agent Harris and I did a joint operation with them earlier this year."

"For the eco-terrorist witch coven thing, right?" I asked rhetorically, knowing exactly which operation he'd been involved in—it was the reason I'd started this conversation. "I heard you got some insight into how DRAFT does things."

Vinny shrugged with faux modesty. "Working with them was definitely an experience. I learned a lot."

I leaned forward, lowering my voice. "Did you learn enough that you might be able to get your hands on some of their old reports from between 2010 and 2013?"

Vinny scrunched up his nose. "DRAFT's activities are usually pretty locked down. I don't know if even Captain Blythe would have the security clearance for it."

"What if you talked to some of the guys you worked with on the eco-terrorism case? Could they help?"

He crossed his arms, eyeing me warily. "I don't know, Kit. Nosing around for something like that …"

"I wouldn't ask if it wasn't important." I leaned closer, meeting his eyes. "I'm looking for reports that mention Agent Kade."

His body language instantly changed, arms dropping and shoulders stiffening. "Kade was a DRAFT agent?"

I nodded. "For three years before he joined Internal Affairs."

"Hmm." Vinny scooted his chair forward and tapped his mouse to wake the computer on his desk. "I'll see what I can do."

"Awesome. Keep me posted, okay?" I backed out of his cubicle. "I'm overdue for a debriefing with Captain Blythe."

I was three steps away before Vinny spoke. "Hey, Kit?"

Pausing, I glanced back. "Yeah?"

"Thanks. You know, for …"

"Don't mention it," I replied. "Seriously. I mean that in the most literal sense."

Not that I regretted giving him a small confidence boost, but I also didn't want to have to think about Vinny's love life ever again.

A few minutes later, I was sitting across from Blythe, the door to her office closed tightly behind me to avoid any prying eyes or eavesdropping ears. She had her elbows braced on her desk, hands clasped, blue gaze laser-beaming across my face.

"Tell me what you learned," she ordered.

"Agent Park has a new girlfriend and deep-seated self-image issues."

She scowled. "You know what I mean."

"Oh, you mean how Kade has been a violent psychopath since adolescence and once murdered his middle school class's beloved pet turtle?"

Blythe's gaze sharpened even more. "Keep going."

I gave her a speedy rundown of my conversation with Miriam Baker, including Kade's "slipperiness." This detail didn't seem particularly revelatory to Blythe; she was less concerned about Kade's powers and more interested in where he was and who he was working for.

"Well, he's in Vancouver," I said. "As of an hour ago, anyway."

Her whole body tensed. "How do you know that?"

"He followed me through Gastown. I managed to give him the slip, but not before I heard his voice in my head." I shrugged. "Methinks he's a secret telepath."

Blythe slowly leaned back, her frown deepening. I watched her, wondering what thoughts and questions were churning in her head—and if they were the same as mine.

"I don't like it," she finally said.

"You don't like that the violent lunatic we've been hunting for the past five months, to no avail, has shown up right in our neighborhood?"

"No."

"Me neither." I chewed my lip in thought. "I can only come up with a few reasons he might return to Vancouver—pretty much all of them of the murder variety. Namely, to kill me, you, and/or Darius, who was his 'primary objective' back in March, if you recall."

Blythe's lips thinned at the mention of Darius.

"But," I continued, "Kade also knows that our whole precinct wants him behind bars, that you and I extra want him behind bars for trying to kill us, and that Darius extra-*extra* wants to stick one of his very sharp daggers into Kade's throat. So even if Kade is back in town, why reveal himself to me like that?"

"And why reveal his telepathy after keeping it so carefully hidden?" she mused darkly. "He could be back for any number of reasons, but the fact he targeted you is … unexpected."

"Because I'm a small fry compared to you and Darius?" I suggested.

"Or because you were getting too close to uncovering something he doesn't want you to know," she countered. "Though his middle school experiences aren't likely to reveal crucial information."

I nodded, fairly certain there was a statute of limitations on turtle murder. On the other hand, the second half of my Arizona adventure *had* included potentially crucial info—Tino's documents—not to mention the three Consilium goons who may or may not have reported my presence on that train to their boss.

The sudden thought that Kade might be said boss had me wishing we hadn't set that trio loose.

Unfortunately, I couldn't tell Blythe about the Consilium assassins or Tino or my side quest with Darius. She knew there was corruption in the MPD, but she wasn't aware of the Consilium's pompous appellation. Lienna and I had included it in our reports, but as Darius had predicted back in March, everything we'd submitted into the MPD system that had included the word "Consilium" had mysteriously vanished.

Blythe, who'd been recovering from her Kade-inflicted stab wound at the time, hadn't gotten a chance to read those reports before we'd submitted them, and on Darius's advice, I hadn't put the Consilium's name into her brain after the fact. Things might go all kinds of sideways if the wrong people heard either of us talking about the Consilium. It was safer to keep that talk between me and Darius—and outside the precinct.

"You mentioned Kade's father," Blythe said, breaking into my thoughts. "Did you get a name?"

"Peter."

"Peter," she murmured to herself, eyes drifting upward in thought. "Peter Kade …"

"Ringing a bell?" I asked hopefully.

She shook her head. "Not that I can recall, but it's another lead worth following."

"I'm already looking into it."

"Good." She drummed her fingers on her desk. "As for Kade, he knows too much about our precinct. I'll put out a notice to all our agents, but it's time to leverage the guilds. I'll double Kade's bounty and personally speak with the GMs of our top bounty guilds to ensure they understand the urgency and danger."

My eyebrows shot up. "All the GMs, you say?"

"Yes," she snapped impatiently.

"Even the Crow and Hammer's GM?"

Her glare intensified. "Anything else, Agent Morris?"

I was going to take that as a "yes, and I hate it with the fire of a thousand jilted lovers." I just hoped Darius was quick on his mental feet when she informed him about Kade, seeing as I'd called him on my way to the precinct to warn him that the assassin who'd almost offed him was back on his turf.

"How's your investigation going?" I asked Blythe, slouching more comfortably in my chair. "I don't suppose *your* persons of interest showed up randomly in Vancouver today too?"

"They did not," she growled, as though this was a great disappointment to her.

This was unsurprising, to say the least, considering her persons of interest were Söze, who was too dead to show up anywhere, and Sparks, whose spot at the top of the Internal Affairs ladder probably prevented him from taking unscheduled trips to Canada's west coast to harass a lowly field agent. Her prying into Söze had given us nothing but dead ends—pun intended—which left only Sparks as a potential line of inquiry.

"I've exhausted all my avenues for insight into the IA department," Blythe continued. "As far as I can determine, Commissioner Sparks is in full control of his subordinates. Everyone has the same opinion: nothing happens in Internal Affairs that Sparks isn't aware of."

I didn't speak, letting that statement settle over us like an unpleasant, chilly blanket. "So, it was Sparks who sent Söze and

Kade to implode our precinct and murder Darius. Or he at least knew about it."

This wasn't exactly a surprise—we'd suspected Commissioner Sparks all along—but channels of power within the MPD were convoluted and always shifting, with inter-department interference, shadowy backdoor influencers, and too many crisscrossing lines of communication to keep track of. Blythe had spent the last five months carefully prodding the IA for insider info about who controlled whom, and she'd needed to tread *very* carefully.

"This is bigger than just one dude," I said, "even if he is the IA's head honcho. If we can go through everyone on the committee that elects the IA Commissioner—"

"No," Blythe interrupted.

"No?"

"The special committee that elects the Internal Affairs commissioner is classified at the highest level. There's no way for us to acquire a list of the members' names."

"No shit," I said quietly, leaning back in my chair.

This revelation flew in the face of everything I knew about how department heads were elected. According to the MPD handbook, each bigwig was voted in by a special committee comprising the experts, influencers, and authority figures of that particular field. Getting an invitation to join a committee was a point of pride for most folks. If you were a hotshot mythic accountant, for example, being invited to vote for the head of the financial department was a real feather in your cap. Or a bead on your abacus. Or whatever.

It reminded me of the Academy Awards: writers nominate writers, editors nominate editors, actors nominate actors, and so on. And no one in Hollywood was shy about proclaiming their official Academy member status.

Which was the opposite of the IA's special committee, apparently. No one outside the committee knew who had put Sparks in charge of one of the most powerful departments in the MPD. How was everyone okay with that?

"Why is it such a big secret?" I asked.

Blythe's expression grew darker and more thundercloud-like. "To protect the committee members from persecution, bribery, undue influence, and so on."

"That's not very helpful if the bastards have already been bribed or corrupted," I observed, frustration hardening my voice.

She nodded in agreement.

"So," I said pointedly, "maybe we should find out who these oh-so-special people are."

Blythe gave me a long, hard, silent stare, during which she was either considering my proposal or reconsidering her opinion of my intelligence.

"Wherever the records of the special committee members are kept," she said, "neither of us has a chance in hell of getting our hands on them. Start with Sparks instead. I want a list of all politically powerful mythics he interacts with, has a past with, or who might have influence over him."

"Got it."

Her lips thinned again as she pulled a folder off the stack on her desk and held it out. "Be careful, Kit. We're wading into even more dangerous waters now."

A chill ran through my limbs. Taking the folder, I flipped it open to give the top page a glance. A photo of Commissioner

Sparks stared up at me. Closing the folder with a snap, I gave a short nod.

"Is that all?" she asked. "Any other details from your trip I should know about?"

Details like ... illegally leaping onto a moving train with her sworn enemy to save a neurotic archivist from a trio of Consilium assassins?

"Nope," I answered. "That's all she wrote."

"Keep me updated."

"You got it, Cap."

I rose from my chair, tucked the folder under my arm, and quickly exited her office, exhaling as soon as the door closed behind me. I'd been performing this dance for five months now—keeping my team-up with Darius King on the DL, avoiding any direct references to the Consilium, inventing excuses to go on "work trips" that had precisely nothing to do with my investigation into Kade.

I was getting real tired of it. Being torn between these two lovers-turned-foes who were both essentially working on the same goddamn case but refusing to speak with each other—it really wore a guy out.

And it left me wondering ... how long could I keep it up?

AS I LOCKED MY APARTMENT DOOR, I let out a huge sigh. Talk about high-tension transportation. I usually walked from the precinct to my old/new condo in Coal Harbor, but with Kade playing cat and mouse with me, I'd decided a little bus roulette was in order. Combined with some well-timed invisi-warps, I hoped I'd sufficiently muddled my trail.

After all, this wasn't just my place of residence—it was the condo Blythe had bought to assemble her own anti-Söze hideout. The last thing I wanted was to lead Kade directly to our center of operations.

Kicking off my shoes, I briefly checked the three monitors of our precinct surveillance setup, ensuring everything was as it should be. Spying on my fellow agents made me feel slightly icky, but we had an unidentified mole among our ranks. Plus, there was the skeevy jerk who'd vanished the hard copies of our reports about Söze and the Consilium, though I had no idea if the culprit had been a precinct employee or an interloper who was long gone.

Heading into the kitchen, I whipped up a taco salad for my late dinner. With extra cheese ... because, well, did I need a reason? Between the serious overtime I was pulling for Blythe and the added workload of teaming up with Darius, I was racking up some serious investigative hours, and now I wanted some Tex-Mex cheddar goodness to fuel the take-home assignment I'd acquired from the captain.

With my dinner and Blythe's folder of info about Commissioner Sparks beside me on the kitchen island, I opened my laptop and got started. The clock crawled from nine to ten to eleven. Sparks had been bouncing around various MPD roles and departments for the better part of thirty years, meaning I had three decades' worth of data to sift through before I could start digging into his personal life.

As the time ticked closer to midnight, I got up to stretch. Needing a break from endless archive reports featuring Sparks's name and a reprieve from the barstool at the kitchen island that was threatening to put my butt cheeks to sleep, I wandered over to the desk in the living room, where a much plushier office chair awaited me. I plugged in the USB stick that Zak, the walking manifestation of sexy danger also known as the Ghost, had given me.

Following the USB stick's instructions, which I now knew by heart, I logged into the sketchy online chat portal I'd been frequenting off and on all spring and summer. It took a few minutes, during which I watched cute cat videos on my phone. A feline-induced dopamine dump couldn't hurt right about now.

Soon enough, green text popped up in the black TOR browser.

>Sugar Glider has logged in.

>Sugar Glider: Who is this?

I pocketed my phone in the middle of a compilation of adorable kittens startling themselves into wild acrobatics and scooted up to the keyboard.

>You: Your favorite customer.

I waited for a moment, just to see, but I knew the faceless rodent on the other end of the connection wouldn't reply until I gave them the response they were waiting for.

>You: Rose Petal

It was the nickname I'd been assigned the first time I'd contacted the mole who lurked within the Vancouver precinct. Yeah, one of my coworkers was a sleazy, classified-information-selling scumbag. But they'd also helped me and Lienna out—for a price—when we'd been in real hot water last March.

>Sugar Glider: Is this another lonely
nighttime chat? I'm a busy person, you
know.

I glanced at the clock in the corner of the screen. It was almost midnight.

>You: Yet here you are, answering my lonely
late-night call.

>Sugar Glider: Don't you have anything
better to do, like planning your next
mysterious out-of-town errand?

I grimaced. I hadn't been sharing my travel schedule with the mole, but at some point during our dealings, they had worked out my identity. They knew who I was, but I still didn't know who they were.

```
>You: I actually have a legit request this
time.
```

```
>Sugar Glider: Can you pay for it?
```

See? Mercenary to their furry, whiskered core.

```
>You: Why don't you hear me out before we
start haggling?
```

"Haggling" was probably the wrong word. The mole had zero sympathy for my mediocre financial situation. In theory, I could ask Blythe for a chunk o' change to pay them, but she was less than thrilled that I'd communicated with the mole in the first place. I imagined she'd be—to put it lightly—violently disappointed in me for bringing the mole into her ultrasecret investigation, no matter how carefully I did it.

```
>Sugar Glider: What do you need?
```

```
>You: I'm looking for information on the
special committee that elects the IA
commissioner.
```

```
>Sugar Glider: Why not ask me for winning
lottery numbers?
```

```
>You: Can you actually do that?
```

```
>Sugar Glider: No. Which is the point.
```

```
>You: What about the Internal Affairs
department itself?
```

```
>Sugar Glider: Slightly closer to a
plausible request.
```

I took that as a "maybe," which surprised me. The IA was an international arm of the MPD. How was our local mole able to glean anything about the IA's business?

```
>You: How about information on other audits
the IA has done like the one they did to
```

```
us? Especially any that involve Agent Söze
or Agent Kade.

>Sugar Glider: Is there something specific
you're looking for?
```

The mole's response was almost instant. Whoever they were, they'd spent considerable time under Agent Söze's oppressive thumb, and they harbored the same resentment we all did on that front.

```
>You: I'm looking for a pattern. I want to
know who else they've been screwing with
and why. Can you do that?

>Sugar Glider: That depends on what you can
pay.

>You: I have an alternative proposal. If
you do this for me, I swear on the grave of
Laurence Olivier not to come after you.
Ever. I won't poke, prod, or probe for your
real-world identity at any point between
now and the heat death of the universe.

>Sugar Glider: That was never a concern for
me.

>You: And now it never has to be.
```

A knock at the door jolted my brain away from the computer monitor and back into the nondigital world of my condo. Who the hell was that?

I turned back to the screen.

```
>You: Do we have a deal?

>Sugar Glider: I'll think about it. Check
back in a few days.

>Sugar Glider has logged out.
```

Another knock. I unplugged the USB key, shoved it into my pocket, and jogged toward the condo's entrance. Squinting through the peephole, I saw the silver fox I should have expected.

I affected a deep frown as I opened the door. "You're not the pizza delivery guy."

Darius didn't wait for me to invite him in, striding through the open door. I locked it behind him, homing in on the brown folder he was carrying.

"Is that what I think it is?" I asked, pointing at it.

"That depends on what you think it is." He headed for the recliner, his seat of choice whenever he stopped by to talk shop—namely, our Consilium investigation. "No further sign of Kade?"

"Nope." I dropped onto the sofa across from him. "But the slippery bastard is bound to turn up sooner or later."

Darius's expression scarcely changed, but I recognized that steely shift in his eyes. If I was reading him right, that was his "I'd like to carve out Kade's spleen with a dull spoon" look.

"Aaron has put together two well-equipped teams," the ex-assassin said, nonchalant as ever. "He's feeling extremely motivated."

"Can't blame him. Kade almost cooked his bacon along with the rest of us. Did you give him a heads-up about Kade's potential telepathy?"

"Yes, he's aware. They'll take precautions."

I tilted my head curiously. "Did Captain Blythe talk to you?"

Darius's expression was completely unreadable now. "She sent a text."

Interesting. I definitely recalled her saying she would "personally speak with" all the GMs.

"Do you two text a lot?" I fished.

He didn't take the bait, instead holding out his brown folder. I hopped up to take it, then settled back into my seat.

I fanned the folder dramatically. "This is either the cocojito recipe I've been pestering you about for months, or you've got a lead. I'm not sure which I want more."

He merely arched his eyebrows.

I flipped open the folder. Front and center on the first page was the headshot of a clean-shaven businessman in the "semiretired" era of his life with a perfectly pressed white collar and black tie. His short, graying hair was neatly parted and styled to one side, and his nose had a charming bend à la Owen Wilson—an old break that looked like it had come from an overly aggressive game of frat boy flag football.

Since it wasn't a drink recipe, that meant it was most definitely a lead.

"Jayce Tyrian is a retired MPD agent," Darius informed me. "A pyromage originally from Pittsburgh. Over the past decade, he's constructed a very successful business empire."

I turned to the next page in the folder, finding a list of all the companies Tyrian either owned outright or had a controlling stake in: real estate ventures, an investment firm, a couple of businesses with names too vague to discern their nature, and a chain of boutique grocery stores. The vast majority of them were headquartered relatively close to his hometown in Pennsylvania.

I grimaced. "So, he's a gazillionaire."

"Well on his way to becoming a billionaire, at least."

"And he's a Consilium stooge?" I guessed.

"Not as far as I can tell. All of his business dealings appear to be above board."

"Then why do we care about him?"

"Page eight."

I flipped forward in the folder until I landed on a page about Tyrian's latest corporate acquisition: Trident Ltd., located in Miami, Florida. That was several hundred miles outside the business magnate's sphere of influence.

"'Florida's Premium Brokerage Firm,'" I read aloud. "Is that supposed to mean something to me? I know I'm ex-KCQ, but I never became fully fluent in venture capital vernacular."

Darius drummed his fingers on his knee, a rare sign of impatience. "That's the very successful front hiding an equally successful mythic artifact brokerage. Again, as far as I can determine, its business activities are entirely legal."

"Then, to revisit my prior question: why the hell do we care?"

"Mickey Gomez," Darius replied. "According to the financial documents we have, he was the owner of Trident Ltd. before Jayce Tyrian acquired it."

I sat up straight. "And Mickey Gomez is a Consilium acolyte! We have a nice big pile of financial documents on him showing all those unexplained deposits."

Said documents were among the piles about to collapse the boardroom table on the Crow and Hammer's third floor.

"To make a convoluted tale much shorter, Mickey got himself into some legal trouble last year that the Consilium was either unable or unwilling to help him escape. Between debt, fines, and lawyer fees, he was forced to sell most of his holdings, and Jayce Tyrian snapped up Trident Ltd. a few months ago."

I leaned forward and braced my elbows on my knees. "Did Tyrian take over Trident for the business opportunity, or did he take over as a Consilium fanboy too?"

Darius's expression was thoughtful. "There's no indication that Jayce Tyrian has any involvement with the Consilium—or anything illegal, for that matter."

"That's boring." I waved the Tyrian folder. "What aren't you telling me?"

"Jayce Tyrian now has access to Trident's records, including all the artifacts that passed through the brokerage while it was under the control of a Consilium lackey. And we"—his mouth curved in a faint smile—"have an extensive list of spells and artifacts that interest the Consilium, all cataloged by Tino."

I let that sink into my gray matter. If we could get Trident's sales records, we could cross-reference them with our list of Big Bad Magic and see if the Consilium had successfully acquired a moon-exploding spell. Or worse.

"Do you think Jayce will be a 'sharing is caring' kind of guy?" I asked.

Darius's smile sharpened. "We're going to find out. He's currently in Miami for a series of meetings with Trident's executives."

I stood up from the couch. "I guess I should pack sunscreen."

"I'll send you my flight details so you can buy a ticket." He also rose to his feet. "I'll see you at the airport at 6:30 a.m."

I groaned. Early morning mission flights were the absolute worst. How was I supposed to be at my warping best when I didn't get enough beauty sleep? And was there a sane person on the planet who could get genuinely restful shut-eye whilst being shuttled across the continent with a Planck length of legroom, in a vibrating metal cylinder going a thousand kilometers per hour, forty thousand feet above the ground?

Darius left me with the folder on Jayce Tyrian and headed home, presumably to prepare for our beachside date with our new potential informant.

As I packed my bag for the trip—sunscreen absolutely included; otherwise, I'd return to Vancouver the color of boiled lobster—I pondered what sort of excuse to give Blythe about my impromptu Miami getaway. I couldn't cherry-pick another Kade-related interviewee, not with that slippery shit stain in Vancouver.

It wasn't until I was stripping down to get ready for bed that I noticed the notification on my phone. I'd missed a text from Lienna.

> How did it go today? Any insights from
> Captain Blythe after your trip?

I'd already filled her in on my interview with Kade's old schoolteacher, but not my perilous adventure aboard the Arizona Express with Darius. He'd been very clear that no lines of communication were safe. She didn't have a clue that I was up to anything besides investigating Kade, and even then, I had to be careful with what I shared. I hated keeping her in the dark.

I sat on the edge of my bed, staring at her message for a minute, debating what I could safely share and what I should hide to keep her concern-o-meter from skyrocketing. If I were in her shoes, I'd want to know that the psychopathic killer who'd planned to slowly torture us to death was back in town. All the bounty guilds in the city knew he was here, so it wasn't a secret.

I started typing.

> No insights from Blythe, but I got a
> mindful from Kade himself. He's back in
> Vancouver, and it looks like his mysterious
> extra magic is telepathy. Blythe has all
> the bounty guilds on the hunt for him.

I read it over before hitting send, hoping I'd successfully walked the line between serious and nonchalant. I didn't want her worrying about me when she had her family to take care of.

A minute passed, but she didn't respond. It was after midnight. She was probably asleep.

I zipped my thumbs across the digital keyboard again.

```
I'm heading out of town first thing in the
morning, so I'll be well out of Kade's way.
But I might not be reachable while I'm on
the road. Call you when I'm back. Hope you
and your family are doing okay.
```

I almost hit send, then stopped to add three more words.

```
I miss you.
```

I sent the message off, set my phone on the nightstand, and rubbed my hands over my face. Long-distance relationships were hard—especially when your exact relationship was so undefined.

Lienna still hadn't replied by the time I set my alarm for an ungodly hour and crawled into bed. A lonely ache burrowed into my chest. Not for the first time over the past five months, a traitorous thought circled my exhausted brain.

Was Lienna ever coming back?

"WHAT DID YOU TELL HER?" Darius asked as he parked our rental convertible on an ocean-side street. Palm trees and sand separated us from the water, and we were half a block away from a marina full of speedboats and yachts. A gentle breeze washed over our faces, keeping the humid heat at bay.

Directly opposite us across the road was the massive white skyscraper that housed Trident Ltd. on the fifty-eighth, fifty-ninth, and sixtieth floors.

It had taken a wee bit of persuasive Kit-charm to convince the distinguished guild master to pick the cherry red convertible off the rental lot instead of a nondescript gray sedan. But we were in Miami! I wore a lightweight, short-sleeved shirt, unbuttoned past my collarbone, a pair of salmon-pink shorts, and a heavy base coat of SPF 60.

The only warm-weather apparel I'd skipped was sandals, just to be safe. The last thing I wanted to do was blow a mission by tripping over my own feet while chasing after a rogue Floridian mage or something.

Darius, on the other hand, had opted for a business casual, white dress shirt and brown belt outfit. It was so simple, yet he still looked like he belonged on the cover of GQ. Everything about him said, "When I tell you this vintage of cabernet franc has notes of smoked raspberry and dried dark cherry, I'm not bluffing—my palate is just that refined." Whereas I looked like I'd ask a bartender for whatever cocktail was fruity enough to mask the taste of vodka.

I adjusted the oversized aviator sunglasses I'd picked up at the airport. "What did I tell who?"

"Your captain."

"With Kade in Vancouver, I couldn't concoct a plausible excuse to travel." I stared down at my shirt, wondering if the number of unbuttoned buttons had crossed the line from suave to skeezy. "I told her I was taking a personal day to catch up on sleep while the guilds got a head start on tracking him down. She seemed suspicious, but that's probably because I've never taken a personal day before."

Darius arched an eyebrow but didn't comment. His gaze turned to the curved architecture of the skyscraper across from us. "Are you ready?"

"We could just enjoy this beautiful day for a smidge. My pale skin aches for the sun."

"I just watched you smother yourself in an entire bottle of sunscreen."

"Yeah, I want vitamin D, not melanoma."

Darius opened his door. "We can sunbathe after we get what we came for."

The skyscraper's lobby had been uglified by an interior designer who clearly thought art deco was the only viable option for a luxury office building. The relentless fusillade of gold-inlaid geometric shapes and crisscrossing lines gave me a headache before Darius and I even reached the elevator. We rode the high-speed lift up to the fifty-eighth floor and emerged just around the corner from the receptionist's desk.

As we walked in, I craned my neck to take a gander at the ceiling forty-five feet above us. Equally tall glass walls revealed the three levels of open office space that surrounded the reception area. In the center, a steel-and-marble spiral staircase wound up to the top floor. I could see workers milling about on the second and third floors above me.

"Whoa," I muttered. "I guess artifact brokering pays the rent, huh?"

"It's time for your badge," Darius replied in an undertone as we approached the receptionist.

"Good morning, gentlemen," she said with a perfectly practiced smile, her gaze shifting from my loud beachcomber garb to Darius's much classier ensemble. "How can I help you today?"

"Hey there." I pulled my badge out of my pocket and flashed it at her. "MPD. We'd like to have a chat with Mr. Tyrian."

The receptionist's smile didn't so much as bobble, but her eyes brightened with interest. "Of course. Let me see if Mr. Tyrian is available."

"Thanks a bunch."

She picked up her phone and tapped a button. Her gaze flicked between us, her curiosity obvious. I guess administrative work at Trident Ltd. didn't offer a lot of excitement.

With the skill only a seasoned receptionist possessed, she spoke into the phone too quietly for me to catch more than a few words, even though I was barely three feet away. But I definitely heard "MagiPol" and "agents" and "ruggedly handsome."

She was probably talking about Darius.

She ended the call and smiled again. "Mr. Tyrian is just finishing up a meeting. Please have a seat while you wait."

The ruggedly handsome GM and I took a seat on the pristine white lounge chairs across from her desk, my gaze scanning the office and its convenient glass walls.

Revving up my psychic engine, I dropped a widespread halluci-bomb that would hide my voice from prying ears.

"Three cameras," I murmured.

Darius nodded absently as he smoothed his beard, four fingers turned toward me. I checked again and spotted the fourth camera half behind the spiral staircase.

"Security?" I asked.

He nodded again, gesturing surreptitiously at a gray-suited man loitering on the second floor. My gaze swept across the enormous space, picking out four more men in identical outfits who were positioned at strategic corners and junctions.

The receptionist circled her desk, her heels clicking against the marble floor, and gestured at us to rise. "Mr. Tyrian will see you now. This way, please."

We nodded our thanks and made our way up the spiral staircase. As we walked, I could see Darius's eagle eyes carefully taking in details across the office. The doors all had security panels beside them, likely requiring a key card or fob, and I was going to go ahead and assume the staff didn't leave their computers unlocked either.

At the top of the stairs, the receptionist stepped aside to reveal the big boss man himself waiting for us with a charming, vaguely questioning smile. He looked almost exactly like his photo, albeit with a bit more white in his hair and a few more wrinkles.

"Agent Garabaldi," I said, shaking his hand.

"Agent Delaware," Darius told him as he also stepped forward for a firm handshake.

As far as off-the-cuff pseudonyms went, it was hard to go wrong with a random state. The same couldn't be said for Canadian provinces. "Agent Newfoundland" sounded more like a shaggy crime-solving cartoon dog than a respectable MPD agent.

I, on the other hand, had put careful thought into my fake name. Agent Gavin Garabaldi was a former extreme athlete turned devil-may-care MagiPol operative who used his world-class skydiving and wakeboarding skills to take down rogue villains across the globe.

Tyrian led us into his office, which took up an entire corner of the top floor. Massive windows offered a picturesque view of the ocean. Conveniently, there were no security cameras in view.

Tyrian sat behind his massive glass-topped desk, while Darius and I took our seats in the plush leather chairs across from him.

"Thank you for making time to speak with us," Darius said in a smooth, professional tone. "We'll keep it quick."

"I appreciate that." Tyrian clasped his hands, focusing entirely on Darius. "It's a pleasure to meet you, Agent Delaware. I thought I knew all the senior agents from our precinct."

And what was Agent Garabaldi? Chopped liver? I guess in the eyes of this aging plutocrat, being young and underdressed disqualified me from any form of respect or acknowledgment.

"I spent the last few years abroad," Darius said, leaning back comfortably. "I was interested to see what opportunities I could find at the international level."

Tyrian looked interested, still maintaining his utter neglect toward me. "Where did you end up?"

Since Darius had this part of the job handled, I would get a head start on our primary objective: finding Trident's artifact files. Dropping a halluci-bomb in case anyone from the lobby below happened to be peeping on their boss, I left a Split Kit to smile vacantly in my seat. The real me stood up, extricating myself from the doldrums of this conversation.

"I joined Special Investigations," Darius answered.

As I circled Tyrian's desk, the businessman sat forward, genuinely intrigued. "Really? I spent a decade in the Finance Department, and the watercooler talk about Special Investigations was always … fascinating."

Before I could worry that Darius was in over his head with this conversation, he answered without hesitation.

"That's what attracted me to the department." He gave Tyrian a sharklike smile as I scooted behind the CEO's desk. "The scope and impact of the cases was highly appealing."

"From what I've heard, Special Investigations doesn't have dull cases. What brought you back stateside?"

I peered at Tyrian's computer monitor—an email from his personal assistant about scheduling a flight back to Pittsburgh—then continued past him to check out the bookshelf behind his desk. The walnut shelves were laden with fat, leather-bound tomes he'd probably never touched.

Darius casually crossed his ankles, oh so relaxed. "You may have heard that Special Investigations utilizes contractors for a lot of their fieldwork. If you think managing employees is tiresome, try headstrong mercenary types."

As Tyrian snorted in amusement, I noticed a book that had been turned around, spine facing inward. Incorporating it into my warp, I slid the book out to read the title: *Forgotten Secrets to Masculine Wealth*.

Cool. Seeing as this bookshelf was a waste of both space and the written word, I continued past it. Where would Tyrian store the secret stuff?

"After a while," Darius went on, matching Tyrian's level of self-importance, "I realized I'd become a middle manager for contractors, and that wasn't to my taste."

"I'm selfishly pleased to have an agent of your experience back in Miami." Tyrian's tone shifted slightly, still amicable but more pointed. "What can I do for you today?"

My ears perked up. The conversation was finally moving from a schmooze-fest toward the heart of why we'd flown across the entire damn continent.

"As you're aware, our precinct did a brief investigation into Mickey Gomez's activities," Darius said, referring to a suspiciously abbreviated report we'd found in the MPD archives.

Tyrian nodded, undoubtedly familiar with his financially fishy predecessor.

As I moved away from the desk, I homed in on what looked like a nifty, supermodern wall with seams that formed a rectangular grid. Layering it into my warp so the masculinely wealthy CEO wouldn't notice me messing around, I pushed on one. It dipped inward, then popped out, revealing a wide drawer stuffed with file folders.

Greetings and salutations, mysterious compartment full of potentially damning documents.

"It seems there was a clerical error," Darius continued, "and certain reports were missed. With your permission, I'd like to collect some documents from Mr. Gomez's tenure."

I couldn't see Tyrian's face, but the displeased "hmm" he emitted was not a good sign. Not knowing how long this interview would last, I hurriedly flipped open the first file folder in the drawer. It was packed to the margins with numbers and graphs that made precisely zero sense to me, but I assumed would make a whole lotta sense to a corporate accountant.

"We have no need to see anything after the acquisition," Darius assured him.

I glanced over my shoulder to see Tyrian lean back in his chair. Despite all the sociable old-boys-club bonding he and Darius had done, the artifact magnate's body language had morphed into a distinctly *un*friendly posture.

Picking up the pace of my search, I risked an array of paper cuts by zipping through the drawer's folders as fast as my fingers would let me—more numbers, more graphs, a handful of charts involving names, dollar signs, and multidigit codes.

Nothing I could make heads or tails of without a calculator and a few hours of spare time. Neither of which I currently possessed.

"Captain Atkinson assured me," Tyrian said after a long, weighty pause, "that the MPD would not subject my company to further nuisance regarding Mr. Gomez's tenure."

The Miami precinct's captain had personally promised to butt out? How much weight did Tyrian's preferences carry with the local MPD? He wasn't even from this state.

"The captain couldn't push the report through in its current condition," Darius said, his tone suggesting this was all a mild inconvenience. "We need to appear a bit more thorough. I'll make sure we're in and out quickly, minimal nuisance, and then we can be done with it for good."

To my ears, that was a solid argument. But I wasn't a multigazillionaire business mogul. Closing the drawer of financial documents, I opened the next one.

"In that case," Tyrian replied, "you must have a warrant."

Yikes. So much for buttering Tyrian up. Figuring this interview would be shortly drawing to a close, I skimmed the file labels in the drawer I had open, shoved it closed, and opened the next.

Darius lowered his voice as though sharing a secret. "A warrant would add to the nuisance factor for both of us, as you know."

Seeing nothing that resembled artifact deals, I closed that drawer and popped a fourth open.

"My apologies, but I don't provide anything to the MPD without a warrant. It's a professional policy." Tyrian's chair rolled across the floor. "It was a pleasure meeting you, Agent Delaware. I hope you can close out the case involving Mr. Gomez without further delay."

That was a not-so-veiled "screw off," if I'd ever heard one. I ran my fingers across the file labels, which were all nonsensical numbers. I pulled one out and peeked inside to find a page labeled "Certificate of Authenticity" and a lovely photo of a very magicky-looking silver dagger with a rune-etched blade.

"I'll do what I can, Mr. Tyrian." Darius scuffed his feet against the floor with unnecessary volume to notify me that he'd stood up. "Thank you for your time."

I shoved the drawer shut, spun around, and made my Split Kit stand up and smile vacantly at Tyrian. Not that it mattered. For all the attention Tyrian was paying me, I could've warped myself into Tony the Tiger and informed him that his cooperation was *grrrrrrreat!* and he still wouldn't have noticed.

I merged with my Split Kit as Tyrian escorted us to the office door. It opened as we reached it, held by one of the gray-suited security guards. He watched passively as we exited, closed the door, then trailed us as we headed down the spiral staircase.

"Have a lovely day, agents," the receptionist said cheerily as we passed her desk.

Positively brimming with a dearth of any discernible personality, the security guard followed us all the way to the elevator, pressed the call button, and stared blankly until the doors chimed and slid open. Darius and I stepped inside, and I gave the expressionless goon a toothy smile as the elevator closed.

Except it hadn't closed. I was holding the "open door" button while simultaneously unleashing a halluci-bomb across all three levels of the Trident office.

"Ready?" I asked Darius.

"Let's go."

I tapped the ground floor button, then Darius and I stepped out of the elevator in unison. The elevator began its lonely, passenger-free descent as we followed the security guard's trail back into the massive office space, completely unseen by any prying eyes—either human or technological.

While I rendered us both invisible to every mind in the vicinity, Darius was utilizing his lumina magic to bend the light around us, screening our existence from the snooping lenses of the four cameras that populated the space.

Over the past five months, I'd mastered the ability to not only make my fashionable friend invisible, but also to exclude his mind from the requisite halluci-bomb. It required an extra dollop of brain effort from me, but it spared him from the disconcerting sensory numbness of his own body being erased from his perception. I was basically doing the work that Lienna's cat's eye necklace normally did for her.

Side by side, we walked back across the reception area and straight up the stairs. I kept close to Darius's elbow so he didn't have to bend as much light to hide me from the cameras. The security guard was a dozen steps ahead, also heading for the top floor.

"That fancy wall in Tyrian's office is full of hidden drawers," I said, my voice audible only to Darius. "I think the fourth one from the left has files with artifact information. You should start there."

Darius nodded. He tended to get very quiet whenever we were up to something covert. Old habits, maybe. He'd done a lot of assassining without a psycho warper around to suppress the noise he made.

Reaching the top level, we shadowed the security guard as he knocked on Tyrian's office door. Inside, the business mogul was on the phone, and he didn't look pleased. He waved at the guard to enter, giving me and Darius the perfect opportunity to slip inside as well.

"Delaware, that's what I said," Tyrian snapped into the phone. "What about Garibaldi? Not a single agent by either name?" His jaw flexed, and his voice dropped ominously low.

"You promised me no interference, Atkinson. Now I have no choice but to deal with these rogue agents myself."

I made a silent "yikes" expression at Darius. Was Tyrian suggesting what I thought he was suggesting?

"I do hope you can keep your end of our deal," Tyrian finished, threat clear in his tone. He dropped the phone back onto its cradle, then looked at his security guard. "Bring those two 'agents' back here. Use the telethesian if you need to."

The guard nodded sharply, turned on his heel, and left the office.

I glanced at my invisible comrade. "I think our time is going to be much shorter than we hoped."

"Keep him distracted," Darius murmured.

"Got it."

As Darius headed for the wall of hidden filing drawers, I added a layer to my halluci-bomb to keep his clandestine inspection concealed. Tyrian, meanwhile, was drumming his fingers against his desk, face hard with anger. With a huff, he stood up.

Son-of-a-pirate-wench. If he was headed for the filing drawers, I'd have no time to stop him from colliding with Darius.

Quickly, I locked onto his mind and made his phone ring, drawing his attention back to his desk.

The CEO dropped into his chair and snatched up the phone. "Yes?"

"Hello, Jayce. Do you know who this is?"

Tyrian frowned. He didn't seem to recognize the slow, ominous drawl of Morpheus from *The Matrix*.

"I've been looking for you, Jayce," my Laurence Fishburne impersonation continued.

"Who is this?" Tyrian snapped, peering at the blank display on his desk phone for a clue about the caller's identity.

I kept half an eye on him and the other half on the rest of the office. Through the glass wall, I could see Tyrian's main security man, now joined by two more gray-suited men. One of them—the telethesian, I assumed—was pacing back and forth in front of the reception desk like a bloodhound trying to catch a scent.

"I don't know if you're ready to see what I want to show you," Morpheus rumbled in Tyrian's ear. "But unfortunately, you and I have run out of time."

It was almost eerie how well Morpheus's movie line matched reality—the trio of blandly attired security stooges were sprinting toward the spiral staircase, following the psychic trail Darius and I had created on our return from the elevator.

Behind me, Darius was rifling through folders at the speed of a professional card shuffler. I really hoped he found something useful in there.

"Who the hell is this?" Tyrian snarled.

"They're coming for you, Jayce," I had Morpheus say as I watched the telethesian lead the two other security guards up the final few steps. "And I don't know what they're going to do."

Tyrian's jaw clenched, a vein pulsing in his cheek. "What the hell are you talking about?"

"Stand up and see for yourself," Morpheus suggested just as the door to the office burst open.

Right on cue, fellas. I was mildly proud of my timing, but more than a trifle concerned that Darius's search efforts would be cut short.

I backed toward the silver fox as Tyrian slammed his phone down and swiveled angrily to face his coterie of intruding security personnel.

"What are you doing?" he barked. "I told you to bring me those agents."

"Their trails lead back up here," the telethesian said. "They're somewhere in this office."

"What? I'm the only one in here."

The telethesian's head whipped around as he searched for us with an unexpected air of desperation. "They have to be here. Maybe they're hiding."

Tyrian scanned his sparsely furnished and mostly glass office with an ounce of exaggeration, as if to emphasize that his interior designer hadn't incorporated an abundance of hidey-holes. I concentrated on my warp as Darius closed a filing drawer and opened another, trusting me to keep him hidden.

"There are two trails leading into your office," the telethesian insisted. "Only one trail out. They couldn't have gone anywhere else."

"Are you certain?" Tyrian asked, a new, acidic note in his voice.

"Yes," the telethesian said with confidence marred by a clear tinge of fear.

"In that case …" Tyrian gestured at his main security guy. "If he doesn't find the two agents in the next ten seconds, shoot him in the head."

The telethesian stiffened. Without so much as a surprised blink, the security guard pulled a black handgun from a holster inside his jacket and pointed it at the telethesian.

Holy shit. I didn't know which was scarier—Tyrian ordering the murder of an employee or the unquestioning obedience of the employee about to murder his coworker. Had Tyrian learned how to run a business from Dr. Evil?

Actually, on second thought, this was probably standard operating procedure straight out of the CEO handbook.

"Oh god," the telethesian gasped, obviously terrified. "Okay, okay, okay."

"Darius …" I muttered, amplifying my voice in his head. The situation was one twitchy index finger away from devolving into a scene out of *Pulp Fiction*, and we needed to get going ASAP.

Darius was leaning over his fourth drawer in the wall, a folder in his hands. I couldn't see what it contained, but it had completely ensnared his attention. Hopefully whatever he was looking at was worth the shitshow we were about to find ourselves in.

The telethesian took a few steps toward me, most likely using his powers to follow the psychic scent I'd left in my wake. I backed up another step.

"Five seconds," Tyrian warned, his expression devoid of empathy as his employee shook with fear. The security guard with the gun hadn't wavered in his aim.

The telethesian stepped closer to me. If I stepped back again, I would collide with Darius, who'd now pulled a second folder from the drawer and was flipping through it at high speed.

"Three," Tyrion snapped.

"Darius?" I said out of the side of my mouth as the telethesian turned in a confused, terrified circle, unable to reconcile what he could sense with what his eyes were telling him.

"Two."

Darius glanced up, giving me a look I could read perfectly. "Just handle it" was more or less the gist.

"One!"

In the split second before he could pull the trigger, I locked onto the gun-toting lackey's brain and flooded his neurons with the sudden, searing sensation of his pistol heating up to approximately a thousand degrees Celsius.

The security guard yelped, dropped the gun, and clutched his hand in agony.

Time for another distraction—a bigger one.

Before Tyrian could pick up the gun and splatter the telethesian's brains all over the wall himself, a deep, booming *whump-whump-whump* sound filled the office. Tyrian and his men looked around in confusion.

From outside the floor-to-ceiling window, a large black helicopter descended to hover on the other side of the glass. A black-clad and grim-looking Keanu Reeves gripped the handles of an M134 Minigun—which, despite its name, was not "mini" at all. Its six-bullet barrel was pointed straight into the office.

"What?" Tyrian gasped, and I was vaguely annoyed that he'd gotten his line wrong.

Keanu—I mean, Neo—opened fire. The window shattered, and all four men dove for nonexistent cover as three thousand rounds per minute tore up the floor. The sound of gunfire was deafening, layered with shattering glass, the roar of the helicopter's blades, and the absolute demolition of Tyrian's book collection.

In short, it was *awesome*.

I aimed the warp at the four men in the room with me, sparing Darius and everyone else from a possible heart attack.

As I added swaths of shattering marble floor tiles across the office, I had to resist the very powerful urge to do it all in dramatic slow motion, which would definitely interfere with the realism.

As Tyrian and his men frantically crawled into the corners of the office, Darius shoved the filing drawer shut. He had a small stack of folders under his arm.

He glanced at the grown men cowering and shouting as they crawled around, shielding their heads from shrapnel that Darius couldn't see.

Eyebrows raised, he looked back at me. "Shall we?"

"Yes," I agreed calmly while making Neo obliterate Tyrian's desk with his never-ending supply of ammunition. "Let's."

And so we did, the ongoing scene of completely innocuous carnage still raging in our wake. It wasn't until we'd reached the bottom of the spiral staircase that I dropped the warp, leaving Tyrian and his men to abruptly discover a pristine, undamaged, and helicopter-free view of his office and the sunny ocean beyond the window, with no sign of the mysterious Agent Gavin Garibaldi and his dashing sidekick Agent Delaware to be found.

DARIUS AND I headed straight back to the airport. With stolen documents in hand and Jayce Tyrian—who clearly had both the aptitude and appetite for cold-blooded murder—on the hunt for us, lying around on a beach wasn't an option.

A few hours later, I was slumped in a cramped seat beside Darius as our direct flight home reached cruising altitude. When we'd first started our globetrotting adventures, I'd expected him to be a Business Class man, but no such luck. He was surprisingly stingy with his hard-earned dollars.

Between rushing to the airport, arranging flights, going through security, and keeping our eyes peeled for any gray-suited Trident goons, we hadn't gotten a chance to discuss, let alone delve into, the small stack of folders Darius had pilfered. Only now was he flipping through the files with thorough scrutiny. I was dying of curiosity, but I kept my mouth shut, letting him concentrate.

Ten minutes later, he closed the last folder. Separating one from the pile, he stuffed the rest into his slim carry-on bag, then opened his folder of choice and tilted it toward me. On the front page was a photo of what looked like a large-ish metal pendant with several concentric rings etched into it.

"This is it," he said, voice pitched so low I could barely hear it over the pervasive drone of jet engines.

"This is what?" I asked, leaning over our shared armrest.

"Do you remember that page from Tino's collection that you asked me about?"

"The one with the weird naked dude surrounded by magic symbols? Sure."

"I couldn't obtain the rest of the documents that went with that illustration," he told me, his gray eyes gleaming. "But this photo—this *exact* photo—was in that briefcase."

"Whoa." I took the sheet to get a closer look. "What is it?"

"I have no idea."

That was anticlimactic.

"But it and everything else in that briefcase I lost," he continued, "were related to the Consilium's efforts to collect powerful, illegal magical weapons—the kinds of weapons the MPD has been trying to suppress for centuries."

"So this thing is probably a weapon," I mused, examining the photo again. Didn't look very scary, but I already knew that meant nothing when it came to artifacts.

"And it's up for sale." Darius tapped the other documents in the folder. "This is Trident's record of the seller's $750,000 deposit to engage their brokerage services. The seller's name is redacted, but if we can track them down, we can steal the artifact before the Consilium can buy it."

"Oh shit. Do you think the Consilium was counting on their goon Gomez to deliver it to them?" I smirked. "They must be scrambling now that Tyrian is in control of Trident. From what we saw of him, even the Consilium would have trouble forcing him to do anything he doesn't want to do."

Darius nodded. "I have contacts who can help me identify the seller. We'll need to move fast. The weapon has been up for sale for five months, but now that Tyrian is in charge of Trident, the Consilium may already be moving to buy it before he can sell it to someone else."

I skimmed the details of the weapon and couldn't glean much of anything beyond it being old. Like, a millennium old. I didn't want to imagine what kind of continent-rifting, soul-devouring power it could unleash if the Consilium got their greasy paws on it.

"You work on that," I said, handing him the page and reclining my seat. "I'm going to recharge the ol' brain battery before we make landfall."

"For anything in particular?"

I heaved a sigh. "Oh, you know, just the usual—leading an investigation into the Consilium without the Consilium, my precinct, or my boss suspecting what I'm up to."

Darius made a noncommittal noise that, all things considered, could have been a little more sympathetic.

LURKING BEHIND A CUBICLE WALL, I watched Vinny swat at the solitary housefly buzzing around his head. He waved an arm in distracted irritation, focused on his monitor.

The fly bravely landed in the middle of his screen. As he reached out to squash it, I skulked toward his cubicle. The fly disappeared under his finger, then reappeared, now behind the screen. It scurried around, climbing over his icons and hiding behind his spreadsheet.

He peered at the fly. "What …?"

Behind him, I leaned close to his ear and whispered, "You might want to call IT. Looks like you've got a bug."

Startled, he spun his chair around, then sighed heavily at the sight of me. "I can't tell if I hate your warps or your puns more."

Ah, sweet normalcy. Agent Park was back to his typical bristly self, not an ounce of puppy love detectable.

He squinted at me. "You look tired. Didn't you take yesterday off?"

"In a manner of speaking." There'd been a takeoff yesterday—two if you counted both planes. I'd arrived home in the middle of the night, crashed for a few hours of restless dreams where I was trapped in a computer program while Neo berated me for getting his outfit wrong in the helicopter warp, before hauling my sorry ass into the precinct around midmorning.

When I didn't reveal any juicy details about my personal day, Vinny swiveled back to his spreadsheet. "What do you want, Kit?"

"How's it going with DRAFT?" I asked, shifting over to lean against his desk where I could see his face.

He shrugged one shoulder. "I'm waiting to hear back from one of the guys I met during that case. He worked with Kade and *definitely* doesn't like him. I think he's going to help, but I might end up having to buy him Canucks tickets."

I let out a low whistle. "Nice work. Did your DRAFT guy have anything interesting to say about Kade from when they worked together?"

"Just that Kade was a bloodthirsty son of …" Vinny cleared his throat. "A lot of profanities, mostly. Anyway, I'll let you know when I hear back from him about the reports."

I nodded. "I appreciate it, Vinny."

"Yeah, yeah," he muttered.

Zipping away from his desk, I angled toward another fellow agent. Agent Vigneault was parked in her cubicle, her thin frame bent over her computer and her tightly curled black hair bobbing along with the rhythm of her keystrokes.

"Hey, Kit," she said, flashing me a smile. "What's up?"

"Same old, same old. You got a minute?"

"Absolutely." She spun her chair to face me. "Official business or something juicier? Girl trouble, maybe? Agent Shen's still in California, right?"

Good gossipy Gabby, was the entire precinct invested in my relationship with Lienna?

"Official business," I told her. "Sort of."

"Sort of? I'm listening."

"I was wondering if you could do some digging for me. I've tried with zero luck, and you're the best agent I know when it comes to uncovering nasty business that no one else can find."

She looked even more intrigued. "Does this have anything to do with whatever secretive case you've been running with Captain Blythe?"

"I can neither confirm nor deny the involvement of our beloved leader."

She snorted. "What do you want me to dig for?"

"Not a 'what' but a 'who,' actually. Peter Kade, father of Benjamin Kade."

Vigneault's expression instantly hardened. If anyone had reason to hate Söze, Kade, and the rest of the IA shitbags who'd made our collective lives a living hell, it was Vigneault. Söze had shut down one of the biggest cases of her career, then thrown her in lockup for calling him out on it.

"Is he as scummy as his son?" she asked darkly.

"That's what I want to find out. Can you help?"

Her look was so vindictive that I half expected her to crack her knuckles. "Happily."

"Thanks, Clarice," I said, genuinely grateful to have a senior agent with hardcore detective skills on my side. "And ... be careful, okay? You know the IA is a quagmire of nasty shit. We don't need any more of their attention."

"I'll be discreet," she promised. "Is there anything else I can help with?"

The smile pulling at my lips took me by surprise. I hadn't expected the other agents in the precinct to be so willing to take on extra work—and risk—to help me. Then again, I'd never tried asking before.

"You're doing more than enough," I told her, then hesitated. "Although ... do you happen to know where Agent Tim is?"

Twenty minutes later, my arm was twisted behind me, and my face was pinned to a mat on the floor of the precinct's training room.

"And that," Agent Tim declared, his knee digging into my back, "is how you disarm and restrain a solo attacker."

From my horizontal position, I could see a dozen fledgling MPD trainees watching Tim intently. He continued speaking without taking his weight off me.

"I know what you're thinking, and not just because I can read your minds."

The students chuckled dutifully. Hardy-har, telepath humor.

The jingle of a chain accompanied his next words. "Your opponent isn't truly subdued without these."

Cold metal cuffs ratcheted closed around my wrists. Instantly, my powers died as though someone had lobotomized my psycho warping control center.

MPD-issued abjuration handcuffs—the kind every agent carried while out in the field, the kind Kade had used to hang Lienna and me from a pipe in the mechanical room of an ice rink, and the kind I had shattered by reality warping the metal into flimsy plastic.

"As you know," Tim told his class, "most Arcana spells require an incantation to activate. These handcuffs, however, are specially designed to activate as soon as the cuff closes. You only need one cuff around a mythic's wrist or ankle to cut off their magic."

And what a *wonderful* feeling it was to have your magic cut off like it had never existed in the first place. I just *loved* it.

Thankfully, Tim didn't keep me down for long. He uncuffed my wrists, and as he stepped back so I could stand, the bright, warm spot in my brain burst back to life.

"All right," Tim said, turning to his students. "We're going to partner up and try this move at half speed to start. Grab your practice cuffs from the bin by the door and get started."

Straightening my shirt, I hastened to join Tim, who was already milling between the pairs of students, observing them as they set up for the exercise.

"Can we talk *now*?" I asked him quietly.

His attention moved over his practicing students. "Until the next demo, sure."

I made a mental note to finish talking to him before he roped me into playing his punching bag again.

"It's about Kade," I said, keeping my voice low so his students wouldn't hear me over the clamor of shouts, yelps, and bodies smacking into the mats.

Tim's eyes jumped to my face. "What about him?"

"Did you notice anything unusual about him?"

The telepath scoffed. "You're gonna need to be more specific."

"I think Kade might be—"

"Hips!" Tim shouted at a nearby pair of trainees. "Use your hips!"

They nodded at their instructor, then performed the drill once more as he watched.

"Better," he said, waving at me to stick close as he wove through the practicing pairs. "Kade might be a what?"

I cleared my throat. "A telepath."

Tim gave me a sharp glance, then shook his head. "Kade's not a telepath."

"You sure?"

"Absolutely."

I frowned. "I'm really actually super certain he's not a plain old sorcerer."

Stopping to face me, Tim nodded slowly. "Yeah, I suspect he has some kind of Psychica ability. But he's definitely not a telepath."

"How can you be so sure?"

I wouldn't normally push back like this, but I had heard that murdery bastard's voice in my head, and as far as I knew, telepaths were the only psychics who could pull that off.

"Telepaths don't fare well against other telepaths," Tim explained, his gaze swinging across the dozen trainees. "Our ability involves reaching out with our thoughts, which makes it impossible for us to simultaneously guard our minds. But Kade was *always* guarded. He's obviously trained in anti-telepathy techniques, and he's very good at it. He never slipped up, not once, not even when he didn't know I was in range of his mind."

I remembered what Kade's middle school teacher had said about his sixth sense for knowing when other people were nearby.

Tim shrugged, a crease between his brows. "He's so guarded that I suspect some kind of psychic power. Something that's honed his mental control. But I don't know what. Mentalism, maybe?"

He sounded less than confident in that theory.

"Are there any abilities besides telepathy that can let a mythic project their voice into someone else's mind?" I asked.

Tim arched his eyebrows. "Of course."

"Which one?" I asked intently.

"Psycho warping, obviously."

Duh. I felt stupid for not figuring that out.

But did that mean … *no*, absolutely not. There was no plausible reality in the infinite multiverse in which Kade was *also* a psycho warper.

I stared into the distance, my vision losing focus. I couldn't detect other people the way Kade could, but I *could* vaguely sense the minds around me. It's how I targeted or excluded other people while warping even when I wasn't looking at them.

"Could he be a telethesian?" Tim asked, yanking me out of my thoughts.

I considered that, then shook my head. "No, it doesn't fit."

Just yesterday, I'd watched a telethesian confusedly search a room for me and Darius while we were only a few feet away. Kade, on the other hand, had unerringly targeted both of us whilst in our respective invisible forms at a much greater distance.

"Kade is something else," I muttered to myself. "Something more powerful."

Tim made a noise of agreement in the back of his throat, then turned to face the trainees. "Bring it in, rookies!"

The trainees pulled themselves out of the various twisted positions they were in and jogged toward us. I inched away, not done with our conversation but also leery of reprising my role as Tim's demo dummy.

"We're going to add a small twist to the exercise." Tim held up a rubber training knife. "All the same movements, but instead of throwing a punch, the attacker will be trying to stab you. The goal is to subdue them without the blade ever touching you."

Near the edge of the group, a trainee set his fingers ablaze and muttered to his neighbor, "Or I could just fry them."

Oh, great, another pyromage. At least this one wasn't a train-hopping Consilium assassin with a cartoonish haircut. He was just an ego-driven chump who thought—pardon the pun—he was hot shit.

As snickers sounded from a few other trainees, Tim clocked the arrogant flame jockey and shot him a glare. "What was that, McMillan?"

"Nothing, sir," McMillan said with zero discomfiture.

"You know what? Change of plans." Tim beckoned me toward him. "Let's do another demo."

Damn it. I should've escaped while I had the chance.

"McMillan," Tim said commandingly, "I want you to attack Agent Morris. Everyone else, stand back."

As Tim and the rest of the trainees retreated ten feet, the pyromage looked between me and his instructor, deeply skeptical.

"You want me to attack him?" he asked.

Tim nodded. "No holds barred. Go all out."

"You mean …?"

"Fire, pyromage," Tim said dryly. "I'd suggest some fire. Unless you want Agent Morris to tie you in a knot."

I raised a questioning eyebrow at the telepath, and he winked.

Okay, I guess we were doing this.

McMillan faced me and took a deep breath. I stared back at him, hands in my pockets, a deliberately bored look plastered on my face. The rookie summoned a meager fireball in the palm of his right hand and threw it at my chest.

I casually sidestepped his attack. "You can do better than that. Hit me with all you got, Charizard."

McMillan smirked. Fire swirled around his hands, and he brought them together, forming a whirling, blazing sphere the size of a basketball, then hurled it at me.

I stretched my arms wide, welcoming his attack. The flames hit me square on, wreathing my chest in orange waves. Instead of shrieking like a scalded banshee, I let out a low, cackling laugh. My body lifted until I was levitating two feet off the floor.

McMillan stared at me, his mouth hanging open. The other trainees gaped.

Maybe I could make this a lesson for all the newbies. If I'd learned anything since becoming a full agent, it was not to underestimate anyone or anything magical. And a hard lesson it'd been.

"You think you're a master of flames, little mage?" the flaming, levitating specter in the middle of the room asked in a beastly rumble. "You don't even know the meaning of fire!"

With the last word, heat roiled through the training room. The walls blackened. The padded mats sizzled, then suddenly plunged downward all around the trainees, who clustered together in sudden panic like extras in *Dante's Peak*.

Hissing, bubbling lava roiled. The room's walls had turned to jagged, blackened stone, and the tiny island of steaming, overheated boulder on which the trainees stood was the only haven amid the seething molten rock. Smoke billowed up toward clouds as dark as the sky above Mordor.

Tim and the trainees cowered in the mouth of a volcano, and the burning specter that had once been Agent Kit Morris had taken on the texture of magma as his jaw expanded, glowing red ooze falling from his mouth.

"This is fire," he boomed as they choked on torrid, sulfuric fumes. "Or more specifically," I added in a normal tone as the whole warp popped like a bubble, everything returning to normal, "this is why you shouldn't underestimate your opponent."

With that, I snapped a pair of practice handcuffs around McMillan's wrists. He twisted to look over his shoulder at me, face drained of all color. I glanced at the rest of the class, seeing the shock permeating the crowd.

I might have gone a tad overboard.

Tim cleared his throat. "All right, back to practicing against an armed opponent. Come on, everyone."

Rather sluggishly and with a lot of huffing and sweating, the students shook off their brief volcanic immersion and split into pairs again. McMillan slunk away without waiting for me to remove the cuffs.

"Holy shit, Morris," Tim muttered, moving to stand beside me. "When the hell did you learn to do *that*?"

"Do what?" I asked, confused. He had a pretty solid understanding of my warping skills, seeing as he'd been my trainer and an opponent during my field tests.

Tim stared at me. "Are you even tired?"

"Tired?" I rubbed a hand through my hair. "I mean, I didn't sleep great last night, but I downed a couple shots of espresso on my way in."

His eyes narrowed, and I could almost feel his telepathic power poking into my brain to check my sincerity.

He shook his head. "Never mind."

I frowned, fully intending to ask what the hell he was going on about, when my phone buzzed in my pocket. As Tim headed toward the trainees, I pulled the device out and unlocked the screen to find a message from Darius.

`How soon can you be here?`

I grinned, all thoughts of Tim's weird probing into my energy levels shoved to the back burner. How soon could I haul ass to the Crow and Hammer to hear what Darius had uncovered about the mysterious weapon the Consilium was so interested in? Why, as soon as I could escape the precinct.

My thumbs zipped across the keyboard, and I hit send as I strode to the door.

`Be there in an hour.`

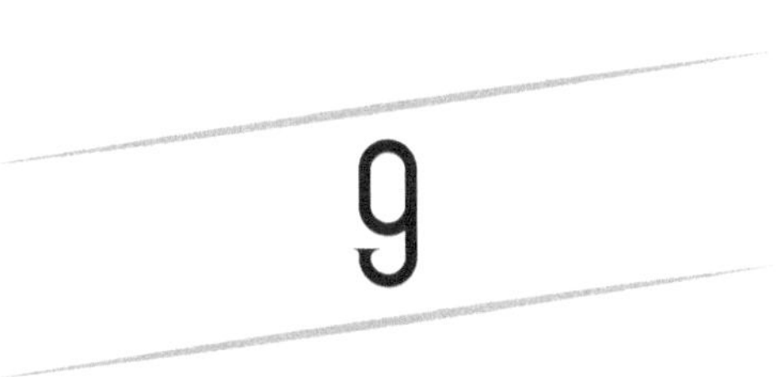

SHOWING MY FACE in public in Vancouver had never been this nerve-racking. I hated Kade even more, if that was possible, for popping up in my town again and making me wary of every shadow that crossed my path.

Before I could join Darius, I needed to swap out my clothes. The precinct's training room had a perpetual stink of newbie sweat that I was sure my outfit had absorbed, not to mention the dusty smudges my white t-shirt had acquired when Tim had flattened me against the training mat. And I kept thinking I could smell the sulfur from my impromptu Krakatoa warp. That was impossible and probably just a product of my overactive imagination, but it was annoying enough that I wanted to shower and change.

I cabbed it to my condo, not only to save time, but also to prevent a certain follicular-challenged psychopath from stalking me through downtown again. If I ever got that bastard behind bars, I'd add my taxi receipts to his tab.

Waving to the doorman on my way past, I rode the elevator up, let myself into the suite, and sighed with relief when I found it empty. Not that I didn't miss my favorite mustachioed human, but Eggsy would've delayed me with a half-hour's worth of congenial discussion about weather, food, and "those young-uns" skateboarding in front of the building. Trevor Eggert was only thirty but had real "grandpa shakes cane at cloud" energy.

Locking the door and dumping my keys on the kitchen island, I stripped off my clothes and made a beeline for the shower. After a hot and speedy scrub, I was out again and de-nuding myself. As I pulled on a hunter-green t-shirt and tugged the hem down over the waist of my jeans, a clatter from the living room pulled me up short.

Adrenaline flashed through me. It was Eggert, I told myself, not Kade. I crept toward the half-closed bedroom door, ready to slam a Blackout warp into the mind of whoever was on the other side if their face didn't come fully equipped with a well-groomed crumb catcher.

A thought popped into my head—the realization that I could, in fact, sense minds. I'd only ever used that ability to pinpoint people for warp-specific purposes, but maybe …

Squinting, I tried to focus. I detected a vague presence somewhere near the kitchen and homed in on it, feeling kind of dumb. What I was supposed to be detecting, exactly? Razor burn on a freshly shorn scalp? A *lack* of razor burn on a fuzzy upper lip? It was just a blurry, wishy-washy blob on my psychic radar.

Huh.

For some reason, my wariness-bordering-on-fear was fading into nothingness. For no real reason, I was absolutely certain that the intruder wasn't Kade. Which was crazy because there was no actual way for me to know that. Something in my subconscious eased with a sense of comfort, rather than tensing at a potential threat.

Frowning deeply, I flung the door open and stepped through it.

The first thing I saw was the six-pack of Dr Pepper on the island. That was followed by a dozen Blu-ray movies stacked beside the fizzy drinks. Finally, I saw a slim, dark-haired woman standing next to the beverage and cinema stacks, staring at me with wide brown eyes.

"Kit," she gasped, a little breathless with a hand pressed to her chest. "You scared me."

I gawked. "Lienna?"

She smiled softly. "I didn't realize you were here. I meant to surprise you ... but I guess I got the surprise."

"Let's call it even," I said, feeling a little breathless myself.

For a stunned moment, I wondered if a latent part of my brain had warped her into existence out of sheer loneliness, but I quickly realized that couldn't be the case. The Lienna I would have pulled from memory had a ponytail and an eclectic array of bangles, bracelets, and other jewelry adorning her wrists and woven into her hair.

This very real Lienna had eschewed all those knickknacks—aside from her cat's eye necklace—in favor of a simple, short-sleeved white blouse and fitted jeans. Her hair, which she wore down, had grown several inches, now a long length of sleek black that fell almost to her elbows.

A fresh, California-inspired look, but the same beautiful sorcerer I knew and loved.

When I didn't say anything else, her smile wavered. Uncertainty crept into her eyes as we stood there, the length of the kitchen between us. The last time we'd been face-to-face, we'd been snuggled up on the sofa while *The Parent Trap* played in the background. Shortly before that, she'd kissed me in a moment of adrenaline-fueled passion after we'd escaped Kade's trap.

She'd also left Vancouver without saying goodbye, and we'd had five months of separation and secrets to really amp up the awkwardness.

I didn't want awkward. Screw it, I wasn't going to *allow* awkward.

Casting my doubts aside, I strode across the distance between us, swept her into my arms, and hugged her. She gasped as I flattened her smaller frame against me, but it only took her a moment to recover. She slung her arms around my neck, her face pressed to my chest as she hugged me back just as tightly.

"I missed you," I admitted in a low voice.

"I missed you too."

We clung to each other for a few more seconds before she loosened her hold. As she leaned back, her face tilted up to mine, her eyes roving across my face as though checking my features against her memories of me. Did I look different?

Her hands slid slowly from my shoulders to my upper arms, and I was intensely aware of her waist under my hands, the warmth of her skin all too noticeable through the thin fabric. I wanted to draw her close again. I wanted to kiss her the way she'd kissed me five months ago.

But it'd been *five months*. I still didn't know why she'd left without a goodbye. Hugging her without permission, sure. Kissing her? Nuh-uh.

Even as I thought that, my disobedient gaze slid down to her mouth, tracing the shape of her soft lips.

"I can't believe you're here," I said, one half of my brain buzzing uselessly with shock while the other half debated whether I should still be holding on to her.

Those inviting lips pursed into a frown. "You say that like you didn't think I was coming back."

I took a moment too long to force a laugh. "It was just a long wait. How's your dad?"

"He's not out of the woods yet, but he's improving. My mom can handle things now, and I …" Her face hardened. "And I wasn't about to leave you on your own with Kade back in Vancouver."

"Shit," I swore, swamped by instant guilt. "I'm sorry, Lienna. I shouldn't've told you. You didn't need to leave your family because—"

"No," she interrupted firmly. "I *did* need to leave. I need to be here. You're my partner."

I'd missed hearing her say that. We were still holding each other—her hands on my shoulders, mine on her waist. She hadn't stepped back, but she also hadn't jumped my bones either, so I was out to sea on what she wanted.

"Besides," she added, that mysterious glint in her eyes. "You've been having all kinds of fun without me, and I'm tired of being left in the dark."

"More fun than you know," I told her, suppressing another wave of guilt, choosing instead to revel in the elation of her return. I arched an eyebrow. "Do you have other plans right now?"

She gave me a quizzical look. "No."

"Then let's walk and talk," I said with a grin as I finally released her waist. "We've got a date with an ex-assassin that we don't want to miss."

WE DIDN'T ACTUALLY WALK OR TALK. Instead, we hailed a cab and rode to the Crow and Hammer in silence. After keeping Lienna in the dark for months on the off chance someone was listening to my phone calls, I wasn't about to spill all that cloak-and-dagger tea within earshot of an anonymous taxi driver.

We disembarked in front of the three-story brick building that housed Darius's guild, and I led the way through the door.

The difference in atmosphere since my last visit was like jumping from a hot tub into a polar vortex. Most of the pub was empty except for a grim-faced group in combat gear loitering near the unmanned bar. They were all excessively armed for a midafternoon spot of bourbon.

"Kit. Agent Shen." Kai, the deadlier-than-average electramage who'd witnessed Kade murdering Söze alongside me and Lienna, peeled away from the group. His dark eyes swept over the two of us. "Any trouble on your way here?"

"Nope." I glanced past him at the combat group. "What's with the walking armory?"

"Kade," he said grimly. "We're not taking any chances. If he attacked the guild once, he might do it again."

My mood, which had been buoyantly floating somewhere in the stratosphere with Lienna's return, came crashing back down to sea level.

"All our combat mythics are on the hunt for him," Kai continued, "and everyone else is lying low. We're rotating guard duty here at the guild. Darius doesn't want the building left empty."

Because all our hard-won documents about the Consilium were being stored here.

"Have you got any leads on Kade's whereabouts?" I asked.

"No leads, but a few ideas," Kai replied. "We haven't seen him yet, though. What about you?"

"Not a peep since he stalked me through Gastown the day before yesterday." I shrugged my shoulders, trying to shake off some tension. "Is Darius upstairs?"

"He had to step out for a few minutes. He's coordinating with the GMs of Pandora Knights and Odin's Eye on the search." Kai waved toward the staircase. "He said you should wait for him."

"Got it."

I grabbed Lienna's hand and tugged her across the pub with me.

"Kit," Lienna said slowly as we climbed toward the third floor. "What's going on? What are we doing here?"

"Do you remember," I began as I led her to the locked door with the old boardroom behind it, "that whiteboard we found in Söze's supervillain lair?"

"The one with all the names?"

"Yeah." I pulled out my keys and unlocked the door. "Remember how Darius's name was in the center? And all the other names were connected to his?"

I pushed the door open and stepped aside, giving her a clear view of the table piled with documents.

"This is why."

Her eyes widened. She stepped past me into the room, taking in our collection of folders and stacks of paper. I closed and locked the door behind us, then joined her.

"Everything here is related to the Consilium in one way or another. Some of it dates back twenty years." I tapped the folder of names. "Like this one. Names of suspected Consilium members, supporters, and cronies."

Moving along the table, I gave her the full tour, explaining each pile and how Darius—or Darius and I—had collected it. The lists of names, the profiles, the financial records. Evidence of crimes, bribes, blackmail, extortion. A rough timeline of the Consilium's activities dating back decades.

"This one," I said, my voice dropping and bitterness weighing on me, "was Georgia Johannesen's. Twenty years ago, she helped Darius compile a record of everything magic-related that the MPD censored without due process—spells, artifacts, people, history, all stuff that disappeared from public record out of nowhere."

Grief pulled at Lienna's features as she looked at the unassuming stack of folders that had gotten the Arcana Historia guild master murdered by Kade five months ago.

"And … Anson Goodman?" she said quietly.

I stepped over to one of our largest piles. "This one. He was an investigative journalist before he became PSFF's editor. He helped Darius uncover the Consilium's top brass the first time."

She turned to me, lips pressed thin. "The first time?"

I nodded. "Yeah. Twenty years ago, Darius went to war with the Consilium."

Her face paled, but before she could respond, the lock clicked. The door opened to reveal the ex-assassin himself, his expression grimly pleased about something—but when he saw Lienna standing beside me, his face shuttered, his eyes cautious.

"Hey Darius," I said, forcing a bright note into my voice. "Look who's back! I was just filling her in on everything."

His gaze raked my face, and I could interpret the subtle "you'd better know what you're doing, Kit" look in his eyes. I gave a short, firm nod.

"Welcome to the madness, Agent Shen," he murmured with the faintest hint of his roguish humor. "I hope you're ready for this."

She pushed her shoulders back. "Absolutely. And you can call me Lienna."

He smiled briefly. "Then I'll get straight to it."

Leading us to the corner of the table beside his laptop, he flipped open a folder to reveal The Weapon. With capital letters. Since we knew less than nothing about its magical properties, all we had was conjecture—but considering it should have been lumped in with Tino's pile of Very Scary Magic, we were going on the assumption that The Weapon was likely something downright apocalyptic. Or at least apocalypse adjacent.

"It took some digging," Darius began, "but a contact of mine was able to link the seller's deposit to an account and trace that account to a person. Her name is Floris Visser."

He flipped open another folder, revealing a mythic profile complete with a grainy black-and-white photo of a lean, sharp-featured woman in her fifties with long, fair hair and narrow eyes. "She's a notorious rogue tempemage who operates throughout Western Europe, primarily in the Netherlands.

She's known for buying and selling dangerous offensive magic."

"So … *weapons*," I translated. "And our plan is to steal one very particular weapon from her—a very expensive one—before the Consilium can get their hands on it. Should be a piece of cake."

"It promises to be our most exciting excursion to date," Darius agreed. He handed me the folder on Visser. "I have a few leads on her current location. Once I confirm her whereabouts, we'll depart immediately. Keep your bags packed."

I glanced at Lienna with a wry grin. "You got it."

Darius and I had spent five months playing investigative catch-up on the Consilium's activities, but now we were finally going to get the jump on them. Visser's ancient weapon would be ours.

10

"I CAN'T BELIEVE you've been doing all this behind Captain Blythe's back."

With my chopsticks halfway to my mouth, I shrugged. Lienna's tone wasn't accusatory or remotely judgmental. If anything, she sounded impressed.

"It hasn't been fun," I admitted after swallowing my mouthful. "I'm supposed to be investigating Commissioner Sparks and figuring out who put his corrupt ass in charge of the IA, but I've barely even had time to sleep the last couple of days."

She nodded sympathetically, her attention split between me and her carton of Pad Thai. We'd spent the last five hours holed up in the Crow and Hammer's boardroom so I could fill Lienna in on all the juicy details of my parallel investigations that I hadn't been able to reveal over the phone. Darius had stuck around for the first hour, then made like an amoeba and split so he could assist with the citywide, multi-guild Kade crusade.

Left to our own devices, we'd divvied up the workload: Lienna and her savant-level Arcana knowledge had taken over Darius's laptop to dig into Floris Visser's mysterious weapon, while I'd read up on Visser herself.

For the record, she was a nasty piece of work; the kind of nastiness that rivaled Charles Manson or Cruella de Vil—she even gave Kade a run for his money in the "psychotic violence" department.

She seemed like a perfect candidate to add to my growing list of enemies.

Around hour four, Lienna and I had ordered in some Thai since the Crow and Hammer's kitchen was currently unstaffed with everyone out hunting for a certain slippery ass-hat. As we munched and worked, we batted around ideas, theories, jokes, and the occasional mildly flirtatious quip.

It felt amazing. Like wrapping yourself up in a warm, fuzzy blanket after a hard day. Or after a long, lonely five months.

I dug my chopsticks into the last of my massaman curry. "What about you? I wasn't the only one holding back while we were apart."

She looked up from Darius's laptop. "What do you mean?"

"You mentioned some hardcore spell research a couple months ago, but I never heard about the finished product."

"Oh, right." She flashed me an excited grin. "I was working on a few new spells for my cube. I got some ideas from my friend, Isla. She's an alchemy genius."

This was the first time I'd ever heard details of Lienna's pre-Vancouver social life. It was strange to think about her having friends in LA. Actually, on second thought, it was stranger to think she *wouldn't* have any friends in LA.

"At one point, we were talking about advanced studies in our Arcana fields," Lienna continued. "Improving our skills, that kind of thing. And she told me about some transmutation stuff she's been working on."

"Wait, I thought the turning-iron-into-gold type of alchemist was a myth."

"Nope, though that's not a very useful application compared to everything else transmutation can do." She gestured with her chopsticks. "It's a branch of Arcana that can get really, *really* advanced."

"Like abjuration?" I ventured. I didn't know a whole hell of a lot about the various difficulty levels of Arcana magic, aside from the fact that Lienna's specialty was Stupid Hard.

"Similar, yes," she agreed. "Abjuration is complex in a different way, though. It requires a fundamental understanding of all magic and how it interacts with abjuration techniques. There's a lot of on-the-spot problem solving, especially if you're using it in the field."

I'd witnessed that a few times, from Lienna using a calculator to plan an array in the middle of a face-off with Quentin to sealing an anti-feminist fae monster back into his human-skull prison while he tried to melt us.

"Transmutation, on the other hand, requires a high level of precision and planning," she explained. "If you don't get it perfect, it won't work and you could end up wasting weeks on a single attempt. But what it can do is incredible—and that got me thinking about your reality warps."

I leaned back in my chair. "What about them?"

"The closest magical comparison to your reality warps—at least the ones you've done so far—is transmutation." Her face lit with excitement. "Turning metal handcuffs into plastic is textbook transmutation."

I nodded slowly, absorbing that.

"You were doing one of the most complex forms of magic that exists, and you did it instantly with just your mind. I think that's why your power disappears afterward."

"I don't follow," I said with a frown. "Arcana mythics don't lose their magic when they do transmutation, do they?"

Lienna shook her head. "But we only make the spell arrays with our inherent magic. The actual magical effect, whether it's creating an artifact or transmuting something, is fueled by the energies of the earth, which are basically limitless. That's why arrays and artifacts need time to charge. They aren't using our magic. They're using the planet's magic."

"And I don't have a whole planet to draw from," I said, catching on. "Just my tiny little brain."

"Exactly. And Arcana transmutation can take days or even weeks to charge, but you do it in an instant. It makes sense that even a simple reality warp will sap all your power at once." She set her empty takeout carton aside. "That's why mages and psychics get tired after using a lot of magic. Their power source is internal and can't be bolstered with an external source like Arcana and Spiritalis."

"Huh." I fiddled with my chopsticks as I connected the proverbial dots. This was a perspective I hadn't considered. I'd been terrified that if I kept screwing with the fabric of reality, someday my powers would vanish permanently, especially since they took longer to return each time I did it.

But maybe that was because my reality warps had become increasingly difficult: when I'd changed a wand into a snake, I'd mostly altered its shape; shifting a grappling hook into an anchor had involved shape and size, including a whole schwack of added mass; and when I'd turned Kade's metal handcuffs into a plastic toy, it'd been a full-on transmutation of its elemental composition.

Thinking about that last bit made me feel a little woozy. Concentrating extra hard should *not* allow a person to rearrange molecules. It was downright unnatural.

"Anyway," Lienna said, pulling Darius's laptop closer, "I've been doing some digging about this weapon the Consilium wants. The Trident file only has basic information—that it was discovered in a Viking tomb twenty years ago and it's estimated to originate from 900 to 1000 CE."

"So real dang old," I concluded helpfully.

She flipped the laptop around to show me some kind of archaeological article on the screen. "I narrowed down all the Viking-related discoveries from around twenty years ago. There were quite a few—mostly these ring forts, which are really fascinating—and I think this is the one."

She scrolled down to a photo of what looked like a very nice field: green grass, a little hilly, the blue sky dotted with fluffy white clouds. It could've been a default Windows wallpaper from 2001.

"Is it an invisible fort?" I asked dubiously.

She rolled her eyes as though that wasn't a completely legitimate question based on the total lack of visible fort in the photo.

"The site is located a short drive southwest of Copenhagen. According to this report from the Nordic Society for Arcane

Archaeology, it was discovered by humans, but when an underground tomb with signs of magic was found beneath the fort, the MPD stepped in and handed it over to a guild to manage."

"Signs of magic? Like ultra deadly weaponry?"

"None of the documents or articles I've looked at mention weapons or artifacts. They're mostly about the remains of the fort."

I sighed. "Interesting, but I don't see how any of that helps us."

"I'll keep looking," she promised, already opening a new search. "Maybe I can find something from the human side—the people who first discovered the tomb."

"Sounds good." I grabbed our empty food containers, fed them to the garbage can, then headed for the opposite end of the table. I gathered Tino's pile of Very Scary Magic and his notes on it and returned to Lienna's side. "I'm going to have another look through here for anything else that could be related to a Viking tomb."

We worked in comfortable silence, the room filled with soft sounds of typing and shuffling paper. I couldn't help smiling, ridiculously content in spite of everything—Kade's return, our dwindling time to steal a weapon from a scary international rogue, and the Consilium's whole "world domination" thing.

As I turned through Tino's notes, I found myself gazing at a familiar page: the unusual drawing of a levitating man surrounded by symbols of magic. I studied it again, my attention lingering on the sunburst symbol filling the man's forehead.

"Hey Lienna." I held up the paper. "What do you make of this?"

She took the page and studied it. "If I had to guess, I'd say it's a depiction of all the mythic types in a single illustration. We've got the elements for mages, nature imagery for Spiritalis, and some of these symbols could represent Arcana."

"Nothing for demons, though."

Lienna shrugged. "Demonica is very old—at least three thousand years, I think—but for most of that time, it was considered a branch of Arcana, not its own magic class."

I grabbed Tino's scant notes on the page and skimmed his neat handwriting. "Our neurotic expert estimated that this drawing dates back to the early sixteenth century."

Lienna tapped her lower lip. "That's around the same time the MPD separated out the Demonica class, but this drawing might predate that change."

"What about that thing?" I tapped my finger on the sun symbol emblazoned on the man's forehead.

She quirked her lips. "Psychic magic, maybe? Why are you so interested in this?"

"That's where I can feel my power." I pressed my fingertip to my forehead. "After I reality warp and lose my powers, I feel this awful emptiness instead—and it's right there."

She made a thoughtful noise. "Do other psychics feel their power in the same place?"

"No idea. I've never asked."

"Hmm." She set down the paper. "What does this illustration have to do with the Consilium?"

"Again, no idea." I gestured to the folder beside her, flipped open to showcase the weapon's photo. "But twenty years ago, the weird magic dude drawing was in a collection of documents along with the weapon, according to Darius. He got the drawing but lost the rest."

Lienna frowned deeply as she looked between the two. "They don't seem connected. A Viking amulet from Denmark a thousand years ago and an illustration from seventeenth century Europe—they have nothing in common."

I eyed that sunburst symbol again, comparing it to the warm, bright feeling of my psychic power. Giving myself a shake, I took the drawing from her and returned it to Tino's pile.

"You know," I said as I set the whole stack down on the table, "we should call it a night. My brain has turned to mush."

Nodding, she closed the laptop, but she didn't get off her chair. Instead, she swiveled to face me. Her eyes looked into mine in an unexpectedly questioning way.

"Kit ..." She seemed to steel herself. "There's something I want to talk about."

A deep feeling of foreboding washed over me. "Okay."

She smiled wanly. "It's nothing bad. I don't think."

That did nothing to reduce my sudden and very acute sense of impending doom.

"When I went home ..." She drew in a slow breath. "I had a lot of time to think. I spent a lot of it worrying about you, and not just because I knew you were hunting Kade, traveling all over by yourself, and doing other dangerous stuff you couldn't tell me about."

I sat in the discomfort of her silence, waiting with dreaded anticipation for her to finish that thought.

She looked down at her lap. "I was also worried that I made a big mistake when I left. The way I left, I mean."

"Sneaking off while I was sleeping without saying goodbye," I clarified.

Her mouth twisted sheepishly. "I thought you might be upset—I mean, I figured you were rightfully upset that I'd left like that when things between us were kind of … up in the air."

That was an apt description—and not just because it was the title of a 2009 George Clooney movie partly about a dude struggling with his love life.

She dragged her gaze back up to me. "Being back home and taking care of my dad, it forced me to think about some stuff. Like how I tend to avoid situations or feelings that make me uncomfortable. I always told myself I was just prioritizing things that are important to me, like my job or my studies."

I watched her, scarcely breathing.

She bit her lip. "But seeing my dad so sick and being so scared that I would lose him—it put all that into perspective. I always thought I'd have time later on to figure out how I really felt about him, whether we could reconcile or not, but suddenly, time with him wasn't guaranteed."

I nodded. That was a lesson I'd learned in the hardest way possible. It was a lesson I carried with me deep in my chest.

She took a moment to collect her thoughts. "My relationship with my dad isn't the only uncomfortable feeling I've been avoiding. There's also … us."

I flinched, and her eyes widened.

"Wait, no—I don't mean that I'm uncomfortable with you. I mean I didn't want to deal with the—the *complications* of us. Because … because I really want there to be an 'us,'" she finished in a small voice.

Oh.

Oh, wow.

I had to swallow twice before I could speak. "You do?"

"Yes." Her confidence returned and she straightened. "I was holding back because of Captain Blythe's warning, and how everyone says not to get involved with coworkers, and I didn't want to ruin our friendship, and … well, we've been dealing with a lot of other stuff—all the life-and-death cases, you know."

"There's been a lot of that," I agreed, my voice a little hoarse.

"But I don't want my fear of complications to hold me back. I don't want to wait until it's too late."

"Too late for what?" I asked softly, not wanting to make any assumptions about her meaning.

A slow flush rose in her cheeks. As she hesitated, I leaned forward, my focus on her intensifying. Was she saying what I thought she was? Had she changed her mind about the possibility of becoming more than friends? More than partners of the work variety?

I needed to know so badly. My heart pounded as I stared at her, my eyes trying to drill straight into her head so I could see what she was thinking.

What if he doesn't want to be with me that way?

Her voice was the faintest whisper, almost too quiet for me to hear.

"I do," I blurted.

She jolted. "What?"

"I really, definitely do," I said in a rush. "I've wanted that for a long time."

"Wanted what?"

My rising hope faltered. "To be with you."

She stared at me like I'd sprouted a face full of tentacles, Davy Jones style.

"You asked … you asked whether I wanted to be with you," I ventured uncertainly. "And I—"

"No, I didn't." She was looking less confused and more freaked out by the second. "I didn't say that. I didn't say anything."

"What? But I heard you—"

"I was *thinking* that, Kit."

"Thinking?" I repeated, feeling stupider by the second. "That doesn't make any sense."

"Kit …" She drew in a deep breath. "What am I thinking?"

If she hadn't looked so deadly serious, I would've made a silly quip about that being an unfair starting point for a romantic relationship.

"Lienna, what are you talking about?"

She leaned forward. "Concentrate, Kit. What am I thinking?"

Unnerved and more than a little confused, I settled into my chair and squinted at her face. This was nuts. I couldn't read her mind, even if I concentrated as hard as I—

—matcha. My grandma's favorite dessert is matcha. My grandma's favorite dessert is matcha. My grandma—

My eyes widened and I jerked back. I could hear her voice, but her mouth wasn't moving. There was no sound in my ears. I could hear her *inside my head.*

"Matcha," I whispered.

Her repetitive stream of grandma sentences stopped, and I caught a sharp "*holy shit*" from her mind before I tore my focus away from her. I turned my chair sideways and stared at the wall instead.

"Lienna," I muttered, feeling like the ground had become dangerously unsteady beneath my feet.

"Kit," she replied. Her breath rushed out. "I don't think Kade has any telepathic ability."

Feeling like I was on the precipice of a very dangerous cliff, I glanced at her, and our eyes met as she dropped the figurative bomb she was holding right on my head.

"I think you do."

"OKAY," I SAID for roughly the zillionth time. "But I'm a psycho warper. Not a telepath."

Lienna and I were walking along a quiet Yaletown street. It was late, and the typically bustling, restaurant-laden neighborhood was almost completely devoid of people. A purple glow cast diffused light over the city as the sun crept below the buildings in the west.

"You read my mind," she pointed out yet again. "Several times. It took you all of ten minutes to figure out how to do it on command."

"All I'm doing is concentrating really hard on the feeling of your mind. I've always been able to vaguely sense minds—but never *read* them. This has never happened before."

"Except with Kade."

We'd left the Crow and Hammer twenty minutes ago, but with my newly discovered, impossible-to-explain mind-reading ability, Lienna hadn't wanted to leave me alone. We were a block away from her apartment, where she would pack a suitcase before we returned to the condo. Depending on when Darius confirmed Floris Visser's location, we might need to leave in a hurry.

"There must be a logical explanation," she muttered.

"There's nothing logical about this." I started ticking things off on my fingers. "Psychics having two completely separate abilities isn't a thing, as far as we know. Psycho warping doesn't include telepathy, as far as we know. And I didn't have this ability before now."

"As far as we know," she added. "Maybe you've had it all along and you only just … unlocked it or something."

"What am I—a video game character? I reached the prerequisite XP level and my next psychic ability popped onto my action bar?"

"I don't know, Kit." She smiled wanly. "It's not a bad thing, though, right? Telepathy is really useful. You should talk to Agent Tim first thing tomorrow."

"No," I said, waving my hands in a negative. "Nope. Nuh-uh. That's a bad idea."

She frowned. "Why?"

"For the same reason we're keeping my reality warping on the DL, and also because spontaneously developing new abilities isn't normal, Lienna. I don't think I should start blabbing about it just yet."

"I guess so," she said, not sounding particularly convinced.

I, on the other hand, was *completely* convinced. Maybe I'd been hanging around a certain cagey ex-assassin too long, but I was more convinced that I shouldn't be revealing my multifaceted psychic skills to anyone than I was about declaring *M*A*S*H* the greatest sitcom ever made.

And that was saying something.

"Let's shift gears," I said, reaching out to take her hand. "The whole telepathy thing derailed us. You were talking about us."

She nodded, quiet for a long moment. We were approaching a small square between rows of restaurants. Tall, heavy trees curled over the square, with an art installation that featured a couple dozen colorful umbrellas strung between them, providing the benches below with whimsical shelter from the city's perpetual drizzle.

"Right," she finally said, curling her fingers more tightly around mine. "I wanted to ask if you—"

With squealing tires, a black Sprinter van came to a sliding halt at the edge of the square across from us. The side door flew open, and two men jumped out. While that alone was rather suspicious, the fact that the men were dressed in black combat gear had us instantly shifting into defensive mode.

"Consilium?" I guessed tersely. "Or a random assassination attempt by one of our many enemies?"

Lienna didn't answer. She'd already pulled out her wooden Rubik's cube and was spinning segments in rapid succession.

With a quick glance around the square and surrounding streets to confirm the four of us were all alone—no passersby, no innocent civilians, no dog walker who might end up with a vampire hand in their poor mutt's jaws—I targeted the two stormtroopers.

One Death-Star-strength Blackout warp, incoming. I slammed the sensory deprivation into their brains, expecting them to seize up, scream, collapse, and plead for me to stop. You know, the usual.

Except they didn't.

"Uh, Lienna?" I muttered. "My warps aren't working on them."

She smiled tightly as she finished twisting her cube. "I'll take care of them. *Ori gravitatis lapido pilis!*"

That wasn't an incantation I'd heard before. As the final syllable left her lips, the cube erupted like a Roman candle, lobbing sparkling, fist-sized shooting stars in rapid succession. Lienna tilted the cube and stepped away from me to adjust her aim as the glowing spots with fizzing orange tails arched toward the goons.

When the first projectile hit the ground, it ballooned for a split second into an eyeball-searing flash that collapsed in on itself like a dying star. Both enemy mythics were yanked violently toward the miniature black hole with the power of a thousand vacuum cleaners.

The next fizzy blob of magic smacked into the ground six feet away, and with a flash, the unprepared goons were sucked toward that one instead. Each subsequent projectile had an equally brutal effect—the moment it connected with a solid surface, it flashed, collapsed, and pulled everything around it toward its center in an awe-inspiring gravity implosion. The men, along with their weapons and other debris, were jerked around like marionettes under the control of a particularly violent puppeteer—left, right, forward, and back. The final magical firework hit one of the suspended umbrellas, and with a flash, it whipped the two men eight feet into the air before dropping them onto the ground with a bone-crunching *thump*. It was the perfect finale to the light show.

"Wow," I murmured.

With a proud grin, Lienna dashed forward to cuff the goons. I followed at an ambling pace, enjoying our fantastical victory.

A quiet pop from somewhere on my right. A flash of movement. A blast of pain through my cheek as something struck me. Then the cold rush of a liquid running down my face—and the terrifying spin of the square as my vision blurred.

I'd been hit with a potion.

Its effect was instant, sucking my brain toward oblivion. As I sagged bonelessly, a hazy figure materialized and a burly pair of hands grabbed my shoulders, dragging me away.

The last thing to penetrate my awareness was the fading shape of Lienna, halfway across the square, screaming my name.

MY FIRST SENSE to awaken was smell. A strong, musty stench of sweat and dust pummeled my nostrils.

Next came pain. My shoulders burned, my hands were numb, and my kneecaps throbbed sharply.

Finally, my sight returned. A bizarre assortment of geometric shapes slowly came into focus. Directly in front of me was a worn workout bench patched with peeling duct tape. A few rusted dumbbells were stacked next to it, and a row of dusty, outdated treadmills, stationary bikes, and ellipticals were lined up against the wall behind it.

Wait … was this actually the afterlife? Maybe there had been some horrible clerical error at the Pearly Gates and I'd been sent to Valhathletica—the Viking graveyard for gym equipment and purgatory for CrossFit enthusiasts, where the rivers ran thick with protein shakes, it only rained creatine, and the angels had six-packs but skipped leg day.

"Agent Morris."

At the sound of that gravelly voice, my woozy contemplation of the hereafter burned away in a surge of adrenaline. This definitely wasn't the afterlife. Or, if it was, it was hell.

Kade stepped into my line of sight. His bald head, broad shoulders, fitted black shirt, black combat pants, and heavy boots were the most unappealing things I'd ever seen.

For the second time this year, I'd been taken captive by this follicle-free fucker.

As I stared at him, battling a flood of fear, my sharpened awareness put together the rest of the intense physical discomfort inundating my body.

My hands were tied above my head. I was on my knees, and my feet were firmly secured behind me. Kade had strung me up so that I was leaning forward, putting extra strain on my shoulders. I couldn't see everything around me, but I guessed I was tied up inside a weight rack, my arms bound to the pull-up bar somewhere above my head.

As my gaze swung sharply around, I saw nothing but fluorescent lights and decaying exercise paraphernalia. I'd been half-right with my afterlife assessment; I was trapped in a gym equipment graveyard.

My only comfort: Lienna wasn't strung up beside me. My woozy recollection placed her halfway across the square and significantly more conscious than yours truly when Kade had snatched me. I hoped she was safe.

"Welcome back," Kade said, sitting down on the old bench in front of me. "I was getting worried you might not wake up."

"Your concern is touching," I grunted. The pain in my shoulders was rapidly climbing toward excruciating, and my back and leg muscles weren't far behind.

"Personally, I'd love to watch the life drain from your eyes," Kade replied, a familiar sadistic glee shining in his unblinking stare, "while you writhe and scream until your body gives up. But fortunately for you, my orders explicitly prohibit that. For now."

Dread spiked in my chest, almost overwhelming my surprise. I'd thought Kade and his superiors wanted me dead for screwing up their attempt to kill Darius and take over the Vancouver precinct five months ago. There was something extra terrifying about this ruthless, powerful mythic cabal not only knowing who I was, but also wanting something from me.

I really didn't need any more terror in my system right now. Knowing Kade, he would have accounted for my psycho warping, so I narrowed my eyes, concentrating on that vague sense of his mind the way I had when I'd accidentally peeked into Lienna's thoughts. If I could snag a snippet of his sadistic internal monologue, I might hit on a clue to help me escape this mess.

But I didn't hear a damn thing.

Kade tilted his head to one side, marginally amused. "What are you attempting, Agent Morris?"

That spike of dread in my chest leaked into the rest of my body, fusing with the agonizing strain on my muscles. I targeted the twisted chunk of gray matter trapped inside his skull and delivered a full-blown sensory deprivation Blackout warp.

Nothing.

Kade raised his left arm, displaying a leather strap around his wrist. "I picked this up at the flea market. It wasn't cheap, but the seller assured me I'd be safe from all psychic attacks."

"Was it Brad?" I asked, trying not to sound like I was grinding my teeth into powder. Stretched out between the ropes, I could only manage shallow inhales.

"I didn't catch his name."

"On the heavier side, unnatural fear of plant life, willing to sell illegal artifacts to hairless psychotic scum?" I prompted.

Sighing, Kade checked his watch. "I wonder if you're not appreciating the seriousness of your situation, Agent Morris."

Oh, I was. I just didn't want him to get the satisfaction of seeing me squirm. It was the only form of resistance I had.

"What were you hoping for?" I asked sardonically. "Weeping and begging for mercy? Would that do me any good?"

That sick smile returned to his face. "No, it wouldn't."

"Then I might as well have a little fun while I'm here," I sneered. "I loved you in *Coneheads*, by the way."

He ignored that, still smiling like a bloodthirsty reptile. "I'm going to be very clear with you, Kit. You can make things much easier for both of us if you cooperate. All I want you to do is answer a few questions."

Something told me that while he might start with a few questions, that wouldn't be the end of it.

"Now, I quite enjoy doing things the hard way," he added, "so it's really up to you."

I clenched my jaw.

He leaned forward slightly. "Let's start with an easy question. Do you know what you are?"

That was vague as hell. I was an agent, an orphan, a psycho warper, and the preeminent expert on early 2000s sitcoms. But with my ragged breath and gasping lungs, I couldn't get all of that out of my mouth.

"Fuck you," I spat. "That's what I am."

"Your wit is failing." His smile widened. "This is my favorite part. Let's try another one. Can you explain the process you used to do *this*?"

He reached into his back pocket and retrieved something. *Two* somethings, in fact: the broken halves of the handcuffs I'd reality warped when he'd chained Lienna and me to a pipe earlier this year. The abjuration symbols still showed against the plastic, making it excessively implausible to pretend they were regular toy cuffs and not transmuted, formerly metal ones.

"We both know there's more to you than those cute illusions," Kade said softly, watching my face with unblinking intensity.

"I was wondering where I left those," I muttered. Sweat had broken out across my skin, but I wasn't sure if it was from the pain in my muscles or the growing panic in my chest. Or both.

Lienna and I had kept my reality warping a secret, but in our hurry to escape Kade's trap and prevent Darius from taking a quick trip to the mortician's table, we'd left the metal-turned-plastic handcuffs behind.

And Kade had found them. Which meant he knew what I could do. Worse, it meant the Consilium knew that too.

I was beginning to get a much clearer picture of what that Assembly of Assholes wanted from me.

"It was an impressive bit of magic," Kade told me, slipping the cuffs back into his pocket. "However, I wouldn't recommend you try it again."

He gestured at something underneath my chest. I could barely move with the way he'd tied me up, but I managed to crane my neck to look downward.

My blood ran cold.

A forty-five-pound plate was lying flat on the floor below me, and fitted into the hole at its center was a broken metal barbell. Where a flat round end should have been, the sheared metal formed a jagged point.

And it was only inches from my chest.

Whether I used reality warping or some other trick, the moment I freed either my arms or legs, I would fall onto that spear-like point—and my body weight would drive it into my chest. Even if I reality warped the bar instead, I'd still be roped up like a rodeo calf without an ounce of magic to free myself. Whether Kade knew I lost my powers after reality warping or not, he'd come up with a brutal solution to the "effective restraints" challenge I presented.

I looked back at Kade to see his sick smile twisting his mouth.

"There's the fear," he breathed. "Excellent."

Desperation on the edge of panic ricocheted through me, and I slammed every warp I hadn't yet tried into his brain—a Swarm layered on a Funhouse accompanied by a Split Kit with a Creature Feature thrown in for good measure—stubbornly hopeful that *something* would break through that goddamn protection spell.

But he just kept smiling, unaffected.

"You might think you're special," he continued blandly, "but you're nothing more than an aberration that shouldn't exist."

"Because I've got looks *and* brains?" I shot back, trying not to sound breathless.

"From where I'm sitting, all I see is a scared little boy with a big mouth."

Maybe he was right. Maybe I was all bark, no bite. Maybe I was so terrified and in such agony that I was on the brink of tears and letting out a wretched, uncontrollable moan.

But I gritted my teeth and swallowed the pain.

"Let's try another question, Kit," he said, bracing his elbows on his knees. "Are you aware that your abilities have changed recently?"

What the hell? How could he possibly know that?

Kade rose from the bench and closed the distance between us, stopping less than a foot from me before crouching so we were at eye level. He stared into my face as though trying to burrow into the recesses of my gray matter.

"I know you've changed." There was no emotion behind his words—no surprise or annoyance or anger or joy—just a monotone statement of fact tinted by the smallest modicum of interest. "I wonder if you've noticed anything."

I couldn't think of a response, and I was afraid that if I opened my mouth, I'd groan or gasp or choke.

When I didn't shoot back with a pithy retort, Kade returned to his spot on the bench. "You may not realize it yet, but sooner or later, you'll tell me everything I want to know."

I sucked in a shallow breath. "Why the hell would I do that?"

"Because you'll soon be meeting a colleague of mine. She's very proficient in the kind of alchemy that turns willpower into obedience. By the time she's finished, you'll do whatever we tell you."

Oh goody. That sounded unambiguously delightful.

Panic was dominating all my thoughts and emotions now, and the pain in my shoulders and knees felt like a thousand white-hot needles had been shoved into my bones. My breathing was growing shakier with each passing moment. I didn't know how much longer I could take it.

"It won't be nearly as much fun for me," Kade added as he checked his watch. "We're out of time. Don't forget I gave you the option of the easy way out. Everything that happens after this was your decision."

Bullshit. I wanted to spit the word at him, but I was panting rapidly and didn't have enough air to speak. Whatever sick shit Kade and his colleagues had planned for me, nothing I said or did would change it.

Kade stood up, straightened his black shirt, rocked his head from side to side to stretch his neck, and turned to walk away.

"Savor these last few minutes of autonomy, Agent Morris," he said over his shoulder. "They'll be the last you ever have."

He crossed the long warehouse and disappeared through a doorway. As soon as he was out of sight, I let all the agony out in a guttural, gasping groan. I sucked in as much oxygen as I could, not caring if it sounded like a ragged sob.

Then I turned my focus inward, doing my damnedest to shut out the pain and panic. I had until Kade returned to escape. Whether it was seconds or minutes, this was my only chance.

12

FROM MY AGONIZING, front-leaning position, I looked down at the steel skewer protruding from the forty-five-pound plate, its sharp point less than a hand's width from my chest.

Psycho warping wouldn't save me. No amount of halluci-bombs or invisi-warps could untie the ropes or move the skewer.

So that left reality warping. Kade had engineered this trap to thwart that very option, but beneath the agonizing strain that threatened to tear my muscles apart and the rushing whitewater of fear that threatened to drown me, I still clung to a tiny glimmer of hope.

Since my conversation with Lienna about my reality warps and transmutation, a silly little idea had been bouncing around in the Kit chaos of my brain: if transmutation was an extra complex form of Arcana, did that mean reality warping also had degrees of difficulty? Had I skipped past the introductory water wings and wading basin to dive straight into the deepest end of the pool?

And if there were easier forms of reality warping than transmutation, could I tap into one to free myself?

The big question was what else reality warping could involve. I was already accomplished at one form of mind magic—psycho warping—and I'd just discovered I had access to another—telepathy.

With as much focus as I could gather, I fixated on the pointy murder stick under my chest. That warm, bright spot in my brain where my powers lived lit up, and I visualized what I wanted, just like when I'd transformed Kade's metal cuffs into brittle plastic.

But I didn't imagine a transmutation. I imagined something much simpler.

I visualized the rod lifting out of the plate that held it in position. I pictured it drifting gently upward with exhaustive detail as though I were projecting the most convincing warp I'd ever done—except I was my own target.

A foreign tension threaded through my muscles, almost lost in the excruciating burn of my arduous position. It felt as though a weight had been added to my shoulders. I could almost feel the cold steel in my hands.

My fingers curled instinctively as I dedicated every neuron of my psychic power toward the rod. The muscles in my hands cramped, forearms straining—

And the rod moved.

With no pomp or circumstance, it rose from its spot, defying gravity to hover above the plate.

Holy shit, it had worked! I could now add "telekinesis" to my expanding CV of psychic skills.

Redoubling my concentration and fighting through the agonizing strain wrenching every inch of my body, I visualized the rod gliding out from under my chest. It followed my thoughts, the process rapidly smoothing until it didn't feel all that different from warping—except for the unsettling additional pressure on my muscles.

I guided the rod up past my head and toward the single line of rope connecting my wrists to the pull-up bar. Craning my neck painfully to bring it into my line of sight, I pushed the sharpened tip into the tensed strand. Stress burned through my muscles as the rod met the rope's resistance.

A telekinetic's psychic strength was linked to their physical power—if they could lift it with their body, they could lift it with their mind—but my body was under excessive duress. The strength I was using to control the rod was little more than the fumes in my proverbial gas tank.

Gritting my teeth, I mentally shoved the tip of the spear into the strands of the rope. The burn and pressure on my muscles intensified, and a groan rattled in my chest.

Snap!

The rope broke and gravity sent me face-first toward the concrete floor. I managed to get my arms in front of my head, breaking my fall and bruising my elbows. The rod clattered noisily to the ground, its metallic clang ringing throughout the warehouse.

"What was that?" a distant, unfamiliar voice barked.

I gasped like a deep-sea free diver coming up for air. My muscles throbbed violently, and all I wanted to do was curl into the fetal position until the pain subsided. Unfortunately, I had no time to rest.

My wrists were still bound together—I'd only severed the piece tying me to the bar—but my fingers were free, so I grabbed the sharpened rod, sat upright, and jammed it into the rope wrapped around my ankles.

A door clanged—the one Kade had used to exit the oversized equipment graveyard. The bald bastard reappeared, flanked by a tall, lanky woman carrying a black case and a short, stocky bruiser with bulging muscles.

I didn't wait for their reactions to my semi-freed state. I twisted back toward my ankles and shoved the rod into the rope with all the force I could muster. Ripping apart my bonds sans telekinesis was a much quicker endeavor, and my restraints snapped cleanly.

I jumped to my feet, whirled around, and swung the sharp end of the rod wildly, forcing Kade to backpedal an instant before he would've tackled me to the floor. Teeth bared, he grabbed for the pseudo-spear, but I whipped it sideways, catching his arm and scoring a shallow cut.

It wasn't much of a weapon, but it was better than fighting empty-handed.

A glimpse of movement caught the corner of my eye—the alchemist lady's beefy sidekick was pulling a black pistol from his belt. I backed into the weight rack, using the steel frame to keep Kade in front of me, and simultaneously unleashed a Blackout halluci-bomb. Kade had already pummeled my body, brain, and soul, so the hefty warp weighed heavier on my psyche than normal.

Both the lanky lady and stocky sir went down, writhing on the gym floor, their confused and terrified shouts echoing off the rusty stationary bikes and dusty rowing machines.

That left me, Kade, and his stupid anti-Kit bracelet. The shiny-scalped shithead faced me as I aimed the very sharp point of the broken rod at his chest. He didn't whip out any deadly decapitation magic, though; by his own admission, he was under strict orders *not* to kill me.

I, on the other hand, had no such orders.

I summoned my inner King Leonidas and attempted a speedy thrust of the pseudo-spear. With the same agility I'd seen from him before, Kade twisted sideways and sprang forward, slipping past my guard and slamming into me.

I crashed over the rear of the weight rack, landing on my ass. Kade ripped the rod out of my roped-up hands. I spun away from him and scrambled awkwardly to my feet.

Standing within the rack that had formerly been my prison, Kade grinned viciously. "You just can't wait for me to make you bleed, can you?"

I didn't waste my breath on a retort. Instead, I sprinted into the maze of deceased fitness equipment. The cluttered storage area had become my advantage—I sprang, zigzagged, and vaulted my way through a haphazard arrangement of dead treadmills. The chaotic obstacles hampered Kade's agility, keeping him two or three steps behind me.

But I couldn't lead him on this wild Kit chase forever. Between the bone-deep muscle aches, physical exhaustion, and continual drain of the Blackout warp, my endurance level was about to hit zero.

I left the treadmill labyrinth and blitzed toward a pile of barbells, dumbbells, kettlebells, and other assorted muscle-growing bells. As soon as I passed them, I spun around, bound hands outstretched as though I was making my final stand.

Kade slowed his advance, smacking the rod against his palm like an all-star batter swaggering up to home plate. At least he wouldn't run me through with it. Probably.

I retreated a few steps, baiting him to attack me—and he did.

Focusing my newly realized telekinetic ability, I locked my psychic fingers on a nearby barbell and yanked it with all my might, throwing it across Kade's path at ankle height.

As he lunged at me with all the aerodynamic power his hairlessness afforded him, his ankles *clonked* into the barbell, and he went down.

I might not have Blythe-level brain brawn, but my greenhorn telekinesis was getting the job done.

As much as I wanted to cave his shiny cranium in with the heaviest weight I could find, my hands were still tied together and every warning light on my internal dashboard was flashing red. I opted to make a break for the exit instead. A loud clang and a frustrated roar from Kade followed me.

As I whipped through the door into a small office area, I spotted Kade's combat gear sitting on a metal chair—and on top of it was a familiar leather wallet, MPD badge, and cellphone.

I grabbed my stuff, slipping and almost falling on the dusty floor in my frenzied haste, then rammed through another door and out into the cool darkness of night.

Where the hell was I?

An industrial area, it seemed. A wide-open parking lot stretched out in front of me, sparsely illuminated by tall streetlamps. Beyond that were the silhouetted shapes of other massive buildings in the distance, but nothing close. Nowhere to hide.

Which meant I needed to run.

I dropped the Blackout warp, feeling the release on my mind, then turned right and sped along the length of the warehouse I'd just escaped, booking it for the nearest road.

As I sprinted, my mind spiraled dangerously close to outright panic. I was on foot, exhausted, and my hands were still tied. Kade would catch me. I couldn't outrun him, I couldn't fight him, and I couldn't hide from his goddamn sixth sense.

As I reached the end of the warehouse, the street just ahead, blinding white light obliterated my vision. For a bleary-eyed second, I thought Darius was attacking me—then I realized it was actually four different beams of light shining directly into my confused pupils.

"Kit?" a semi-familiar voice shouted in surprise.

I squinted, my exhausted brain failing to identify the voice but recognizing the speaker as a friendly. The lights flashed wildly, and I was abruptly surrounded by black-clad mythics with a veritable crapload of weapons.

"Holy shit, Kit." The bright beam directly in front of me shut off. "Where did you come from?"

I blinked a ginger-haired, freckled face into focus—Aaron Sinclair, the only pyromage I'd actually *want* to meet in a back alley.

"Oh, you know," I said, hoarse and breathless, "just some casual, late-night escaping."

A Crow and Hammer combat team had encircled me, and the realization that I was safe hit me like a monster-sized bucket of liquid exhaustion. Tremors shook my limbs, and my knees threatened to forgo their lifelong duty of holding me upright.

Aaron grabbed my elbow before I pitched over. "Drew, Venus, get him back to the van and call Darius. Kit, where is Kade?"

I tipped my head toward the warehouse. "In there with an alchemist and some other stooge. Both armed."

Aaron barked a few more orders, and moments later, I was being led across the street by two very capable mythics. Drew was keeping me steady while Venus sorted through her alchemy supplies for a potion that would be much friendlier than whatever Kade's lady friend had prepared for me.

The other four locked-and-loaded combat mythics, led by the top pyromage in Vancouver, were storming the CrossFit castle. In a couple of minutes, they'd come striding back out with Kade's head on a proverbial pike, and this part of the saga would be over.

Deep inside, I knew that wouldn't happen. There was no way that slippery bastard would go down this easily. There was no way this was the last I'd see of Benjamin Kade.

13

LIENNA HANDED ME a tall, steaming cup of fragrant anti-fatigue. "A Sleepy Kit Special."

I wrapped both hands around it, inhaling the aroma as I warmed my hands. It was eight in the morning, and despite the seven or so hours since my escape, my every muscle and bone still ached.

Kade, as I'd expected, had vanished along with the alchemist and the beefcake. The Crow and Hammer team had transported me to the precinct, where Scooter had declared I was exhausted, bruised, and in need of serious rest. He'd given me some painkillers and a salve for the rope burns on my wrists and ankles, then sent me home to recuperate.

Being the rebellious rapscallion I am, I'd defied the healer's orders and reunited with Lienna and Blythe instead, hopeful they'd been able to squeeze some critical insight out of the two goons my partner had gravity bombed damn near into the afterlife. What I'd learned, however, was that when Lienna had seen our nemesis dragging me away, she'd pursued the van on foot for several blocks. By the time she'd returned to the square, there'd been no sign of either goon or their vehicle.

Our only chance of gaining anything useful from this entire shitshow rested on my severely sore shoulders. So I'd spilled my guts, telling them everything.

Okay, not *everything*. I'd glossed over a few details, like Kade's comments about my mutating abilities, the reality-warped handcuffs, and my newfound telekinesis. Blythe didn't have a clue that I was anything but a hallucination magician, and I wasn't planning on enlightening her—not yet.

Thus, the only real takeaway for Blythe was that Kade had abducted me on behalf of his superiors—a revelation she was less than thrilled about.

"How are you feeling?" Lienna asked softly as she sat on the chair beside me. We were camped out in the glass-walled conference room on the fifth floor, where Blythe had often skulked during Söze's tenure as interloper extraordinaire.

I gingerly touched the rope burns on my wrists. "Like an exhausted, traumatized rodeo calf."

She smiled at my attempted humor, but it didn't reach her eyes. She was tired too. We'd both tried to catch a few hours of sleep in the infirmary beds, but the cardboard-esque mattresses and antiseptic décor had made getting some much-needed shut-eye all but impossible. On the plus side, it had given me a chance to fill Lienna in on all the details I'd kept from Blythe.

"It's a mess," I muttered, taking a sip of the life-giving java juice my partner had provided. "Kade and the Consilium know about the reality warping—and my new telekinesis. Even before he witnessed me tossing gym equipment around with my mind, he knew. He could sense that my powers had changed."

Okay, so maybe "tossing gym equipment" was hyperbolic—haphazardly repositioning a barbell was more accurate—but my point stood, nonetheless.

I raised my eyes to hers. "Not that I'm complaining about the sudden boost in brain power, but *why*? Why is this happening to me?"

She shifted her weight. "Your abilities have been evolving since we started working together. Remember how you could only really do sight and sound with your warps at first? Now you can disable an entire room full of people with just a thought."

I frowned. "That's still just a psycho warp. Bigger and better, but not different."

"It looks really different to me." She gave a small shrug. "When you changed the handcuffs, that was the first time you reality warped on purpose, right? Maybe that unlocked something for you."

I rubbed my eyes, wishing I could massage the freshly imbibed caffeine straight into my frontal lobe to help me figure out what the hell was going on. "So you're saying I've been a psycho warping telepathic telekinetic who can also break the immutable laws of physics all along and I just didn't realize it?"

"I don't know, Kit. I'm just guessing."

"Kade knows something," I muttered. "He also said I was an aberration that shouldn't exist. He must've been referring to my magic."

Lienna pressed her lips into an anxious line, but before she could respond, the conference room's glass door opened. Captain Blythe entered, along with Vinny, Vigneault, and

Tim. Last in line was Agent Jack Cutter, a bearded telethesian who perpetually wore plaid and failed to understand why I made so many lumberjack jokes at his expense.

The other agents took spots at the table with me and Lienna, while Blythe moved to the front of the room.

"You all know why you're here," she began, her blue eyes steely. "Agent Morris has already involved most of you in our investigation into the IA, and now that Kade is back and moving against us, it's time to reveal the rest."

The surrounding agents all sat up straighter, their gazes intent despite the early morning.

"Söze, Kade, and their subordinates are part of a corrupt faction within the IA—a faction that likely extends beyond the IA and into the rest of the MPD."

"Hold on," Tim said skeptically. "Isn't that a big leap? What about all the reports and testimonies we submitted about Söze's illegal actions?"

"The IA has already dismissed the investigation," Blythe stated simply.

"What?" Vigneault barked. "But Söze was clearly abusing his power and—"

"It doesn't matter," the captain interrupted. "It isn't surprising that the IA chose not to investigate itself. Our task— the case Kit and I have been working on for five months—is to uncover the depths of the corruption. It doesn't end with Söze and Kade."

Vinny glanced at me. "Is that why you had me looking into Kade's history with DRAFT?"

"Bingo," I said with a nod. "The cap and I are trying to map the web of influence that connects Kade, Söze, the Internal Affairs Commissioner, and anyone else involved in their scheming."

I knew a whole helluva lot more about that scheming than I was letting on, but everything Darius had revealed about the Consilium and its history was for my ears alone—and Lienna's.

"On that note," I said to my former cubicle-mate, "have you learned anything?"

Vinny nodded. "I convinced a couple of DRAFT guys who worked with Kade to send me classified reports, but they were pretty standard. Nothing in particular about Kade. Just that he was present for the missions."

I crumpled my empty coffee cup in my fist. "Damn it."

"That wasn't all they gave me." The mohawked kryomage paused for dramatic effect. "According to my DRAFT contacts, Kade was often assigned to reconnaissance. On more than one mission, he provided detailed information on the targets—locations, numbers, stuff like that. But when the team got to the site, it was obvious he couldn't have known those details without touring the entire building first, which should have been impossible."

Tim swore so suddenly and creatively that everyone turned to look at him.

"That slimy bastard is a clairsentient," the telepath snarled. "How did I miss that?"

"A di-mythic?" Jack Cutter asked. "Arcana *and* Psychica?"

"Or the whole Arcana thing is bullshit," I suggested. "Anyone can use artifacts. Unless he's been doing public array-building demonstrations, how would anyone know whether he's a genuine sorcerer?"

"Clairsentient," Vigneault mused darkly. "What does that ability involve, exactly?"

"He can perceive the psychic energy of anyone close to him," Tim confirmed. "It overlaps telethesian and empath abilities to a degree, but clairsentience is its own beast. He can sense minds more clearly, accurately, and at greater distances than a telethesian, but he can't track people once they're out of his range. And he can't affect emotions, but he can get a feel for someone's mental state, mood, or even strong intentions—like, say, if they're about to attack."

That made more sense than a wishing well outside a penny factory. Clairsentience explained the bald bastard's slipperiness to an absolute tee—how he could see me coming, how he could pinpoint Darius amidst his lumina-driven invisibility, and how he'd murdered Georgia Johannsen and Anson Goodman while they were alone and with zero witnesses.

"And the stronger the clairsentient is," Tim added, "the more they can perceive. There have been a few famous clairsentients who could even determine someone's mythic class."

Well, shit. If Kade could sense the shift in my powers, then he had to be a virtuoso-level clairsentient. Because of course he was. Why couldn't I, just for once, make enemies with an evil idiot who was mediocre at magic?

"What about hearing Kade's voice in your head?" Blythe asked me. "That doesn't fit clairsentience."

"Oh, that." I scrambled for an explanation. "That was my bad. Psycho warping paranoia playing tricks on me. He's definitely a clairsentient."

Blythe gave me a hard squint rife with skepticism, and I hastily turned to Lienna and changed the subject.

"Is there any way to defend against clairsentience?" I asked her. "An artifact we can use to keep us off his radar?"

"There are potions that can mask your psychic trail," she mused. "I'll look into it and see what I can find."

If anyone could break Kade's magic or shield us from his prying mind, it was the Abjuration Queen Supreme, Lienna Shen.

"Okay," I said with an exhale, turning to Agent Vigneault. "Any luck on your front, Clarice?"

"I think so," she answered. "The only 'Peter' I could find in connection with Kade that seemed at all relevant was a document from the former head of the IA back in 2011, when Kade first applied for a job with Internal Affairs."

"He applied more than once?" Blythe asked.

Vigneault nodded. "Twice. He was rejected in 2011 because of 'a conflict of interest.' It didn't specify *what* conflict, so I kept digging. That's when I discovered that the IA was investigating the Obscura Influentia department at that time, and its commissioner happens to be a Peter."

"Peter Druthers," Blythe hissed.

"Peter Druthers," Vigneault confirmed. "He's the right age to be Kade's father."

Oh shit. I hadn't considered that Kade and his father might not share a surname. I was even less excited at the prospect of Daddy Kade controlling an international MPD department—and not just any department. Obscura Influentia literally meant "secret influence," and its main purpose was manipulating and controlling human governments and organizations for the benefit of mythics.

"If the IA was investigating Obscura Influentia," Blythe said, "the director's son joining the IA and having access to the investigation files would be a glaring conflict of interest."

"Yep," Vigneault agreed. "But less than six months later, while Obscura Influentia was still under investigation, the IA commissioner abruptly retired, and Commissioner Sparks got the job. Kade reapplied to the IA and got in."

"So Commissioner Sparks didn't care that Kade could be reporting to his pop?" I asked.

"Apparently not." Vigneault arched her eyebrows. "To add some extra spice to the stew, within a few months of Sparks and Kade entering the IA, the investigation into Peter Druthers's department was all buttoned up. I can't access the IA's reports, but I didn't find anything that suggested the IA acted against Obscura Influentia. The investigation simply ended."

I caught Blythe's eye. She was frowning, and assuming we were on the same mental page, she was also thinking that Peter Druthers was eyeballs-deep in corruption alongside his son and Commissioner Sparks—which made for not one but *two* Consilium-affiliated department heads.

I needed to tell Darius about this.

"Vincent," Vigneault said, swiveling her chair to face the kryomage, "have you still got those DRAFT reports handy? We should compare notes."

Vinny straightened. "Of course."

"I'd like to see them too," Tim added. "If Kade is coming after us, we need to strategize. Whatever defense Shen comes up with is a good first step, but we should have a real tactical plan in place."

Blythe nodded in approval. "Make that your priority. That goes for everyone in this room."

"I'd like to pick up Kade's trail," Cutter said, running his fingers through his rugged face fuzz.

Blythe shook her head. "The guilds are already handling that."

"They're tracking where he went," Cutter said. "I want to find out where he's been. I'll start with the location where he took Kit, then follow his path in reverse. Maybe I can determine what he's been up to in between abduction attempts."

The captain considered this. "Given the circumstances, I don't want you out there on your own. Take Agent Wolfe with you."

Wolfe was a senior agent and a formidable terramage, but I'd also noticed his conspicuous absence from our secretive soiree. "Are we bringing Wolfe in on the investigation?"

"He's a good agent, but it's too risky," Blythe replied. "Cutter, tell him you're following a lead, but don't say a word about Kade, Söze, or any of what we've discussed here today."

Cutter frowned. "What kind of lead?"

"Make something up."

The telethesian's brows furrowed so deep they formed an uppercase V on his forehead. Clearly, his beard–enshrouded brain was more in tune with chopping wood than concocting believable fabrications.

"I heard there's a rogue tempemage named Faustus Trivium on the loose in that area," I offered. "You'll recognize him by his triangular smile and penchant for screeching when provoked."

Cutter gave a slow, slightly confused nod. "I guess that will work."

Lienna rolled her eyes at me. Hey, it was a plausible story that would hold up if Wolfe took the initiative to type their target's name into the MPD database. And if they coincidentally stumbled across my former foe and made his day a little extra miserable, I wouldn't complain.

After everyone else had filed out of the meeting room to commence their respective assignments, leaving only Lienna, the cap, and me, I sprawled out on one of the chairs and prayed for a refill of my Sleepy Kit Special.

"What about me?" I asked. "What's my assignment?"

"You got your assignment from Scooter," Blythe replied. "Rest, and lots of it."

I straightened out of my sprawl. "Rest? While everyone else is—"

"You need to recover physically and mentally from Kade's abduction," she said implacably. "Apparently, you're so stressed you've been hearing voices."

Touché. I wanted to explain that I wasn't *really* hearing voices, but I also wasn't keen on explaining my burgeoning psychic capabilities. But I also *also* wasn't interested in sitting on my ass doing desk work for the next week.

Reading the mutiny in my expression, Blythe crossed her arms. "Kade is out to get you, and you'll be of absolutely no use to me or this investigation if you get yourself kidnapped again—or killed."

"At least give me something to do while I sit around," I grumbled.

"Have you forgotten you're supposed to be investigating the people around Commissioner Sparks? Or is memory loss another of your symptoms?"

I chose not to comment.

Blythe snapped her glare to Lienna. "Keep him under control, Agent Shen."

She nodded, and I felt a quiet flicker of betrayal that disappeared the moment she caught my gaze—and I saw the conspiratorial gleam in her eyes.

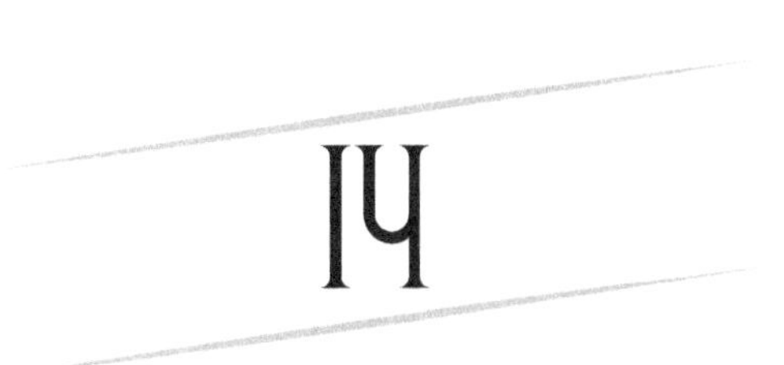

LIENNA WASN'T the by-the-book, unswerving-obedience-to-her-superiors agent she'd once been, which in my books was a change for the better—and one I took full credit for.

Instead of escorting me back to the condo, she ushered me out of the precinct and straight to the Crow and Hammer. Not that I'd had any inclination to retreat to the condo anyway, but I was delighted to have Lienna operating on my wavelength.

At the guild, I spent a few minutes assuring various concerned members that I was totally fine post-abduction. Then Darius arrived, and in short order we were locked in our secret boardroom of documents while I brought Darius up to speed on my involuntary excursion into the bodybuilding afterlife.

When I reached the part where Kade had pulled out the plastic handcuffs, however, I hesitated. Way back when, after I'd morphed Quentin's super-Psychica stick into a snake, Lienna and I had decided it was the best course of action to remain extremely hush-hush about the whole thing. People knowing I had the ability to alter the fabric of reality with nothing but imagination and stubbornness was a recipe for a slew of disasters.

But if I didn't tell Darius the entire story, I'd have to leave out potentially crucial details about the whole Kade encounter, which seemed downright unwise.

Darius had entrusted me with some of his most dangerous secrets. I could do the same.

"There's this thing," I said, scrambling for the right words. "A thing I can do. A pretty crazy thing I've only done a few times. But I happened to do that thing to escape Kade back in March, and I accidentally left evidence of the thing for Kade to find."

Holy thesaurus, Kit, what happened to your vocabulary?

Darius arched an eyebrow, silently pointing out the obvious: that had been a nonsensical explanation of nothing. Lienna also didn't comment, seeming surprised that I was willing to reveal my biggest secret to him.

I exhaled. "The thing is reality warping—that's what Lienna and I call it. On rare occasions, three total by my last count, my psycho warps have become real. Case in point: right before he tried to murder you, Kade used very real metal handcuffs to hang us both from a pipe … and I turned them into plastic so we could break free."

Darius's expression didn't change, and I found that oddly ominous.

"You turned metal into plastic with your psychic power?" he asked in a neutral tone.

"Yep."

"Was it a temporary change? Or—"

"Permanent," I said. "Kade has the plastic ones. I also reshaped a silver wand into a snake and turned a grappling hook into an anchor."

Darius leaned back in his chair, placing me under the hefty weight of his steely gray eyes. If I hadn't known him so well by this point, I would've said he looked thoughtful—but I knew better. He was totally nonplussed.

"Before meeting you," he said, "I'd never heard of a psycho warper. Are there any records of other psycho warpers being able to warp reality?"

"No," Lienna answered for me. "I've searched high and low over the past year. Psycho warpers are only mentioned in passing and never with much detail."

"Kade called me 'an aberration that shouldn't exist.'" I fidgeted with a loose thread on my jeans. "It makes me think he knows more about it than we do."

Darius's expression finally changed, darkening with grimness. "Then so does the Consilium."

"Which is a delightful thought." I cleared my throat. "The thing is, I've got a few more tricks up my sleeve. In the past couple days, I've also discovered I can use telepathy and telekinesis."

Darius's gaze swept over me from head to toe as though looking for signs that I was actually a well-disguised alien. "You *just* discovered this? How?"

"The telepathy happened first, by accident." I rubbed my jaw, feeling the stubble I hadn't had the time to shave. "My working theory is that it's a variation of reality warping. I can fake a one-sided telepathy convo easily enough—maybe I just made it real. So, when Kade had me tied up and I was out of options, I decided to give telekinesis a whirl."

"And it worked?"

I shrugged. "Enough to cut me loose."

Darius's eyes narrowed. "Do you know what I'm thinking right now?"

"That I've completely lost my marbles, and this is just a stress-induced fever dream? Because, believe me, I've considered that, but—"

"No, Kit," he said firmly. "Can you use your new telepathy on me?"

"Oh." I adjusted my position in my chair, resting my forearms on my knees. It took me a moment to recreate the mind-magic I'd accomplished in this very room only a day earlier. I homed in on the presence of Darius's mind and focused. "You're counting up in multiples of three?"

The silver fox's eyebrows lifted no more than a millimeter, but by Darius standards, that was an expression of outright shock. He said nothing, needing a moment to process.

To fill the awkward silence, I launched back into the tale of my escape, including all of Kade's creepy remarks about my abilities changing. When I finished, Darius slowly shook his head.

"I assumed Kade was targeting you for your knowledge," he said, choosing his words carefully. "The Consilium wants to know what we've been up to over the past few months. They don't know how much I know, and that's a risk factor I'm sure they'd prefer to eliminate."

I was always impressed by Darius's ability to talk about murder without ever actually using the word "murder."

He braced his elbows on the table and steepled his fingers. "However, Kade's focus on your magic suggests otherwise. Psychica is one of the least understood classes, and what you can do might not be exclusive to you alone. But there's no arguing that it's *extremely* rare, and the Consilium has a taste for rare, dangerous magic."

He tilted his chin toward Tino's pile of scary magic to emphasize his point.

"I'll never go to the Dark Side," I said emphatically. "They've got to know that."

"Not willingly, but even the best of us will trample our morals into the ground given enough motivation."

I opened my mouth to disagree, then glanced surreptitiously at Lienna. If the Consilium used her as a hostage against me…

Would I kill for them—or worse—to save her? The hypothetical made me nauseous.

Darius tapped his fingers on the table. "Unfortunately, we don't have much time to unravel Kade's intentions or let you rest as Aurelia wants. I got word on my way here that Trident Ltd. just received a deposit of \$31,245,000."

I blinked dumbly. Darius had someone tracking Trident's bank accounts?

"As you probably recall, Floris Visser's asking price for the weapon was thirty million." He smiled grimly. "The extra one-point-two million is likely the remainder of Trident's brokerage fee."

I snapped straight in my chair. "Oh, shit."

"She's selling the weapon?" Lienna asked sharply. "Now?"

"Now," Darius echoed. "I suspect the Consilium is aware that Trident had unwelcome visitors. They may even know which files were stolen. They're trying to get the weapon before we do."

I swore again. "They're going to beat us to it. Do you know where Visser is yet?"

"The last location I've been able to confirm is Amsterdam, but that information is five weeks out of date. I'm waiting for her current location, and in the worst-case scenario, we'll get the details of the sale from Trident."

"I'm assuming you won't be asking them nicely to hand over their records."

Darius slanted a mysterious look at me. "I sent someone to keep a close eye on Jayce Tyrian."

I let out a low whistle. Holy hell, this man had connections. I knew better than to ask for details. Darius had a PhD in not sinking ships with loose lips.

"So the moment we get a location," Lienna began, "we're going to rush there to steal the artifact before Visser hands it off to the Consilium? That's a dangerously tight timeline."

Darius nodded. "Unfortunately, we don't have a better option."

I pushed off my chair, too restless to sit. My muscles were still aching, and I stifled a groan as I rolled my shoulders. Lienna and Darius began discussing what preparations we should make for a short-notice heist, but I tuned them out. I wasn't in the right headspace for logistics, tactics, and plane tickets. Pacing the length of the room, I half closed my eyes, mentally juggling all the pieces.

To kick it off, we had Kade and his affinity for abduction, which had previously been focused on Darius—with a side dish of attempted murder—but was now concentrated on yours truly. Was I easier prey? Was he after my knowledge? My powers? Both?

Then there were Commissioner Sparks and Peter Druthers, two influential men sitting at the tippy-top of the MPD power pyramid, and who were probably in the Consilium's pocket.

Finally, we had this weapon—whatever it was. We knew the Consilium wanted it, to the tune of thirty million smackeroos and twenty years of waiting. But did they actively need it, or was it another evil item to add to their magic collection of antique nightmares?

I stopped at Tino's pile of documents. The levitating man drawing was on top, where I'd last left it. I picked it up, staring moodily at the sun symbol on the illustrated man's forehead. The stolen Trident folder sat beside Tino's notes, open to the photo of the weapon.

Still holding the drawing, I spun to face my two partners in anti-crime. At my sudden movement, they both shot me questioning looks.

"We don't know what Visser's weapon does," I said, "but we know where it came from. Lienna, you figured out which Viking site the weapon was found at, right?"

"Yeah," she agreed. "It's in Denmark."

"And Denmark is a whole ocean and continent closer to Amsterdam than it is to Vancouver. If Kade is so intent on hunting me down on my home turf, why don't I get the hell out of town? Lienna and I can scope out the Viking tomb and see if we can learn anything about the weapon"—I looked at Darius—"and as soon as you have Visser's location, we can hop, skip, and jump right over to her doorstep."

Darius nodded. "I can meet you there."

"Perfect." I grinned at Lienna. "How do you feel about some Lara Croft-style tomb raiding?"

She returned my grin. "I'll book us on the next flight to Copenhagen."

15

"DO YOU THINK there's more you can do?" Lienna mused.

We were seated outside a cute coffee shop not far from a waterway with a Danish name so unpronounceable it might as well have been my neighbor's Wi-Fi password. The early birds of Copenhagen walked past, and I didn't see any obvious tourists aside from us. Seven a.m. was a tad early for sightseeing.

"Telepathy and telekinesis aren't enough for you?" I asked, then pitched my voice up into an admittedly flawed Lienna Shen impersonation. "My partner's okay, I guess. He's the only psycho warper I've ever heard of, he can read minds and move objects without touching them, but sometimes I wish he could do *more*."

She shot me a playful scowl. "I'm just saying, there are a lot of psychic powers. Have you tried anything else?"

I shrugged. "I don't even know what to attempt."

"What about clairsentience?"

Pondering that, I took a big gulp of my Danish coffee, which was a lot like Canadian coffee, just accompanied by a delicious flaky pastry. "It'd be handy to sense Kade coming so I don't jump out of my skin every time I spot a bald dude on the street. I can sort of feel minds—I think that's how I accidentally telepathed you—but it's all pretty fuzzy."

Lienna pursed her lips in thought. "Agent Tim said clairsentience overlaps with empath and telethesian abilities. What about those? Maybe they're easier."

I fidgeted with my mug, swirling the dregs of my coffee into an unpleasantly brown vortex. "Every magical stunt I've ever pulled has come from my imagination. If I can dream it up, I can make a hallucination out of it. Reality warping, telekinesis, telepathy—they're just extensions of that. I can imagine turning metal into plastic or moving a barbell with my mind or hearing your thoughts, but those other abilities … I can't begin to imagine what it'd be like to sense a person's psychic waves."

Lienna nodded, a slight frown knitting her brows together. "That rules out a lot of Psychica abilities."

"Yeah, I won't be taking over Cutter's job anytime soon."

"Mmm," she replied vaguely, her gaze traveling around. The architecture along the street featured flat-faced buildings painted in a pastel rainbow of blues, yellows, pinks, and greens, all with white-framed windows on every floor. With the clear sky broken only by the odd whisp of cloud, it was like we'd wandered onto the set of a cozy, coastal fairy tale.

I watched her, trying not to look too mesmerized by the early morning sun lighting her glossy black hair. She was wearing it down again, and it softened her face in a way that kept drawing my gaze. Or maybe I wasn't over the fact that we were together again after five months of separation.

She abruptly swiveled her head back to face me. "Kit, should we finish that talk we started the other night?"

I simultaneously tensed and tried not to look tense, which was a muscular paradox that reminded my shoulders of how sore they were from being tied to a pull-up bar. I'd been dying to finish that conversation. Lienna's statement that she wanted there to be an "us" had been playing on a permanent loop in the back of my head like a busted record player ever since the sentence had left her lips.

Between inadvertent mind reading, Kade kidnappings, secret meetings, and last-minute travel plans, that conversation hadn't had the chance to reach its conclusion. We'd had more than half a day on the cross-Atlantic plane ride to revive the subject, but as far as I was concerned, the only people who carried out heartfelt relationship talks over the never-ending drone of a jet engine were flight attendants and boomers who shouted their side of every phone conversation.

"Yes." I cleared my throat, trying not to sound too eager. "We definitely should."

She nodded again, looking both hopeful and unbearably nervous. Her teeth scraped over her lower lip.

Wait, why the hell was I trying to sound *not* eager? This was no time for "cool guy" tomfoolery. I *was* eager.

"Lienna." I leaned forward, holding her gaze. "I've been wildly attracted to you ever since you tackled me in LAX. I've wanted to date you since the days of you dragging my handcuffed ass around the city in our very first smart car. And for the past five months, I haven't stopped thinking about how much I've missed you."

Her face went beet red, but a small smile pulled at her lips. "Yeah?"

"Oh yeah." I sat back in my chair. "So, yes, I absolutely, inarguably, and unequivocally want there to be an 'us.' I just need to know where to start."

"What do you mean?"

"Am I competing for your favor, Robin Hood and Maid Marian style? Do I need to prove my capabilities as a boyfriend first? Or can we skip straight to exclusive power couple?"

Her blush deepened. "I … I mean, exclusive would be good."

Grinning, I leaned back in my chair. "You know, that actually makes a lot of sense, now that I think about it."

"What does?" she asked with a frown.

"Your determination for me to add more powers to my arsenal," I said with a shrug. "You don't want a 'rare psychic ability' partner. You want a hotshot trophy boyfriend."

She rolled her eyes but couldn't contain her smile. "Boyfriend?"

"I don't care what you call me. Your beau, your arm candy, your personal first aid Kit, whatever."

"My personal first aid Kit," she echoed lightly. "I like the sound of that."

"Does that mean I can ask you out? Officially?"

She bobbed her chin, hiding half of her expression behind her coffee mug.

I drew in a deep breath. Then with only partially exaggerated seriousness, I said, "Lienna, would you like to go tomb raiding with me today?"

She choked on a sip of coffee. "You're asking me on a tomb-raiding date? When we were already planning to go?"

"Any activity can be a date with the right mindset," I said brightly. "Also, can I take you to dinner afterward? Assuming we don't get eaten by a Danish grave-robbing demon or something."

She laughed. "All right. It's a date."

We quickly downed the last of our hot beverages, and twenty minutes later, we were cruising down the highway southwest of Copenhagen in our luxury rental sedan. We'd made sure to buy all the collision, demolition, and destruction insurance available—just in case.

The morning sun beamed through the back window, heating the car's interior and bamboozling my internal clock. Beyond the suburbs and industrial areas, we found ourselves in the Danish countryside, farmland stretching out as far as we could see.

Lienna pulled the car off the main thoroughfare and onto a small two-lane road, which we followed until she turned us onto a dirt track that ended at a dusty patch of earth overlooking a rather unremarkable field.

A sign beside the ad hoc parking lot informed us this was a closed site, and trespassers would be heavily fined. Or more accurately, my phone's translator app told us when I held the camera up to the sign.

A grassy ridge nearby featured a set of wooden stairs leading up and over it, but otherwise, the scene felt overwhelmingly plain.

"This is it?" I asked, standing beside Lienna in front of the crude stairs.

"I hope so."

Her investigative efforts hadn't turned up much information about the tomb beyond what she'd already told me: it had been discovered twenty years ago by humans, taken over by the MPD, and assigned to a local archeological guild.

"They're called ring fortresses," she informed me as we started up the wooden steps. "Or Trelleborg-type fortresses, named after the first one that was excavated by archeologists back in the nineteen thirties."

At the top of the stairs, we paused to take in the midmorning view. The grassy mound formed a perfect circle at least a hundred yards in diameter. Two paths intersected at the center of the ring, creating four identical quadrants, all of which were dotted with depressions and knolls that I presumed meant more to an archaeologist than they did to me.

It was bigger than I'd expected, but it also didn't seem like the kind of place that would hide the tomb of a magical Viking monarch.

"Not much of a fortress," I muttered. "Unless the enemy really hated charging uphill."

Lienna rolled her eyes. "There would've been ramparts made of wood and stone built on top, around five meters tall and more than ten meters wide."

"Oh." I imagined massive fortifications rising high above us. "Yeah, that'd do the trick."

Lienna pointed across the former fortress. In the empty field beside it, a plain trailer with a door and a single window had been set up. "That's probably where the archeological team works when they aren't in the tomb."

"Speaking of going in the tomb ..." I looked all around. "Where's the entrance?"

"Near the trailer, most likely. Let's check it out."

The stairs continued down into the earthen ring, and Lienna began her descent. I took in our surroundings one more time before following her, but there wasn't another soul in sight. Too early for archeologists? I would've thought they were go-getter types. Maybe there wasn't much left to study after twenty years.

At the intersection of the two paths, a flat rock was embedded in the ground. There was a circle etched into it, as well as numerous symbols I recognized as Old Norse runes.

"Is *this* the entrance?" I asked. "How do you say 'open sesame' in Old Norse?"

Crouching, Lienna pulled out her phone and snapped a photo of the engraved rock. "I recognize some Arcana elements here. This might be a seal."

"A seal against what?" I raised my eyebrows. "Did Vikings like to be buried with heaps of gold like Egyptian pharaohs?"

"Not necessarily. They were buried with whatever their loved ones thought they might need in the afterlife, like weapons or clothes." Lienna traced an array of circles, her fingertip hovering just above the rock. "I could be wrong, but this seems backward, like the seal acts as protection against something breaking out, not someone breaking in."

"Uh." I inched back. "You weren't planning to open that, were you? Because the last time you cracked open a seal, I was almost melted by fae acid."

"I don't think we need to break it," she said calmly, rising to her feet. "The archaeologists must have found a different way in. Come on."

She skirted around the stone tablet and headed toward the trailer. I hastened after her.

"Okay, but aren't you a little worried about the seal that keeps scary things locked inside the tomb? There are so many cinematic parallels that I don't even know where to start."

"This tomb was excavated twenty years ago, Kit. Besides that, superstitious beliefs about the dead were common in this time period. The seal is probably to keep the deceased monarch from rising."

"Oh, that's fine, then." I nodded. "Just a Viking zombie king, no biggie."

We used another crude set of wooden steps to climb back out of the ring. As we reached the top and the trailer came into view, I jerked to a halt and threw up an invisi-warp, excluding Lienna's mind so her body didn't suddenly vanish from her own senses.

Sitting on the steps of the trailer, with a cigarette hanging from his lips, was a man wearing dark jeans and a black t-shirt. He looked like he'd either popped a few sleeping pills or just endured an unabridged screening of Andy Warhol's *Empire*.

Lienna had frozen beside me. When the overwhelmingly bored man didn't react to us, she glanced at me questioningly.

"I'm invisi-warping us," I told her.

"But I haven't activated my cat's eye."

I shrugged. "You might as well save it for when I need to break out the big warp guns. As long as I have some spare concentration, I can exclude your mind so you don't see anything I'm warping."

She seemed impressed. "When did you learn to do that?"

"I was starting to get the hang of it before you left, but I perfected it while working with Darius. He does all right sans senses, but it was safer to learn to exclude him."

"It's definitely handy. Let me know if you want to switch to me using my spell."

"Got it."

We approached the trailer, getting a better look at the dude guarding the door. He didn't look like an archaeologist, and he was also in our way. Lienna and I were discussing what warp I should use to lure him off the trailer doorstep so we could sneak inside when I caught the sound of voices.

I expanded the range of my warp, and maybe because I was thinking about Lienna's questions about clairsentience, I got a clearer sense than usual of the minds I was warping—three of them.

Appearing from the west side of the ring, a middle-aged woman was accompanied by two younger assistants around my age. Chatting casually as they tromped toward the trailer, all three women were dressed in wide-brimmed hats and pants with so many pockets they'd make Vincent Park nostalgic for his khaki days.

Lienna and I retreated to a safe distance, watching the small team approach Mr. Sleepy. They greeted him, he replied and got out of their way, and they went inside. Then he plunked himself back down on the step, looking more bored than before.

"I think he might be a guard from the guild in charge of this site," Lienna whispered. "They wouldn't want to leave it unprotected."

"That makes sense." Plus, the Dissimulation Department would be very unhappy if scientific proof of actual Viking magic suddenly came to light. This was a strictly "no humans allowed" tomb.

I pointed westward. "Think the entrance is over there?"

We ventured twenty yards farther around the outside of the grassy ring, and there, carved into the earth, was a downward-sloping passageway reinforced with wooden supports. Extension cords ran out from it, snaking toward the trailer, and LED lights beckoned us inside.

"Our tomb raid begins," I declared dramatically. "Should we hold hands? This is our first date, after all."

Rolling her eyes, she marched into the tunnel, and I followed behind her with a grin.

16

AS I FOLLOWED LIENNA down the dank, uncomfortably narrow tunnel, I reminded myself that this was on my secret agent bucket list: an Indiana Jones-style adventure into the heart of a cryptic haunt full of archaic treasure.

Hopefully there'd be no booby traps, cannibalistic cults, or snakes awaiting me.

A clump of heavy-duty extension cords paralleled our path, and the odd LED kept our course visible. Unlike a human worksite, there were no signs of shovels or heavy machinery. The tunnel was precisely cut; it was likely the work of a terramage—or a team of terramages.

Since we were now out of sight, I dropped my invisi-warp, instead keeping my ears alert for any warning signs of life, either from within the tunnel or from the mythic workers returning after their break. The passageway went on for dozens of meters, and unless my internal GPS had gone offline, we were headed toward the center of the former ring fortress—awfully close to that portentous seal designed to entrap whatever subterranean eldritch horror we were about to visit.

The passageway bent abruptly sideways, as though the terramage excavator had missed the mark by six feet. We rounded the corner and stopped.

"Woah," was all I could muster.

The crypt was about the size of my condo's living area, with a couple feet of headroom—but its shape was the real oddity. The rock slabs that created the walls were angled in such a way as to create a long, narrow oval. It was like we were in the belly of a stony, underground ship with an iron sarcophagus in the middle. The metal coffin was raised up on a massive slab of granite with Old Norse runes etched into it.

In fact, almost every square inch of the tomb's slanted walls was covered in the ancient writing, accompanied by a handful of carved illustrations. At about head height, small stone ledges jutted out, around two dozen of them, like empty shelves.

More work lights were propped up on wooden scaffolding, and power cords snaked off into the dimly lit corners, where I spotted two fresh-looking passageways that would force me to walk in a half crouch. A six-foot-wide folding table was set up against the wall, with several binders and notebooks sitting on it, waiting for the archaeologists to return.

Speaking of which, we couldn't waste any time on our crypt-creeping adventure.

Lienna's eyes, alight with scholarly intrigue, were sweeping over the walls. "It's amazing to think that all of this is over a thousand years old."

That was very cool and all, but my attention was locked on that giant iron sarcophagus. "They didn't open that, did they?

And please tell me an overzealous librarian didn't read from any suspiciously evil-looking black books."

I didn't see Lienna's eye roll, but I heard it in her tone. "Of course they opened it, Kit. That's how archeology works."

Creeping forward, I stepped onto the stone base and leaned over the sarcophagus, prepared to flee for my life—but the interior was empty. A thin layer of dust covered the iron bottom.

"Great," I muttered darkly. "So the Viking mummy has already been resurrected. Did you notice any locusts on our way here?"

"Vikings didn't mummify their dead." Lienna threw me a scolding look. "Now quit wasting time and start taking photos of everything. I'll start here."

She parked herself in front of the table while I walked slowly around the perimeter of the room, snapping copious photos with my phone, half my attention on the three passageways, perpetually paranoid of unwanted visitors—either living or undead.

While the carefully etched ancient Norse writing meant less than nothing to me, the perfectly rock-carved illustrations provided some details: sword-wielding soldiers, giant serpents, violent birds of prey, and a *lot* of fire all told a very violent, very deadly tale. As I stepped closer to one particular carving of a Viking warrior impaled on a lance, I noticed how strangely precise each line was. It was as if this tomb's interior decorator had time-traveled a laser cutter to create the design. Assuming an H. G. Wells explanation was off the table, that left one possibility.

Magic. A right-brained terramage with an eye for detail, to be precise.

The uncomfortable feeling of being very small and unimportant amidst the endless flow of time and history swept over me. I knew magic was old, of course, but seeing the ancient remains of a mythic life and a mythic culture really drove it home. We were blips on the timeline, there and gone, only to be remembered by our giant metal sarcophagi.

On my left, Lienna was taking photos of each page in a binder, skim-reading as she went. Not wanting to break her concentration or hover annoyingly over her shoulder—I could *not* read that fast and I wouldn't even try—I stepped into the side tunnels to check what else was down here and found several small niches but no more script-walls.

Returning to the below-ground burial boat, I made another slow circle. This was where the Consilium's weapon had been discovered, the one they'd been trying to acquire for twenty years, but the more I looked around, the less this seemed like a place where a terrible weapon of doom and destruction would be found.

"A queen," Lienna whispered.

I turned to her. "What?"

"This is the tomb of a Viking *queen*. And this"—she waved at the script etched into the walls—"is the story of her life and death. As told by the victors, at least."

"What victors?"

She flipped to another page and snapped a photo. "The queen—she's called Bodil—was born a peasant but rose to power because of her magical ability. She conquered most of Denmark before she was slain in battle."

"So whoever created this tomb and sealed her body inside was also the one who killed her?"

"Yeah. The opposing king is called 'god killer' in the text. He brought an entire army to battle and defeat Bodil."

My eyebrows rose. Just how powerful had Bodil been? I faced the sarcophagus, reassessing it. "Any mention of an artifact or weapon?"

"Not yet. These notes are all about various possible interpretations of the wall text." Lienna turned another page. "It's mostly a big warning about Bodil and 'her kind.' It talks about her and her partner wreaking havoc with their magic, and how 'monsters' like them should be slain at the first sign of their evil power."

"Harsh," I muttered. "Who's this partner? Did they have the same magic?"

"I'm not sure. Her partner is called 'the sha'ir' and it isn't clear if he's a companion, lover, husband. Again, this was written by the king who killed her, so we can't expect it to be terribly accurate."

"The sha'ir?" I asked. "That doesn't sound like a Norse word, not that I'm an expert."

Lienna shook her head. "It's Arabic, actually. The sha'ir were poets who were believed to be endowed with supernatural power."

"That's an ancient mythic if I've ever heard of one." I wandered around the near side of the sarcophagus. "If this dude was an Arabic poet, what the hell was he doing fighting battles with a Viking queen in eastern Denmark?"

"I don't know yet."

I peered toward the entrance tunnel, wondering how long we had until Team Science returned. "Does any of this describe Bodil's 'evil powers'?"

Lienna studied the page in front of her. "The archeologists are uncertain about that part of the translation. They aren't sure if the descriptions are exaggerations, old Viking expressions, or intended to be literal. Firestorms that burned men alive, thunder that struck down dozens of soldiers with each strike, maelstroms of wind, great chasms opening in the earth ..."

"Sounds like magery. Really intense magery."

Lienna nodded. "But mages only have one elemental ability, or maybe two if they develop a combination skill, like a heliomage or volcanomage. But those aren't common."

"And no mage can use *all* the elements."

"There are more descriptions, too. Hordes of beasts and horrendous visions that drove men insane." She shook her head. "It sounds like a pile of hyperbole meant to spawn fear."

"Or Bodil was using a ridiculously powerful artifact that rightfully spawned fear in *her* enemies," I countered, stepping up beside her at the table. "We need to find information about the artifacts they found here."

Nodding, she returned her attention to the binder. I took over photo duty, digitally documenting each page while she skimmed the text. The binder was filled with plastic protector sheets into which pages of handwritten notes, printouts, diagrams, and photos had been inserted. Everything seemed to be focused on the wall script.

We switched to a fat notebook. It was full of archeological mumbo jumbo about soil samples and rock types and estimates of how old everything was, reminding me that archaeology wasn't just bullwhips and cursed treasures. A lot of it was just plain ol' geology and math.

Feeling the pressure of each minute that ticked past, I slid the notebook aside as Lienna opened another binder. On the first page was a photo of one of the shelves that lined the tomb's walls, but it wasn't empty. Sitting on it was a small silver sculpture of a woman warrior, a shield in one hand and a heavy sword in the other.

"Bingo," I whispered.

We went through the binder at top speed, snapping photos as we searched for an artifact that resembled the image from our stolen Trident file. Page after page flipped past, and I was about to lose hope when we reached the last one.

There it was: a copy of the same photo Darius had hijacked from Jayce Tyrian's office of a large, circular amulet with intricate and delicate lines etched in a swirling pattern across its surface.

I started snapping rapid photos while Lienna leaned over a page ripped from a notebook that had been tucked into a protective plastic sleeve.

"This was written by the site's first archeologist," Lienna murmured. "He says here all the markings on the sarcophagus are about never opening it for fear of unleashing the horror of her power upon the world."

"And he opened it anyway," I growled. "What's with scholarly types and ignoring ancient warnings?"

Lienna didn't seem to be listening, her eyes zipping across the page. "When he opened the sarcophagus, he found this artifact. It had been placed inside with Bodil's remains."

"Of course it was." A spiral of dread pulled at my gut. "Since they buried it with her, can we assume it's what gave her crazy powers? And that's why the Consilium wants it?"

"Maybe." Lienna tapped the page. "The archeologist was shocked to find that the artifact didn't have any Old Norse on it. The markings are all in Ancient Greek, Latin, and Arabic."

My eyebrows arched up. "Arabic?"

"Like the sha'ir. Maybe it originally belonged to him."

"And he just handed it over to Bodil so she could use it to conquer Denmark?"

"I don't know." Lienna's attention moved to the bottom of the page. "The last thing the archeologist wrote is that while he was waiting for instructions on where to transport the artifact for further study, it was stolen."

"By Floris Visser?" I guessed.

"Seems likely, since she's the one who has it." Lienna flipped the page over, but there was nothing else in the binder. "This is the only page I saw with this person's handwriting. Did the archeologist quit after the artifact was stolen?"

"Maybe he was fired for the lax security on his worksite," I suggested. "Either way, I'm more concerned about the artifact itself, AKA the weapon the Consilium is a scant thirty million bucks from acquiring. The archaeologist didn't say anything about what it does?"

Lienna straightened with a sigh. "It was stolen before he could study it in earnest. It can take years to work out what an artifact does and how to use it, and even longer when they're this old."

Something niggled at my brain, and I rolled my shoulders as I chased down the thought. "If the artifact was stolen before it could be studied and its purpose could be determined …"

"Then how did the Consilium know it was something they wanted?" Lienna finished for me. "Are they assuming it's a deadly weapon because Bodil was so powerful?"

"Maybe, but the story on the walls is pretty suspect. Even if the Consilium is hoping the artifact granted Bodil super-mage powers, that seems like flimsy evidence for an eight-figure purchase."

"We must be missing something."

We were definitely missing something. I turned away from the table, my gaze sliding over the hulking iron sarcophagus. The eyes of the figures carved on the walls watched me as I scanned the script. The "god killer" had been so terrified of Bodil and her artifact that he'd built all of this to keep her power from ever rising again.

Tension built inside me. The shadows seemed darker, the subtle flickering of the lights creating darts of movement in my peripheral vision. Had Bodil just been one ultra powerful mythic? Or had something truly evil been sealed away here?

Bing!

The loud chime made me leap half a foot off the ground. My shoes reconnected with the stone floor, and I realized the sound had been a text notification. Damn, I was getting jumpy.

I pulled out my phone. A message from Darius awaited me.

```
She isn't in Europe.
```

I blinked at the inadequately informative four words. Another message popped up.

```
A flight from Copenhagen to Ho Chi Minh
City departs in three hours. Don't miss it.
```

"What was that?" Lienna asked.

"Darius found Floris Visser." I pocketed my phone. "It looks like we're going to Vietnam."

And there, we'd find out just how badly the Consilium wanted a Viking queen's mysterious weapon of war.

I WAS NOW ON MY THIRD CONTINENT, sixth country, and seventh city—if you ignored the smaller towns, villages, and suburbs I'd passed through—in less than a week. After a nearly twenty-four-hour flight that had stopped in Frankfurt, then again in Singapore, Lienna and I finally met up with Darius outside of arrivals at Tan Son Nhat International Airport in Ho Chi Minh City, Vietnam.

I'd spent over twenty years of my life confined to a single ketchup-chip-loving nation, and now I was a jet-setting international man of mystery. I wished I'd had more opportunities to collect a tacky memento at each pit stop to add to my collection of case souvenirs currently cluttering up my desk. Maybe a set of goofy patches to adorn the worn and fraying backpack I'd been hauling around with me.

An hour after landing, we were cruising westward, away from the city formerly known as Saigon, in the back of a silver minivan. Our driver, Khuong, was a local mythic with thinning black hair and deep laugh lines around his eyes. He was either one of Darius's old contacts or someone the GM had found through his vast global network of eyes and ears. I wasn't fully in the know regarding their relationship.

As the urban environment of Vietnam's most populated metropolis disappeared behind us, overtaken by the lush greenery and occasional cluster of industrial buildings that dotted the countryside, Khuong gave us a rundown on what he knew about Floris Visser.

"Floris Visser arrived about a month ago and formed an alliance with Lửa và Băng," he said, his tone grim. "'Fire and Ice' in English. They're a notorious criminal guild, all of them mages. Their GM owns a private airfield where Visser has been spending a fair bit of time."

"Is that where the handoff is happening?" Lienna asked.

"According to the rogue I bribed for information, yeah," our driver confirmed. "It's supposed to happen tonight, but they didn't know the exact time."

I glanced out the window at the sun dipping below the horizon, its few remaining streaks of light silhouetting the roadside vegetation. "Tonight" could be an hour from now, which meant our mission clock was ticking.

In the passenger seat, Darius glanced from the road to Khuong. "What can you tell us about the airfield?"

"Heavily guarded by the Fire and Ice crew. At least thirty of them, probably more. There's an electric fence around the perimeter, so the only way in or out is the front gate. That means you'll have to get past the guardhouse, which always has at least two men on duty."

Sneaking past unsuspecting sentries? We could handle that.

"I'll drop you off down the road from the guardhouse, but after that, you're on your own." Khuong glanced at Darius. "I can't help you with the layout inside the fence, but I did hear that Visser has her own protection detail that never leaves her side. That's all I know."

"We'll figure it out," Darius murmured.

Khuong nervously adjusted his grip on the steering wheel. "Fire and Ice isn't like the rogue guilds you're used to. They're constantly at war with other gangs, mythic *and* human. They'll be armed with magic and non-magical weapons, and they won't hesitate to kill a trespasser on sight."

Sounded like a real welcoming batch of baddies.

"They're one of the deadliest rogue guilds in the country," Khuong went on, doing his best to ensure my nerves were wound as tight as possible. "I know you're good, Darius, but one misstep and ..."

"We'll manage, Khuong."

Our driver said nothing more, but his doubt hung in the van's interior like an extra humid cloud of doom.

For the next forty minutes, as nighttime closed in around us and all signs of civilization faded away, Darius, Lienna, and I hashed out our plan. Though we had a whole host of sorcery, psychic, and lumina magic at our fingertips, we collectively agreed that in a situation like this—where information was limited and the stakes were high—it was best to keep it simple.

"We'll only engage if absolutely necessary," Darius said. "Nothing attracts attention faster than a dead body."

Words of wisdom the former assassin had mentioned once or twice before.

Our plan was to sneak onto the airfield using our respective invisifying powers—Darius taking care of himself, and me keeping Lienna and her cat's eye safe from prying eyes. Once inside the airfield proper, we'd split up to search for Visser.

From there, it was only a matter of remaining unseen, locating the weapon, and retreating back to Khuong and his getaway van before Visser—or anyone else—was the wiser.

Our contingency was even simpler: if it all went south or we couldn't steal the weapon undetected, we'd spam the entire airfield with the most potent forms of our collective magic—Blackouts, blinding flashes, and Lienna's new gravity bomb spell—then use the ensuing chaos to snatch what we came for, avoid death or capture, and peace out.

Through the windshield, a tall metal fence came into view—and if a fence could look mean, this one was maximum nasty, with bars too thick to cut and barbed wire coiled along the top. A ways ahead, the guardhouse was a dark shape in the deepening twilight.

Khuong brought the minivan to a stop on the side of the road. Darius, Lienna, and I climbed out, our wireless earpieces tucked into their required head holes.

We circled to the back of the van, where Darius opened the hatch. We covered our vital organs with bulletproof combat vests. Darius buckled a weapons belt around his waist, two sets of long daggers neatly sheathed against his hips. Dressed in all-black civvies, he didn't look like a combat-ready soldier, but he sure as hell looked dangerous.

I added a potion-filled gun to my belt, and Lienna strapped her satchel over her vest before adding two new necklaces and an engraved gold ring, slipped onto her right index finger, to her arsenal. We were ready.

"Well," Darius murmured, "this should be—"

"Don't say it." I squinted a warning in his direction. "So help me Zeus, if you tell us this should be a very straightforward mission."

"… fun," he finished delicately.

Together, we began our trek down the dirt road to the airfield, leaving Khuong to wait in the dark van on the side of the road. The sun had completely set, and the moon competed with the bright, beckoning lights that lit the airfield.

A hundred feet from the guardhouse, Darius gave the signal. Lienna whispered her cat's eye incantation, and all three of us vanished.

As we approached the guardhouse, I heard the low murmur of men talking in Vietnamese. They didn't notice as we slunk through the shadows toward the well-lit entrance, harsh white lights directed at the dirt drive.

As we ducked under the boom barrier, I glimpsed the men inside the guardhouse: black fatigues, bulletproof vests, and machine guns hanging from their shoulders. Holy soldiery shit. They looked more like military black ops than mythics.

Feeling both highly grateful for the miracle that was my invisi-warp and increasingly apprehensive, I surveyed the airfield. Dead ahead, across a wide expanse of tarmac, we had a clear view of the single runway, its length marked by orange lights. On our right was a cluster of smaller single-story buildings, and on our left, beyond a couple of corroded aluminum sheds, was a long, bulky structure—the hangar, large enough to house half a dozen medium-sized aircraft.

I knew Darius was only a few feet away. I could sense his mind, and my ability to gauge distance was improving. Handy, but also low-key alarming.

"Going left," I whispered.

"*Heading right,*" Darius replied, his voice crackling faintly through my earpiece.

My faint awareness of his presence veered away from us. So weird.

Lienna and I peeled off to the left, straight toward the colossal rectangular hangar. Pairs of goons patrolled along the fenced perimeter and between the buildings. Some were easy to spot, while others were dark shapes in the shadows between lights. Out on the tarmac, a handful of them were leaning against a maintenance truck. My adrenaline steadily rose as I subconsciously counted them. Eighteen mythics. All mages.

When it came to classes of magic, the consensus was inarguable: mages represented the most dangerous combination of firepower and flexibility, especially when you grouped up several elements.

This might be the deadliest band of rogues I'd ever encountered.

Even though my halluci-bomb hid both my and Lienna's footfalls, I still felt the urge to tiptoe as we snuck past the sheds and approached the nearest side of the hangar. I wasn't super keen on getting burned, iced, blasted, and crushed into nonexistence by a violent melee of the elements.

We found a door partway along the hangar's exterior wall, but it was locked. Lienna dug into her satchel, searching for a bolt-busting artifact, and I pressed the mic button on my earpiece.

"Darius," I whispered. "Anything yet?"

"*No,*" came a short, terse reply.

"How many rogues have you counted?" I had no doubt he'd been tallying them up, just like I was.

"*Twenty-three.*"

That brought the total to over forty. These guys weren't merely dressed like soldiers; they had the numbers too.

Footsteps crunched, heading our way from around the backside of the building. I put a hand on Lienna's arm, halting her quiet rustling.

Two mythics appeared, patrolling the shadows between the hangar and the electrified fence. They turned the corner and moved toward us, conversing in a low tone.

We pressed ourselves against the building, holding our breath as the two men passed within a couple feet of us. One had daggers strapped to his thighs, while the other carried a polearm. Based on Khuong's intel that these guys were all mages, I assumed those were their switches.

"Should we break open the door?" Lienna whispered once the guards were well past us.

I shook my head, not wanting to linger too long in one spot. "There's got to be an easier way in. Let's keep moving."

We crept along the wall until we reached the front corner, then peered around it, my head above hers like two of the three stooges spying down a hallway they weren't supposed to be in.

The first thing I saw was the tail end of a steel-gray, transport-style military plane waiting just outside the hangar, its cargo bay opened into a long ramp that rested on the pavement. Inside the bay, I spotted a jacked-up blond dude with the kind of hair and beard that gave off definite Thor vibes, which got me thinking that this plane wasn't owned by the Fire and Ice guild.

Did it belong to Floris Visser? Or the Consilium buyer?

A dozen or so black-garbed mythics stood around the entrance of the open hangar door, about fifty feet away from us. Past their heads, I could see a tall woman: Floris Visser. Her long hair was white-blond and her face sharp and angular under the bright illumination.

Behind her, four hulking bodyguards formed a protective semicircle. Each one looked like they could run a marathon, rip your head from your body to use as an improvised shot put, then wrestle a puma as a cooldown.

Sitting at Visser's feet, right in the middle of all that muscle, was a black Pelican case. It was pretty large for a single amulet-style artifact, but maybe she wanted her thirty-million-dollar weapon to seem more weighty and impressive.

Lienna tapped her earpiece. "Darius? We have eyes on Visser. She has a case that probably contains the weapon."

There was a crackle across the mic.

"*Copy. I'll join you … in a few minutes.*"

Was it just me, or did he sound a touch out of breath?

Lienna must have noticed too because she asked, "Are you okay?"

Another crackling pause.

"*A minor setback,*" he replied. "*I just need to hide some bodies.*"

Once an assassin …

Assuming our time was about to run short, I refocused on the obstacles in front of me. Between Floris, her personal guard, and the assortment of rogue mages meeting with her, over a dozen mythics were loitering in the hangar. A couple of spiffy six-seater planes looked remarkably small beneath the high ceiling, while tool chests, rolling staircases, spare parts, and other supplies cluttered the space along the walls. My eyes zipped across the collection of enemies and objects, mapping a path.

"I think I can grab it," I whispered to Lienna. "I can slip between those muscle heads, lift the case, and we can skedaddle before anyone notices Darius's bodies."

"Are you sure?" Lienna shifted anxiously. "Maybe we should—"

"We don't have time." I straightened from my crouch. "I'm going for it. Wait here."

I sucked in a breath and focused my mind on my invisi-bomb, paying special attention to the play of light and shadow created by the eyeball-abusing illumination in and around the hangar. Then I launched forward.

I got exactly one step before Lienna grabbed my arm and hauled me back. Her nails dug painfully into my elbow.

"Kit, *look.*"

The barely tempered horror in her voice sent a wave of fear rushing down my spine. I followed the direction of her pointing finger, and that fear morphed into a zero-Kelvin cold spell that turned my blood to solid ice.

"You've got to be shitting me," I muttered.

Descending the ramp of the transport plane was another man. A familiar man. A chrome-domed, psychotically sadistic, resistant-to-my-powers, bane-of-my-existence man.

Benjamin. Fucking. Kade.

18

Kade was the buyer. What a surprise. Who else would the Consilium send to pick up their apocalyptic artifact? Who else could possibly play the role of glorified deliveryman? Apparently, that bald bastard didn't have enough on his plate with trying to kidnap me.

While I swore like a sailor with a stubbed toe, Lienna dragged me back around the corner of the hangar as though that might shield us from his clairsentience.

"Are we far enough away?" she asked urgently. "Do you think he can sense us from here? Will he recognize us with all the other people around?"

I answered with an unhelpful curse. My actual answers, if I'd been coherent enough to share them, would've been, "Probably not," "Probably yes," "Definitely yes," and to the final question she hadn't yet voiced, "*Absolutely* yes, we are so fucked."

Did we have a Plan C? Because if it somehow involved taking that asshole on a ride up to thirty thousand feet in his own plane, then sending him ground side without a parachute, I'd happily volunteer for the job of Primary Pusher.

Teeth gritted, I poked my head around the corner. Kade had joined the group surrounding Visser, and he was speaking to her with almost deferential body language—which put me that much more on edge. How tough was Visser that even Kade didn't want to tick her off?

Kade wasn't looking our way. Could I assume we were outside the radius of his clairsentient powers? Regardless, the moment we got any closer, he'd know we were here and why.

I tapped my earpiece. "Darius, where are you? We found the buyer, and it's Kade."

"*Kade?*" Darius repeated after a brief pause. "*Where are you?*"

"Near side of the hangar. Front corner."

"I'll be there in three minutes. Wait for me."

Three minutes wasn't long, but it felt like an eternity. I leaned out to take another quick peek. Visser was now holding the black case with the artifact. Kade extended his hand to take it.

Shiiiiit.

"Darius," I muttered, "they aren't wasting any time. We don't have three minutes."

His voice didn't pop into my ears. Had he run into trouble?

"We can't wait," I told Lienna. "Kade could get on that plane any second now. We have to move."

Her eyes were wide with trepidation. "But how? Kade will sense us."

"I don't need to get that close." I waved my hand. "I'm a telekinetic. I can yank the case away from him, Blythe-style."

One more glance around the corner—the case was in Kade's hand.

It was now or never.

"Cover me," I said, then rushed into the hangar.

Cursing, Lienna stepped out behind me as I made a beeline for the group of mythics, invisible to everyone but Kade. He was handing something to Visser and didn't so much as glance my way.

I narrowed my focus to the black case in his other hand, imagining my psychic grip wrapping around it. Faint pressure pulled at the muscles in my arms.

"*Ori gravitatis maximum inicio globum!*" Lienna chanted, somewhere behind me.

I yanked as hard as I could with my telekinetic powers.

Three things happened at once: the case wrenched from Kade's hand, he and Visser both turned sharply toward me, and a giant, fizzy orange star soared over my head.

Lienna's spell looked like the Roman-candle sparkler barrage she'd used on Kade's goons, the one that had erupted into mini black holes. Except this spell emitted a single shot—a Hulk-sized, hopped-up-on-steroids shot.

Sparkling brightly, the scintillating spell flew in a beautiful arc, reaching its peak halfway between me and its targets, its trajectory perfectly aimed to land smack-dab in the middle of the goon convention. The Pelican case flew through the air just above the ground in the opposite direction, racing toward me.

Visser threw her hand up. A volley of monstrous ice shards carried on a howling gust of wind hurtled into Lienna's magical projectile.

The moment the ice touched it, Lienna's spell flashed blindingly bright, then erupted into a swirling black orb.

Everything nearby was sucked toward it—including the artifact case I was zooming toward my waiting hands.

It was wrenched from my telekinetic grip with cosmic force, flying into the air along with a few unfortunate mythics and their various belongings. Its gravitational pull dragged me several feet toward it, but I was far enough away to resist its supercharged yank.

Unfortunately, so were Kade, Visser, and most of the Fire and Ice rogues.

Staggering against the pull of the spell, I reinforced my invisi-bomb and tried to spot the black case amidst the swirling black gravity orb the size of a smart car. The spell waned, and several men fell out of it, landing with thuds on the concrete floor of the hangar.

A blast of icy wind hit me hard. Lienna grabbed my arm as we both stumbled, slipping on the suddenly slick floor. Ice was spreading across it, and the wind gusted harder as the air hazed.

Standing beside Kade, Visser had her arm outstretched toward me and Lienna. *Invisible* me and Lienna.

Belatedly, I noticed the new piece of jewelry around her wrist—the item Kade had given her. A leather bracelet just like his anti-Psychica one.

Visser was immune to my warps.

Had Kade bought a whole goddamn six-pack of those things at the flea market?

Dark, angry clouds roiled across the ceiling, spinning ominously as the spiraling wind picked up in velocity. It whipped sharp pellets of ice into my face, half blinding me. Lienna ducked behind me, frantically spinning her cube.

"*Ori te formo cupolam!*" she cried.

Her blue shield shimmered into being around us a moment before three white-hot streaks of lightning blasted down from a vortex of clouds, hitting the watery dome with ear-splitting cracks of thunder. The shrieking wind whipped into a tight maelstrom that closed around us—a tornado.

Visser had called down a *tornado*. For a split second, all I felt was jilted fury at yet another way Faustus Trivium had screwed with me: his pathetic example of tempe magic had given me a wholly inadequate idea of what Visser could do. Faustus was an incompetent cretin on every possible level.

Visser's weather-from-hell battered Lienna's shield, and it rippled wildly under the onslaught. I couldn't see anything outside it but wind, clouds, and ice.

Thunder rumbled directly overhead. Another lightning bolt slammed down onto the shield, and it burst apart.

The weathery assault crashed into us—ice and dirt whipping into our faces, the wind almost shoving us off our feet. Eyes scrunched, I grabbed Lienna and threw us down, trying to protect her with my body, my arms over my head.

The battering wind died to an ominously cyclonic breeze. I shoved up into a crouch, took a look around—and went still, my pulse hammering in my throat. Beside me, Lienna had pushed onto her hands and knees, but she didn't make a move either.

We were trapped.

Visser stood fifteen feet away, a hand raised casually toward us. She'd pulled out her switch at some point—a nasty-looking stiletto dagger with a curved cross guard. Her sunken, hooded eyes watched us with zero mercy.

Arrayed behind her was her personal guard of muscle-headed mythics, and completing the semi-circle that cut off our exit and hemmed us in against the hangar wall were a solid twenty Fire and Ice mages.

For a petrified moment, I wondered if my psycho warping powers were working at all. I was still invisi-bombing the shit out of every mind here to make me and Lienna undetectable, yet everyone was looking our way.

I glanced at my partner out of the side of my eye and realized my mistake. Visser's arctic storm had left frost and bits of ice clinging to us—and I hadn't incorporated that into my warp.

Visser could see us, thanks to the artifact Kade had given her, and she'd passed that gift on to everyone else with her polar assault.

Speaking of Kade, the billiard-headed bastard was lingering a few steps behind Visser, watching with mild curiosity as two dozen mages prepared to obliterate me and Lienna. The black artifact case was safely back in his hand.

Shit.

"Tell me who you work for," Visser ordered, her accented voice rough like a chain-smoker's.

Double, triple, quadruple *shit*.

Kade arched his eyebrows as if asking what I intended to do now.

Visser waited a moment longer, then twirled her blade. "Then you can just die. Kill them!"

Not waiting for the inevitable onslaught of the rogue guild's eponymous magic, I dropped a Funhouse halluci-bomb over the entire hangar. Everyone—save Visser and Kade—reeled, but it wasn't enough to stop them. Fire, ice, wind, water, and weather launched at us from every angle.

"*Ori elementa diffundo!*" Lienna shouted.

A shimmering orb, almost transparent, billowed out from one of Lienna's new necklaces. As it expanded around us, the incoming elemental missiles met the shimmering barrier and fizzled. Instead of electric bolts and fireballs, we were lightly dusted with sparks and ash. Even Visser's wind-propelled ice blades had diffused into snowflakes.

It was one of the craziest abjuration spells I'd ever seen from my partner, but it was already fading—and the mages had lots of juice left.

I fractured everyone's perceptions by several more degrees, straining to make it complex enough to mess with a bunch of brains at once. I pulled my potion gun and fired indiscriminately at the surrounding enemies, dropping a couple of them before they could launch a second attack.

It wasn't enough—there were too many of them and Visser was ramping up for another wave of tempestuous weather, totally unperturbed by my warps.

This was the end of the road.

A voice crackled through my ear. "*Going dark.*"

Darius's warning came an instant before his magic struck.

My vision went black.

Not merely *dark*. It was a total absence of any illumination whatsoever, more encompassing than the deepest moonless night, more impenetrable than a sealed subterranean cave.

Lienna's gasp and the sudden eruption of alarmed shouts from the enemy mythics told me I wasn't the only one who'd gone blind. Darius must've blanketed the entire hangar in this absolute eclipse.

With our imminent deaths marginally averted, one thought dominated my brain: get to Kade.

But where in all this utter pandemonium was he?

I concentrated. It only took me a moment to find Kade's mind among all the strangers—he'd given me a real clear picture of the psychotic slimeball he was, so I knew which gross, glutinous brain to feel for. The moment I locked onto him, I realized he was moving away from me.

"Lienna!" I yelled, reaching blindly for her. "Kade's this way!"

Our hands connected in the darkness, and I pulled her forward—right as the darkness popped. Light poured into my unprepared pupils, revealing Visser and two muscle heads mere steps away from us.

"Kit, go!" Lienna raised her hand as Visser swiped her dagger through the air. "*Ori repercutio!*"

The gold ring on Lienna's hand flashed faintly as an ice-shard-laden gust erupted from Visser's dagger. The elemental attack met the shimmering glow of Lienna's ring and rebounded, blasting Visser and her minions.

Half impressed by yet another new spell and half panicking at the thought of leaving Lienna alone in this hellish magic brawl, I invisi-warped myself and ran toward the open hangar door.

I sped past a cluster of enraged, confused mages—mages who appeared to be blind. As shouts rang out, I glimpsed a flicker of a certain silver fox as he slit a man's throat and vanished. The rogues were going down fast, unable to defend against the assassin in all the chaos.

Breaking free of the melee, I sprinted onto the tarmac outside the hangar. Ahead of me, Kade was all alone, striding toward the ramp into the plane's cargo bay. Its engines were starting up, their roar growing louder and louder.

I couldn't warp his mind. I couldn't sneak up on him. So I would charge that bastard down and use my fists instead.

Kade glanced back over his shoulder then broke into a run.

I pumped my arms, pushing my muscles for more speed. Concentrating hard, I locked my telekinetic grip around the black case and wrenched it toward me.

Kade lurched, almost losing his grip. At the foot of the ramp, he whirled around to face me. His grin was sharp and taunting.

"Want this?" he called, holding up the case.

I gave it another telekinetic yank, throwing everything into it. The sudden weight on all my muscles made me stumble, and I almost fell.

Kade still held the case. Telekinetic strength was limited by physical strength, and Kade, with his linebacker build, was stronger than me. This was a tug o' war I would lose.

So, I let go. The sudden release of tension caused Kade to recoil and fall backward.

I reached him as he jumped to his feet. He lifted the case, and my swinging fist crashed into it instead of his solar plexus. Pain splintered through my knuckles.

Kade backed up the ramp as I lunged for him, slamming into his middle. He went down, and I drove my fist into his kidney before he threw me off. I rolled away, afraid he'd try to pin me.

As I leaped up, unsteady on the steep ramp, Kade tossed the case into the cargo hold, where the blond Thor-esque minion caught it.

Baring my teeth, I hit the man with a Blackout warp—but he didn't go down. Damn the bald creep for arming all his underlings with anti-Kit artifacts.

A fistfight it would be.

I rushed Kade again, thankful that his "don't kill the psycho warper" orders prevented him from pulling a weapon on me. We came together with fists swinging, the slant of the ramp giving him an extra foot of height. He blocked my first hit, but I smashed his kneecap with my second. I tried to tackle him again, but he got a grip on my vest. With a grunt of effort, he hauled me up and flipped me over his shoulder.

I hit the metal floor with a gasp, my earpiece dislodging from its spot and skittering away. Damn, I should have remembered Obi-Wan's wisdom about the high ground.

Kade's foot hit my gut, the blow tempered by my bulletproof vest. I rolled sideways to get away from him.

"Go," Kade barked. Not at me, I assumed, since I wasn't going anywhere without that case.

I shoved up, ready to leap at Kade again, when the floor rumbled violently. A loud motor sound filled the back of the cargo bay, and the plane lurched forward.

The plane was moving?

Kade sneered at me, our positions reversed—I was inside the plane, facing the cargo bay ramp. Sickening fear rippled down my spine and weakened my legs.

Behind Kade, the cargo ramp was lifting. It was *closing*. The plane was picking up speed, moving away from the hangar—toward the runway.

My gaze jumped to Kade, who grinned like a shark smelling blood in the water and knowing his dinner was moments away.

Oh hell no. He was abducting me again, and I hadn't even realized it.

I looked back over my shoulder, where the blond minion had retreated with the case. Two more dark-clad goons waited.

I was outnumbered and trapped, and pretty soon I'd be several thousand feet in the air.

"So nice of you to save me a trip back to Vancouver," Kade said, cruel humor weighing down his voice. "I'm afraid we'll have to make a quick pit stop in New York before I can hand you over to my superiors."

I faced him again, my heart hammering in the vicinity of my Adam's apple. I couldn't take them all, not without warps—but I couldn't leave the artifact.

Kade read the conflict on my face. "You'll be our property one way or another, Kit. It's up to you how much you want to suffer first."

The decision I had to make felt like a tearing pain in my chest. I let out a wordless shout, thrust out my arm, and made a hooking motion.

The back of Kade's shirt whipped up and pulled over his head, covering his eyes and restricting his arms. I charged straight into him, ramming my shoulder into his stomach. We slammed down and rolled onto the half-closed cargo ramp. It kept rising, tilting us back into the plane.

Kade pulled his shirt off his eyes and grabbed for me as I lunged toward the ramp. His fingers grazed my arm as I used telekinesis to shove myself away from him.

His laughter reached my ears as I rolled off the ramp. I dropped, arms clamped around my head, and hit the tarmac.

I'd seen a hundred versions of the "bail from a moving vehicle and roll across the pavement" move performed by stunt doubles and adrenaline-addicted action stars, but holy shit, I hadn't realized how much it hurt. Like getting body-slammed by a brick wall.

I rolled until my momentum flagged, then sprawled against the tarmac. The transport plane's engines thundered, painfully blasting my eardrums, and I lifted my head to see the aircraft accelerating down the runway, its cargo hatch fully closed. The nose lifted and the plane was away.

The weapon was gone.

Anger boiled through me—at Kade and at myself. But I didn't have time to marinate in self-pity. This wasn't over yet.

Shoving to my feet, I forced my aching body into a limping run. A couple hundred yards away, magic burst and flashed in the hangar. A pillar of terramage-shifted earth had sprouted from the tarmac like an ugly tree.

I pushed myself faster. I'd left Lienna and Darius alone to fight a horde of mages. If they were hurt—if they'd been killed—

Another flash of fire, and then a sudden, earth-shaking boom blasted outward. The silhouetted figures in and around the hangar were knocked off their feet. A roiling fireball that looked way more like burning jet fuel than pyro magic exploded, belching smoke into the air.

What the hell had happened?

Cursing my lost earpiece, I kept running, closing in on the action. From out of the smoke, the tall, lanky form of Floris Visser appeared, backing away from something as she lashed her switch through the air, frosty wind spiraling around her like a shield.

Before whatever magic she'd been about to unleash could manifest, a barrage of black darts fired out of the smoke and peppered Visser. They went right through her, but they weren't harmless. She dropped to her knees, all signs of her weather magic dissipating.

Lienna charged out of the hangar, clutching her wooden cube, her hair tangled and her satchel bouncing at her side. Soot and blood streaked her face.

"Lienna!" I yelled, veering toward her.

One of Visser's bodyguards jumped between his boss and my partner, slamming his pike-shaped switch into the ground. A wall of earth erupted up through the tarmac around Visser, creating a circular barrier.

Lienna spotted me amidst the bedlam and ran toward me. "Kit!"

I caught her with both arms, holding her tightly. "Where's Darius?"

"Here."

In a blink, he appeared. He was sootier than Lienna, and his clothes were scorched on one side. I had a sudden idea of who'd been responsible for the huge-ass explosion—though I had no idea *how*.

I took a deep breath, settling my lungs and taking in the warzone around us. Through the ash, ice, and smoke, I could see at least ten rogue mages homing in on us, unwilling to give up the fight.

My jaw clenched. Keeping Lienna and Darius out of my halluci-bomb, I unleashed a Blackout that cascaded through the entire hangar. With a clarity I'd never experienced before, I felt every mind—every single one, dozens of them—buckle under the all-consuming emptiness. I could feel their emotions flash into terror as their senses vanished into the void.

The weight of the warp crushed my mind. Foggy, dizzy numbness rolled over me, but I would hold it until we were safe. Every mythic in sight collapsed, writhing on the ground, the air filling with screams and begging cries for help.

Only Visser stayed as she was, staring at us from behind her crumbled earthy shield, her magic wiped out by Lienna's spell.

"Time to go." Darius placed a hand on my shoulder. "I'll hide us."

Panting, I dropped the warp. Darius took my elbow with one hand and Lienna's with the other. He steered us away from the hangar as the screams stopped, leaving only the roar of the blazing fuel tanks. Visser kept staring at the spot where we'd disappeared, her face twisted with fury and fear.

Invisible and empty-handed, we left the burning hangar and vacant runway behind.

19

FROM THE SIXTH-FLOOR WINDOW of our hotel, the glowing nightlife of Ho Chi Minh City seemed inappropriately cheerful. A fitful rain shower had dampened the city, and the streetlamps reflected off the puddles. Even the persistent headlights of traffic appeared brighter than they should have.

This juxtaposed brutally with the mood inside our room.

Three rooms, actually—Darius had booked one for each of us. When the receptionist quoted him a price of three million Vietnamese dong, I'd about choked. After the shitshow we'd endured, the last thing Darius needed was to remortgage his house to pay for hotel rooms.

Then I'd learned that a million dong was equivalent to less than sixty Canadian loonies.

We'd gathered in the first room we'd reached, our belongings dumped on the floor in the entryway and our tired bodies slouched on the furniture—Lienna on the edge of the queen bed, me on an ottoman beside the window, and Darius in an uncomfortable-looking armchair.

Lienna rubbed her hands over her soot-smudged face. "That was …"

I shifted away from the window. "A disaster?"

Darius didn't comment. He had his elbows braced on his knees, and it seemed like all his remaining brain power was dedicated to keeping his head from lolling side to side. Of all the magic classes, Elementaria took the most brutal toll on its users. Darius had pushed himself to his limit.

And it had all been for nothing. Kade was gone, and the weapon was gone with him. Not exactly a mission to write home about.

"What do we do now?" Lienna muttered. "Kade could take the weapon anywhere. Do we just … give up?"

"I don't know where he's taking the weapon." I leaned back against the cool glass of the window. "But his next stop is New York."

Darius lifted his head. Haggard exhaustion had grayed his complexion. "How do you know that?"

"He told me." I shrugged. "I don't think he was lying since he was pretty sure he'd trapped me on that plane with him when he said it. I barely managed to jump out before it took off."

There was a moment of silence in which Darius and Lienna were either contemplating why Kade would go to New York or wondering how I'd messed up so badly that I'd almost gotten abducted again while *also* failing to steal the weapon.

"Should we go to New York?" Lienna suggested.

"Unless we recruit the world's largest team of telethesians, we'll never find him. Besides, all he said was 'New York.' He could've meant the whole damn state, not the city."

"What about the New York MPD?" my partner suggested. "Could we ask them for help?"

"Can we trust them?" I countered. "Our little Canadian precinct has a mole. Who knows what kind of Manhattan sewer rat or Consilium infestation is lurking in one of the world's largest precincts?"

Lienna sagged, her shoulders drooping with hopelessness.

I glanced at Darius. "I don't suppose you have any contacts in NYC we can call in for backup?"

"Not for this." He pushed to his feet as though every muscle in his body was three seconds from atrophying. "There's nothing we can do right now. We should get some sleep. In the morning …"

He trailed off in a not-very-Darius way.

I jumped up. My bones ached, and my flesh was bruised from tumbling across the runway, but I was nowhere near as exhausted as the luminamage. I helped carry his luggage to the room next door, made sure he didn't need anything, then left him to collapse in privacy.

As I walked the ten steps back to the first room, ugly emotions churned in my gut. Darius had given that fight everything—I doubted Lienna and I would be alive if he hadn't—but I still had psychic gas in the tank.

Which meant I *hadn't* given that fight everything. I should have done more. I should have found a way to beat Kade.

I let myself back into our original room and found Lienna digging first aid supplies out of her luggage. I took them from her hands.

"Let me," I said quietly. "Come on."

I led her into the reasonably spacious—for a cheap hotel room—bathroom, where she leaned on the counter. Wetting a cloth, I started wiping the soot off her face.

"I can do it," she murmured.

"I'm your first aid Kit, remember?"

She smiled, offering no more protest. When I'd removed the signs of battle from her face, she pulled her long-sleeved shirt off, revealing a fitted black tank top underneath. Scrapes and smears of blood marked her arms. I carefully cleaned them, finding more bruises, as well as a burn on her left wrist.

I exhaled roughly as I opened a jar of neatly labeled burn ointment. "I'm sorry."

"For what?"

I dipped my fingertips into the white salve, unable to meet her eyes. "Kade got the better of me—*again*. It's my fault we lost the weapon."

"It's no one's fault." She watched me gently smooth the cream over her blistered wrist. "Nothing went according to plan, and the odds were stacked against us from the start."

I swapped the cream for a pack of big Band-Aids, which I applied to the scrapes on her arms. "You could have died. I should have done more."

"Kit." She pulled the bandages from my hands, set them on the counter, then grasped my wrists. "Fighting the Consilium, stopping them—you aren't solely responsible. I know it feels that way, especially since you've been working with both Darius and Blythe, but you can't carry the weight of it all on your shoulders alone."

My hands curled into fists. She was right that I felt ultimately responsible, but that's because I *was* responsible. Bouncing back and forth between Darius and Blythe had forced me into the uncomfortable role of being the only person who knew everything that was really going on. If I didn't take on that responsibility, who would?

"The Consilium has the weapon." I looked down at her fingers curled around my wrists. "I can't prove it, but I think they're going to use it soon. They didn't drop thirty million dollars and pull Kade off his 'abduct Kit' mission for something they might not need."

Lienna gave a small nod. "Probably not."

I dragged my gaze back up to hers. "By the time we wake up tomorrow, Kade might have leveled half of Manhattan with super-mage magic."

She released my wrists and brought her hands to my face, pressing her warm palms to my cheeks. "That won't happen, Kit. The Consilium operates in secret. Causing mass destruction isn't their MO."

She didn't know that. None of us knew what the Consilium planned to do.

Her hands slid down to my shoulders, and she pulled me closer. When she draped her arms around my neck, I wrapped her in an embrace. We held each other, oblivious to the dirt on our clothes or the lingering smell of smoke and blood in our hair.

I wanted to hold her like this forever. I wanted to never leave this room so we wouldn't have to face more danger, more threats, more unanswerable questions, and more Consilium bullshit that we shouldn't have been responsible for stopping, but somehow we were.

An ex-conman with inexplicably growing powers, an abjuration prodigy trying to make up for her father's corruption, and a former assassin who'd fought this battle once before.

We were up against a cabal of ruthless, untouchable, anonymous power players in the upper echelon of the world's most powerful organization.

Lienna combed her fingers through my hair, probably trying to soften the rigid tension in my shoulders. I settled my hands on her waist, leaning back slightly to bring her face into view.

Her eyes were gentle with understanding and dampened by weariness, but behind both was that mysterious glint. I'd wondered since the day I met her what that glint meant, and for the first time, I had a real inkling.

It was the determination and passion, the sheer force of her personality that drove her to keep reaching for the impossibly high standards she set for herself. She wasn't giving up.

Neither would I.

My fingers brushed across her cheek as I slid my hand into her hair. She tilted her face up, cheeks flushing and lips parting with anticipation. I leaned down.

The kiss started slow, building with gradual, inevitable intensity. Finally, there was no danger, no undue influence, no adrenaline rush. It was just the two of us, arms around each other, bodies pressed close, mouths locked.

It was the kind of kiss I thought I'd never get with Lienna. It was exactly a thousand times better than I'd imagined.

Our lips parted, her warm breath whispering over my skin. I rubbed my thumb against her cheek.

"You should get ready for bed," I told her softly. "We need sleep."

She nodded, her cheeks flushed and her eyes a little wide. She pushed up onto her toes, pressing one more kiss to my lips.

I left her in the bathroom and took over the chair Darius had vacated. As the sounds of running water filled the bathroom, my thoughts wandered back to my failed attempt to steal the weapon—but hating every iota of Kade's miserable existence wouldn't accomplish anything except ruining the memory of that kiss with Lienna.

Levering back to my feet, I grabbed my laptop and keys. Sitting on the bed with my legs stretched out, I inserted the USB stick and raced through the TOR browser setup until a green cursor blinked on a black screen, waiting for the mole to join the chat.

Only after a log-in message from "Degu" had appeared did I bother considering what time it was in Vancouver.

```
>Degu: Who is this?

>You: Rose Petal.

>Degu: Word around the precinct is you're
on an extended vacation. In my experience,
that's usually code for a forced leave of
absence because you're a screwup.
```

Okay, dude, hit me where it hurts, why don't you.

While my few days of globetrotting were not, in fact, the result of a work-related snafu, I couldn't deny that "screwup" was an appropriate assessment of my current state—on a scale the mole couldn't even fathom.

```
>You: Not exactly. Have you found anything
on the IA audits I asked about?

>Degu: This is a give-and-take
relationship. Satisfy my curiosity on your
whereabouts and I'll tell you what I've
uncovered.
```

I groaned aloud. I was so not in the mood for this underhanded furball's games.

```
>You: If I tell you I'm in a time zone 14
hours ahead of you, is that good enough?

>Degu: I'd prefer GPS coordinates, but I'll
take what I can get.
```

```
>You: Asia is lovely this time of year.

>Degu: Fine.
```

The cursor blinked for several long seconds. I waited, hoping the mole was busy typing up all sorts of juicy IA details for me.

```
>Degu: Considering what I had to do to get
this info, you owe me big. For starters,
Söze's audit on our precinct? Those orders
came straight from Sparks.
```

Oh shit. So Commissioner Sparks wasn't merely *aware* of Söze and Kade's nefarious intentions; he'd sicced the two murderous slimeballs on us.

```
>Degu: Sparks personally ordered 9 precinct
audits, including ours, over the past 2
yrs. The audits he DIDN'T order seemed
legit, but the others had no real history
of corruption or incompetence. But the IA
still went in and dismantled their
leadership. Söze was involved in 5 of the
audits, and we were the only precinct to
come out the other end still functioning.
```

Holy chaotic crap. Sparks was deliberately unraveling entire precincts.

Scratch that.

The *Consilium* was deliberately unraveling entire precincts.

"That can't be good," I muttered, reaching for the keyboard.

"What can't be good?"

I jolted, looking up to find Lienna standing beside me, her hair tied up in a bun and an oversized t-shirt making her look extra cozy. I'd been so focused on the mole's information that I hadn't heard her leave the bathroom.

I scooted into the middle of the bed, tilting the laptop invitingly. She sat beside me and leaned close to read what

"Degu" had said. Her eyebrows scrunched tighter and tighter as her gaze zipped across the text.

"This *definitely* isn't good."

"Seems to be a running theme with these guys." I straightened the laptop on my thighs and typed a quick question.

```
>You: What happened to the other eight
precincts?

>Degu: People quit or were fired or
disappeared. Inexperienced agents got
promoted to positions of power. Admin roles
were left vacant. Post-audits, the affected
cities saw reported mythic crimes up 200%,
bounty completions down 40%, guild
compliance down 35%, and incidents of
public magic exposure up 1600%. The
Dissimulation Department had to scramble to
get things under control.
```

"You know it's bad when the DD shows up," I remarked grimly.

Lienna nodded. "But why? What's the point of messing up precincts?"

A damn good question. Yeah, Sparks and the Consilium were colossal bags of week-old elephant shit, but even the baddest of bad guys generally had a reason for their evil misdeeds.

```
>Degu: Now get this. Over the same 2 yr
period, Sparks tried to launch an
investigation into the DD six separate
times. His justification: the DD's poor
performance in the same cities where the IA
sent the precincts into a death spiral. He
blamed the DD for not doing a good enough
job at handling the rise in magic exposure.
```

"That's bullshit," Lienna said, scowling at the screen. "The IA created the problem, and besides that, it's never been the DD's job to police mythics."

I nodded in agreement. Local agents were the first line of defense when something went wrong with magic secrecy, and only when shit got too big or too messy did the DD step in. Say what you will about the authoritarian regime of one Captain Aurelia Blythe, but she ran a ship so tight, the only time I'd seen DD agents on the streets of Vancouver was a particularly memorable day when two angry super-fae re-enacted *King Kong vs. Godzilla* in broad daylight.

My fingers zipped over the keyboard, adding another question.

```
>You: What happened to the investigation
attempts?

>Degu: Nothing. The DD shut that shit down
each time. The department is too powerful
to get pushed around by the IA, and
Ashbluff has been in charge for 20 yrs. He
knows what he's doing.
```

"Ashbluff?" I muttered, rifling through my memory banks for the name.

"Director of the DD," Lienna informed me. "My dad said he's the only department head who is well-liked by all the GM coalitions."

I drummed my fingers on the side of the laptop. "Was the purpose of all the precinct audits to disrupt the DD and get rid of Ashbluff? Does Sparks just have a burning hatred for this guy, or was there some other reason?"

"It can't be that simple. When Sparks sent Söze and Kade to destroy our precinct, they were also ordered to capture and/or kill Darius and his allies."

"Right," I muttered, my head aching with all the unanswered questions. I thought for a moment, then typed in a reply.

```
>You: What's YOUR take on all this?

>Degu: That's your job, Sherlock. I just
provide the information. If you want more,
I suggest you bring me back a souvenir.

>You: There's a shop here with cute little
mugs that have different names on them.
What name should I look for?

>Degu has logged out.
```

Oh well, it was worth a try.

I unplugged the USB stick and tossed my keys into my open bag, where it sat beside the bed. "We can assume the Consilium isn't particularly fond of Director Ashbluff."

"That sounds like a safe bet." Lienna pulled the laptop onto her legs and opened the MPD archives. "The Consilium already controls the head of the IA, and if Kade's father is also involved with the Consilium, they control the head of the Obscura Influentia department too. That's two of the four most powerful MPD departments."

"What are the other two?"

"According to my dad, Special Investigations ..."

I remembered that one—Darius had fictitiously worked for it while pretending to be a senior MPD agent during his chat with Jayce Tyrian.

"... and the Dissimulation Department," Lienna finished, typing its name into the search bar as she spoke.

She hit the enter key. The loading wheel spun, and then we were dumped onto a subpage for the DD. The first thing on the page was a big "report an incident" button. Under that was the contact information for the department's HQ.

"Shit," I whispered, cold sinking through my gut. "Lienna, look."

I pointed at the DD's address: a building in New York, New York. Our eyes met, shared trepidation zinging between us.

"It could be a coincidence that Kade is going to New York," she said quickly. "It's the biggest city in America, and one of the big hubs of the international MPD. The DD isn't the only department in that building."

"Right," I agreed, wishing her logic could calm the "doom is imminent" pounding of my heart. "He could be going to New York for anything. Maybe he wants to go to Coney Island."

She nodded emphatically as she clicked a few more times. The DD's basic info page, accessible to any mythic, was replaced by the agent-only information board. A big notice with a red title sat pretty at the top, and its glaring letters assaulted my widening eyes.

That feeling of impending doom increased tenfold, and no logic on our good green planet could convince me that the mythic world as we knew it wasn't about to end.

"Lienna," I croaked.

"Yeah," she agreed, her voice a whisper of dread.

"What do we do?"

She pushed the computer onto my lap and swung her legs off the bed. "I'll go wake up Darius." She grabbed my phone off the nightstand and held it out to me. "You call Captain Blythe."

I took the phone with numb fingers. As Lienna speed-walked for the hotel room door, I scrolled through my contacts until I found Blythe's private number. A single call from Vietnam to Canada would absolutely wreck my upcoming phone bill.

I hit her number and lifted the phone to my ear. It rang a handful of times before the cap's familiar voice barked at me from half a world away.

"Agent Morris, are you following orders?"

Well, hello to you too, dear captain. "What orders?"

"You're supposed to be resting. Where the hell are you?"

There were so many ways I could answer that: "I swear on the grave of Charlie Chaplain that I haven't set a single foot on the streets of Vancouver," or "I definitely did not engage in a life-or-death brawl against an international criminal and her army of mercenaries," but I opted for the truth instead.

"I'm in Vietnam."

There was a very long, very heavy pause.

"Why?"

I inhaled deeply and let it out. "Captain, we have a problem. A really big problem." I glanced at the open laptop screen and that bold headline in red. "We need to go to New York City."

"Kit." Her utterance of my name was layered with all kinds of questions. "What the hell are you up to?"

"Oh, nothing much." I snapped the laptop shut. "Just trying to prevent the apocalypse."

20

SOMEWHERE OVER the Pacific Ocean, I realized I was nearing the end of a trip quite literally around the world. Vancouver to Copenhagen to Ho Chi Minh City and back to Vancouver, crossing three different continents and spanning two oceans.

My biggest regret—other than the general suckiness of letting Kade escape with the weapon—was that I'd been too busy being an agent to be a tourist. I'd hit one Viking ruin in Denmark but missed out on Legoland and a whole schwack of castles and museums. Don't even get me started on Vietnam: Halong Bay, the Golden Bridge, Ban Gioc waterfall, not to mention the multitudinous markets, street vendors, national parks, and restaurants.

Instead, I was heading back to Canada for the briefest of moments before jetting off to New York City. There were no shows on Broadway, views from the Empire State Building, or strolls through Central Park in my future.

When we landed at the Vancouver International Airport, we didn't even get that universal pleasure of exiting the airport with maximum haste enjoyed by every long-haul flight passenger. Instead, Lienna and I followed Darius to a small, out-of-the-way gate at the opposite end of the terminal where a private charter plane awaited us.

The ex-assassin had made some calls before we vacated Vietnam, and to absolutely no one's surprise, he knew a guy who knew a guy who knew a filthy rich guy who was willing to loan us his private jet to save the world. Though if Mr. Big Bucks had known our history of road-vehicle-related destruction, he'd have been less than keen at offering up his luxurious Bombardier aircraft.

Anyway, that's how I found myself standing under a dreary noon sky, squinting at the sleek white jet with bloodshot eyes, wondering if it included a bed. Hell, I'd sleep on the floor as long as no one drove a drink cart over my slumbering form.

Darius had ditched us on the tarmac with his luggage, vanishing back into the airport for some mysterious errand. Maybe he wanted to buy one of those cushy neck pillows that prevent your head from bobbing weirdly while you slowly lose consciousness from sleep deprivation.

Sweet Somnus, I needed some shut-eye.

Unfortunately, I wouldn't be getting any sleep—not until our team had properly assembled and we were on our way to the Big Apple.

Sitting beside Lienna at the foot of the steps leading up to the plane, I fantasized about pillows, blankets, and king-sized mattresses. Maybe there was an obscure sleep-related psychic ability I could tap into. "Allucinators" could control others' dreams, but maybe there was a skill that would allow my mind to enter a state of much-needed dormancy while still fulfilling my day-to-day duties. Clairnappience? Hibernesis? Teletorpidity?

Lienna nudged my foot with hers. "They're here."

I looked up. Captain Blythe was striding across the tarmac toward us, a carry-on suitcase rolling along beside her and her blue glare laser-beaming into my skull. Vinny and Tim followed in her wake.

"Kit!" she barked. "You'd better be ready with that 'full explanation' you promised me."

Before I could summon a response from the foggy recesses of my lethargic mind, her attention snapped to Lienna.

"Agent Shen," she said with noticeably less venom.

The juxtaposition between our respective greetings was both stark and strange: the colloquialism of my first name versus Lienna's formal address; and Blythe's tone of "I am one wrong word away from spit-roasting you over a vat of nuclear waste" for the psycho warper, while the abjuration sorceress had received words with notes of respect.

The captain was a complicated—and often terrifying—enigma.

I pushed to my feet and stepped aside, gesturing grandly for the newly arrived trio to approach. "Welcome aboard. Where are Vigneault and Cutter?"

"They're keeping the precinct running while I'm gone." Blythe stalked past me. When she reached the bottom step, she released her suitcase, and it floated ahead of her as she ascended.

"Where did you get a private jet?" Vinny hissed, gingerly kicking the stairs as though he suspected it was all an elaborate warp.

I wiggled my fingers at him. "I work in mysterious ways, Agent Park."

He squinted suspiciously at me as he followed Blythe upward. Tim didn't say anything; he just arched his eyebrows so high they almost detached from his face.

Lienna and I boarded last. The jet's interior was about as swanky as you'd expect: varnished wood paneling, a fully stocked bar, which we would unfortunately not be taking advantage of, and cushy leather chairs. There were only eight seats, which, in a space that a commercial airliner would have packed the population of a small country into, amounted to enough legroom for Robert Wadlow to fully stretch out.

After tucking their bags away in the dedicated baggage compartment next to the bathroom, Blythe, Vinny, and Tim swiftly selected seats. I plonked onto a cushy chair across from my fellow agents, and Lienna took the spot next to me. This opulent sky wagon had clearly been designed with socializing and/or business dealing in mind, because all the chairs could swivel, allowing for easy conversation.

"Were you able to reach Ashbluff?" I asked before Blythe could launch into a tirade about my insubordinate secret-keeping.

She crossed her legs at the knee. "I spoke with half a dozen assistants, managers, and security personnel and left a message with Ashbluff's office."

"That's it?" I asked, my gut sinking. "Didn't you tell them that a rogue agent with a potential weapon of mass magical destruction is going to—"

"Of course I did. I was assured that they take security 'very seriously.'" She hit the air quotes so hard I almost expected them to manifest on either side of her head like one of my warps. "But as I pointed out on our call, you haven't sufficiently explained what this weapon is, how you know Kade's plans, or how we're supposed to do a damn thing about either."

"Been wondering all that myself," Tim remarked dryly.

Beside him, Vinny nodded.

"Well, you see …" I hedged. "I've been working on this investigation from a few different angles. Not all those angles have been, shall we say, wholly aboveboard."

Blythe's eyes blazed, but before she could comment, footsteps sounded on the plane's stairs. A moment later, two men stepped into view.

Darius boarded first, a duffel bag slung over his shoulder. Accompanying him was the Crow and Hammer's first officer. Girard was around Darius's age, but where the ex-assassin was a well-dressed silver fox, Girard had a "Western gentlemen circa 1920" air to him, with chin-length, steel-gray hair, a short beard, and a mustache that challenged Eggert's for magnificence.

Blythe lurched out of her seat, face twisting at the sight of Darius. "What the *hell* are you doing here?"

I cleared my throat. "He's one of those not 'wholly aboveboard' angles I mentioned."

Her glare flashed to me then back to Darius. The awkwardness in the ensuing silence was so palpable it made my very soul cringe.

"Aurelia," Darius murmured. "If you can allow me a moment to talk to the crew, once we take off, I'll explain."

"Explain what?" she snapped.

"Everything."

Her eyes widened briefly before she controlled her expression. Jaw clenched, she dropped back into her chair and folded her arms.

Darius handed his duffel bag to Girard, then disappeared through a curtain at the front of the plane.

You're in deep shit. Tim's voice in my head was half amused, half intrigued. *How long have you been playing double agent?*

It's not like that, I retorted with a sharp internal thought, then swiveled toward Girard. "Did Darius volunteer you for this wacky adventure?"

Girard grinned through his mustache as he selected a seat, leaving the one beside me empty for Darius.

"He figured we could use some extra Arcana expertise—and firepower." He nodded at Lienna. "Not to suggest you aren't an expert, but I've developed something of a specialty when it comes to weapons."

"We're happy to have you," Lienna replied graciously.

Some of us were. Blythe looked ready to test whether her telekinesis could yank a man's intestines out of his nose, which was about as far away from "happy" as one could be on any imaginable spectrum of emotion.

The plane's engines started a moment later, and Darius reappeared. He sat between me and Girard, and I belatedly realized we'd created an unfortunate "Darius's team versus Blythe's team" vibe with the center aisle as no man's land.

The appreciable awkwardness clouding the cabin increased steadily while we waited to speed down the runway and whoosh up into the sky. Blythe's seething disposition suggested she was continuing to contemplate the variety of ways she could disassemble Darius's innards, while the GM himself remained so still I was briefly concerned he'd been zapped by a holding spell.

When the seat belt light blinked off, Blythe shucked off her safety strap and spun her chair to face Darius.

"What do *you* have to do with Kade and this weapon Morris reported?" she demanded.

Ah crap, I was back to "Morris" again. Not even *Agent* Morris. How far down her shit list had I fallen?

The deepest shit, Tim whispered helpfully in my mind.

Darius's gaze moved across Blythe's face in a searching look layered with unspoken things I couldn't even guess at. With that inscrutable glance, the airborne awkwardness that was damn near suffocating me morphed into brusque anticipation. I realized I was holding my breath—and it looked like everyone else had forgotten to exhale as well.

"I've thought about this a thousand times over the last twenty years," Darius began in a slow, measured voice, as though weighing each word. "And a thousand times, I decided there were countless reasons to keep my silence and only one reason to break it."

Despite the fact that six people were hanging on his every word, he was speaking only to Blythe. Her eyes had gone wide again.

"But that's changed," he continued. "Now, I have every reason to tell you, and only one to stay silent—the fear that the truth won't make a difference, not after this long."

Blythe held completely still. A subtle shift had come over her features: an open, naked vulnerability I'd never seen before and couldn't have imagined on my harsh, commanding captain's face.

"Now?" she said hoarsely. "You're going to tell me *now*? Because of this?"

"Yes."

His answer was simple, and fury burned across her face, overtaking the vulnerability. She gripped her seat's armrests, the ferocity of her glare back in full force.

"This all began with what seemed like a routine contract twenty-three years ago," Darius said. "A former Special Investigations agent had gone rogue and was selling classified information. I tracked him down in Chicago and eliminated him. As I was cleaning the scene, I found correspondence between him and his buyers. What caught my attention was the information he was leaking: details of illegal actions by certain agents within Special Investigations.

"The rogue was selling the information to be used to blackmail SI members. I collected everything I could find and turned it over. I assumed it would trigger an internal probe into the bad actors within the SI. Instead, the evidence I submitted disappeared. The hard copies vanished from evidence storage, and when I pulled up my report, all references to it were gone."

"Why didn't you ever mention that?" Blythe asked tersely. "I was working in Special Investigations. I could have looked into it."

Hold up—Blythe had worked in Special Investigations too? How the hell had I never come across that tidbit? Was that how she and Darius had met?

Darius studied her for a moment. "I didn't know the extent of what I'd stumbled on. If someone could make evidence and reports disappear from the SI, could they make an SI analyst disappear too?"

Blythe grimaced. "But—"

"I didn't want to risk your life, Aurelia. I didn't tell you—and I didn't tell anyone else either." His shoulders shifted in a sigh that was absorbed by the drone of the jet engines. "I started paying closer attention to the contracts I was offered. I began asking careful questions. I talked to other contractors, and they told me about unlikely targets and flimsy rationales."

He paused, eyes distant for a few seconds before he refocused on Blythe. "The deeper I dug, the more I found. Espionage and assassination contracts that couldn't be traced back to whatever SI agents had ordered them. Bogus investigations with falsified evidence. Paper trails that dissolved into nothing. The other contractors and I were spying on and assassinating people we thought were dangerous criminals, when in reality, there was no evidence, no transparency, and no accountability.

"I eventually connected with Anson Goodman. He was an investigative journalist, and he'd been hunting whispers of MPD corruption for several years already but didn't have a way to dig for information within the upper echelon of the MPD. I did.

"I brought in others—connections I'd made, fellow contractors, MPD agents and administrators, even anti-MPD radicals. Anyone I thought I could get information from. Some knew what I was doing, some didn't. The picture that formed, the pieces we connected ..."

A rumble of turbulence shook the plane, and we all sat silently, waiting for it to subside.

"They called themselves the Consilium." Darius entwined his fingers, elbows on his knees, eyes on Blythe. "A group of politically and financially powerful mythics inside and outside of the MPD's upper ranks. We identified some of them, but not all—not the ones at the very top. They had spies, acolytes, and minions everywhere. They had a death grip on the SI. They controlled or influenced multiple MPD departments, international guilds, and GM coalitions. They were taking over."

His words eerily echoed the present we now faced.

"My allies tried to bring the MPD's inbuilt system of checks and balances into play. They reported the corruption and submitted the evidence we'd gathered." His mouth pressed into a thin line. "Then they started to disappear."

Blythe's shoulders stiffened.

"In the space of three months, sixteen people I had involved in my investigation were missing or dead. The evidence they'd helped provide disappeared and the cases were closed.

"I sent out warnings to everyone I'd ever talked to about possible corruption, and almost all of them went into hiding. Only a few remained, but we were moving more carefully now. I was the only one who knew the names of everyone connected to my investigation, and the Consilium didn't know I was behind it—not yet.

"About three years had passed by that point. Only a few of us were still tracking the Consilium's moves. That's when ..." His gaze broke from Blythe's, moving across the gathered mythics one by one. "We identified the leaders of the Consilium."

Even knowing how this story went, I found myself dreading the next part.

"A new member had been appointed to the Supreme Judiciary Council—the former Director of Special Investigations, whom we knew to be near the top of the Consilium's hierarchy. He'd already turned the SI department into an extension of the Consilium's will, and having him at the highest judicial level of the MPD was potentially catastrophic. We started tracking his every move—everywhere he went, everyone he met with, all his correspondents and flunkies—and we began to realize that not only was he a leader of the Consilium, but so were five of his fellow Supreme Judiciary Council members."

Blythe's face paled to a ghostly white, all vestiges of her trademarked glare having drained away.

"They occupied a full half of the Council," Darius continued heavily. "They had the power to block or push through laws, pardon their allies and followers, and consolidate their hold on the MPD and, through it, the mythic world.

"The Supreme Judiciary Council meets twice a year to ratify new and amended laws for the mythic world, and the controversial law dominating mythic discussion at that time was a revival of the Senatus Consultum Ultimum, a decree dating back to the Roman Republic that granted unchecked power to the Senate—or in this case, the unchecked power to create and deploy a military force of mythics."

I could feel the muscles in my neck tense, just as they had five months ago when Darius had first explained the Ultimum to me. The reasoning behind it was that the mythic community needed a reserve force in case of a major conflict with human militaries. The reality would have been a large-scale, personal army for the Consilium to control.

"There was no way to postpone the ruling and no time to expose the corrupt Council members. To prevent them from turning the Ultimum into reality, I had one option left."

Blythe balled her hands into fists, but that didn't hide the faint tremor in her limbs.

Darius leaned back in his seat. "I had started this, and I owed it to my allies to see it through. I knew I would be a suspect—for the MPD and the Consilium both. But who else could do it? So, the night before the Council met, I killed the corrupt members and collected whatever evidence of their crimes or plans I could find."

He said the last part so simply that he could have been talking about making a pot of coffee before work. His expression, however, was stony and closed off, his emotions tightly controlled.

"It almost went to plan. Almost." His eyes were locked on Blythe. "I didn't account for news of the first two deaths reaching you, or for you to figure out I was responsible and confront me in the last Consilium member's hotel room."

Woah.

Darius had *not* included that rather glaring detail when he'd told me the tale of the Consilium of twenty years past. No wonder Blythe had always been so dead-set convinced that Darius was a traitor and guilty of those six murders. She'd caught him red-handed.

Blythe pressed her lips into thin white lines, saying nothing.

"No one in the MPD could prove I was the killer," Darius continued abruptly, and I got the distinct impression he'd skipped over something. "And the Consilium was leaderless. What was left of their organization fell into chaos—or so it appeared based on the behavior of the remaining Consilium supporters we'd identified."

He rolled his shoulders. "Expecting that the MPD would investigate me, I split all the evidence I had gathered and sent it to my allies-in-hiding for safekeeping. Then I retired as an MPD contractor and joined the Crow and Hammer as a bartender."

"In *Vancouver*." Blythe's voice cracked. "You aren't even from Vancouver."

Another biographical datapoint I hadn't known. Darius was Canadian—according to his passport, which I'd seen during our globetrotting travels—but I couldn't guess his province of origin.

"I wanted to be close," he said. "I'd beheaded the Consilium, but I hadn't eradicated it. Anson and Georgia came with me, and we kept our ears to the ground, listening for any sign that the Consilium was resurrecting itself."

Which, as we were all painfully aware, it had.

Vinny shifted uncomfortably, then asked in a small voice, "Um, I'm sorry, but you wanted to be close to what?"

Darius didn't reply, his gaze on Blythe. Her throat moved as she swallowed.

"He wanted to be close to *me*," she said through gritted teeth. "After he murdered half the Council, I resigned from Special Investigations and returned home to Vancouver to be a regular agent."

"But … why?" Vinny asked gormlessly.

"I didn't want anything more to do with the shady ethics of the SI. I wanted to put criminals behind bars, not watch them walk away scot-free after murdering six high-ranked MPD leaders." Her jaw tightened further, as though she were steeling herself for the worst part. "In the SI, I would have always been known as the Mage Assassin's jilted fiancée."

Fiancée? Holy Shakespearean Tragedy. I'd assumed they were ex-lovers, but *engaged* was a whole different level of wrecked passion and bitter leftovers.

"You let me believe you'd been bought," she said to Darius, the words a barely audible hiss as though she didn't want the rest of us to hear. "You didn't even have the guts to break off our engagement before your unexplained killing spree."

"I couldn't risk it," he said just as quietly. "The Consilium was watching me, and I couldn't afford any sudden changes in behavior that would put up their guard."

"That hasn't been a concern for two decades now. Why keep it from me?"

"Because I was guilty." His gray eyes were shadowed, hinting at the grief and regret he kept buried. "If I confessed, you would have had to choose between concealing a murderer and keeping your integrity as an MPD agent. I couldn't put you in that position."

She opened her mouth furiously, glanced around at her rapt audience, then snapped it shut without speaking.

Darius took a deep breath as though centering himself. "The Consilium went quiet after that. I kept track of known affiliates for years, but when there were no signs of coordinated activity, I grew complacent."

He said the last words with acerbic bitterness. Silence fell.

"Then earlier this year," I said, picking up the tale, "Söze showed up at our precinct and ordered Damnation-o Moria—"

"*Damnatio memoriae,*" Lienna corrected.

"—against the Crow and Hammer."

Darius settled back in his chair. "It was such an overreach of power that I immediately suspected the Consilium, or some surviving piece of it. They wanted to eliminate me and my guild."

"Right after we averted said mass annihilation of his guild, Darius met with Anson and Georgia to warn them that the Consilium was up to some shady shit again," I filled in, directing the words at Blythe. "But the Consilium had done their homework. Söze and Kade already knew Anson and Georgia were his allies."

"They moved far faster than I expected," Darius agreed, grief and anger darkening his eyes. "Even after Anson and

Georgia were killed, I still wasn't prepared. I would have died that night in March if not for Agent Morris and Agent Shen."

"Meanwhile," I added, "you had picked up on some major corruption inside the IA. Darius figured out I was working with you on that—"

"—and I recruited him to help me," Darius finished. "Without revealing to you what we were doing."

Blythe was glaring again, her wrath flipping back and forth between me and Darius.

Holy shit, Morris, Tim remarked, sounding kind of impressed.

Would you quit with the commentary? I retorted silently.

Tim glanced at me, a curious furrow in his brows. *When did you—*

"Wait," Vinny said, interrupting Tim's telepathic remark. The kryomage swiveled toward me. "You've been investigating the Consilium with Captain Blythe *and* with Darius at the same time?"

"Yup."

"And you kept it a secret from all of us?" He scowled. "*How?*"

In Vinny's case, it hadn't been difficult, but I didn't mention that.

"Your discovery of Kade's plans with this weapon came from your investigation with Darius?" Blythe asked me, still looking as though she'd like to dice me up and shove little Kit bits out the airplane window to scatter across several miles of uninhabited Midwestern wilderness thirty thousand feet below.

I launched into a hasty recap of our visit to Jayce Tyrian's skyscraper, the stolen files, and Floris Visser selling her ill-gotten artifact to the Consilium. I may or may not have glossed over certain specifics regarding my outright inability to defeat Kade in a cargo-hold, bare-knuckle brawl. They didn't need to know that.

"Now Kade is taking it to New York," I summed up. "And we know his target." I plucked a folded printout from my pocket, almost dislodging the other piece of paper tucked against my buttocks for safekeeping. "This."

I unfolded the page and held it out with a flourish. Everyone—minus Darius and Lienna—squinted at the big red letters.

"A security notice?" Tim said. "For—oh hell."

"Tonight at eight o'clock"—I waved the paper in emphasis—"is the vote for the Director of the Dissimulation Department. Three hundred Special Committee invitees will be descending on the North American MPD headquarters, along with Director Ashbluff, the other candidates for the job, and any number of high rollers and schmoozers of the mythic elite."

"It's the perfect opportunity to destroy Ashbluff and destabilize the DD," Lienna added. "That's where Kade is taking the weapon."

Vinny fidgeted with his seat belt, which he'd kept snug across his torso for the entire duration of the flight. Was it a fear of flying or a fear of Kit warps while hurtling through the atmosphere at nine hundred kilometers an hour?

"What does the Consilium get out of messing with the DD?" he asked.

"It's one of the most influential departments in the MPD," Darius explained. "The Consilium already controls Internal Affairs through Commissioner Sparks. We can assume they have influence over the Obscura Influentia department through Kade's father, Peter Druthers. Although I killed the former

Special Investigations Director two decades ago, I now assume his successor was equally loyal to the Consilium."

That was three of the four Boss Departments of the MPD: Internal Affairs, which oversaw—and could interfere with—all other departments; Obscura Influentia, which interfaced with human political regimes across the planet; and Special Investigations, which wielded unchecked intelligence gathering, espionage, and "disappear troublemakers" powers.

That left the Dissimulation Department, which controlled all information about mythics—the masters of propaganda, the suppressors of truth, and the only thing that stood between mythics and full-on public exposure, aka total apocalyptic anarchy.

"Twenty years ago," Darius said grimly, "the Consilium took control of the Supreme Judiciary Council. While that allowed them almost unfettered influence over the MPD and worldwide mythic community, it came with an inherent weakness."

"They had to gather together." Blythe's expression matched her ex-fiancé's level of grimness. "It created an opportunity for you to wipe them out."

Darius nodded. "This time, they've set their sights on the most powerful MPD departments. If they gain control of the Dissimulation Department, they'll have de facto control of the entire MPD. Whatever they intend to do at the vote tonight, we can't let it happen."

Our small party exchanged looks ranging from jittery to determined to downright anxious. Somehow, it was up to us— a ragtag band of misfits from Vancouver pitted against the seemingly unstoppable tide of the Consilium and its secret faction of the MPD's most powerful leaders.

I'd never wished that "the underdog always wins" movie magic applied to real life more than I did now.

21

THE MPD'S NORTH AMERICAN HQ was situated in the heart of Manhattan's Financial District, only a few scant blocks from the actual, literal Wall Street. The impressive skyscraper boasted an all-glass exterior, with a vaguely oval shape except for the top three floors, which were black, perfectly circular, and sat on the rest of the structure like a fancy hat.

That was where the vote to determine the leadership of the Dissimulation Department would begin in a few minutes.

We were cutting it extremely close considering Kade was probably mingling with the mythic elites on the top floors and could unleash the weapon—and any other nefarious Consilium orders he was following—at any moment.

Captain Blythe, Vinny, and Tim had gone in. The vote was taking place on the upper three floors—right inside the skyscraper's stylish concrete chapeau—and they would head straight for the topmost level. Darius and Girard would scope out the second-to-top level, but they'd opted to use an "unofficial" entrance instead of the front doors. I had no idea which entrance that was, but I assumed it wouldn't involve any friendly discussions about their various weaponry with helpful security personnel.

Lienna and I would cover the bottom level of the hat, which itself was still upwards of sixty floors off the ground.

Our primary target was Benjamin Kade. Director Ashbluff of the DD was our secondary target, and our tertiary targets were Commissioner Ruben Sparks of the IA, Director Peter Druthers of Obscura Influentia, and Director Stavros Griva of Special Investigations.

Tim, who'd taken the role of our strategist, had drilled all of us on the names and faces of said targets on the way to New York. He'd also compiled all the details we knew about Kade's crimes and his clairsentient slipperiness, as well as the information Vinny had acquired about the bastard's time with DRAFT. He'd created an unsettling behavior profile of our main target and a short list of likely scenarios to unfold during the vote. At the very top of the list was the expectation that Kade, blood-loving psychopath that he was, would want a front-row seat for whatever violence and mayhem he induced.

I exhaled slowly as Lienna and I ascended the wide steps to the main entrance of the towering skyscraper. Deep evening shadows sucked up the fading warmth as the sun slipped out of sight behind the famous Manhattan skyline.

Our lack of knowledge about the danger was the worst part. How many of the Consilium faithful were lingering among the harmless vote attendees? How and where would Kade make his move? Did he plan to unleash the Viking queen's super elemental magic on the Special Committee while they tried to place their votes? Or would he go after Director Ashbluff?

Inside the spacious lobby, the security was downright robust: multitudinous MPD agents with protective gear searching bags, giving pat-downs, and employing detectors of both the metal and magic variety. There was even a pair of K-9 agents, which, assuming you enjoyed having five fingers on each hand, didn't look like the kind of pooches you'd want to pet.

This was one of the rare occasions where MagiPol subtlety was not required: each agent wore a ball cap with the MPD logo emblazoned on the front, making it clear to everyone who was in charge.

An agent scanned my badge, which brought my face up onto a screen at her station. She compared it to my own real-life face then waved me toward another agent who scanned me with his dual detectors. I wasn't carrying any artifacts, but when Lienna's turn came, they hauled her aside to inspect her satchel.

After a series of questions, during which my partner vastly downplayed the lethal nature of her magical trinkets, and a close examination of her Rubik's cube, she was let through. Carrying artifacts on your person wasn't prohibited, even in a tightly secured venue like this, but out-and-out weapons were a no-go.

Lienna and I rode the elevator up to the sixty-second level, which was the lowest of the triple-layered event center, with half a dozen men in suits speaking rapid Italian.

My partner and I were dressed for the occasion as well. Blythe had grudgingly stopped at both our places to grab an appropriate change of clothes: for me, the expensive three-piece threads from my Quebec adventure with Darius, and for Lienna, a perfectly respectable—but not nearly as wallet-draining—charcoal pantsuit paired with a silky powder-blue blouse.

The elevator doors slid open, letting us out onto a ring-shaped concourse that surrounded the circular auditorium where the main event would occur. At least a hundred well-dressed mythic elites milled about and made small talk. Stationed at regular intervals were more geared agents, ready for trouble. Did these votes always have so much security, or had they taken Blythe's warning seriously?

Lienna caught my eye, then pulled a wireless earpiece from her pocket and tucked it into place. Following suit, I stuffed mine into my ear. A few quick taps on my phone connected me to the rest of the team.

"Jack Bauer, reporting for duty," I said, scanning the ever-moving crowd for bald heads. Surprisingly, everyone in sight had hair.

"Any sign of our targets?" Lienna asked like a proper professional agent on a secret mission.

"*Not yet,*" Blythe responded. "*We've covered half of the third level.*"

"*Nothing on the second level,*" came Darius's smooth voice.

"We're starting our search," Lienna informed them.

"*Remember Kade's profile,*" Tim added. "*He might be hiding in plain sight.*"

I offered my arm to Lienna, and she tucked her fingers into the crook of my elbow as we started a clockwise trek around the ring. The curved hallway was almost pure white—a pearlescent marble that made up the ceiling, floor, and walls. We passed a cocktail bar with a short queue of black-suited mythics. This event felt more like a highfalutin shindig for the one percent than a secretive political election.

That wasn't strictly a problem, except it had attracted an inconvenient number of strangers to the upper levels of the building. The Special Committee had around three hundred members, but there were easily twice as many mythics here.

Any of them could be a Consilium goon ready to lend a helping hand to Kade's inevitable havoc-wreaking.

Lienna and I made our way slowly through the clusters of chatting attendees. My gaze snapped from face to face, looking for anything suspicious, and I was hyper-aware of everyone who looked my way. Were their gazes lingering too long? Were they tracking my progress along the concourse? Were they enemies who recognized me as the psycho warper the Consilium inexplicably wanted to capture?

Part of me really hoped I could remain anonymous. The other part of me knew our best shot at stopping Kade hinged on my presence being known.

Over the course of our continent-hopping world tour, Lienna hadn't had enough downtime to concoct a spell that would undermine Kade's clairsentience. Thus, on Darius's orders, Girard had brought some extra supplies from the Crow and Hammer.

The first helpful addition was a universal antidote, which would protect us from the most common potions Kade or anyone else might try to splatter us with. The second was an anti-telethesian potion. Since anti-clairsentient tonics weren't something the average alchemist had kicking around, Lienna had suggested an alternative that would dampen our brainwaves enough to significantly reduce Kade's ability to sense all of us.

Well, *almost* all of us. I'd skipped the anti-brainwaves brew. We didn't want to smother my Morris essence; we were letting it shine bright and bold for any psychic to see.

Because I was the bait.

Lienna and I passed an art exhibition featuring a medley of paintings and sculptures, presumably detailing the MPD's many victories in the abstract. I twitched my shoulders, itching from the paranoid feeling of eyes watching me. Under the guise of stopping to admire the bronze bust of a medieval MPD visionary, I looked back the way we'd come, scanning the ever-shifting crowd.

Minutes ticked past as we painstakingly navigated toward the opposite end of the concourse. My pulse drummed, gradually increasing in tempo like an EDM song revving up for its bassy breakdown. Kade could unleash the weapon at any moment. I wanted to sprint down the corridor, shouting for everyone to get the hell out of here before it was too late.

"*I have eyes on Commissioner Sparks,*" Girard said abruptly. "*He's walking with two other men—his aides, I think.*"

"*Stay on his tail,*" Darius replied. "*I'll keep searching for the other targets.*"

Splitting up sounded like a terrible idea, but I wouldn't agent-splain covert operations to the Mage Assassin and his first officer.

"Nothing yet on this level," I said as Lienna turned slowly to survey every angle of the concourse. "You got anything, Blythe?"

Several seconds of silence on the earpiece dragged by. Then a few seconds more. Lienna turned to me, her eyes darkening with unease.

An eardrum-piercing crackle burst through the tiny speaker in my ear, the sound blown out beyond recognition.

"Captain Blythe?" I repeated sharply. "Vinny? Tim? Are you there?"

Nothing.

Urgency and adrenaline surged through me. "Darius?"

"*Still connected,*" he replied, a new tension in his voice. "*I'm heading for the upper level to find the others.*"

I swore under my breath. What the hell was going on? What could've silenced our level-three team simultaneously without warning? Had they lost signal?

"We have to finish our pass around this level before we can help them," Lienna whispered, gripping my arm. "This is where we're most likely to find Kade."

I glanced toward the inner wall of the concourse, where two black-suited agents flanked a wide doorway. Through the open auditorium doors, I could glimpse a few hundred evenly spaced chairs, a raised dais in the center, and the bold black lines of a massive Arcana array that spanned the entire floor—a spell that, according to Darius, might cause future Kit a considerable headache.

"*I'm on the third floor.*" Darius's low voice crackled. "*I'm being followed. Two men in black suits.*"

Followed? I looked back over my shoulder. There were dozens of men in suits. How in the name of Fred Astaire was I supposed to discern which of them were enemies?

"I can't tell if we have a tail," I muttered. "Any sign of the others?"

"*Not yet. Girard, where is Sparks now?*"

For the second time, we were met with silence instead of an ally's voice.

"Shit," I hissed. "Something is wrong."

Lienna grabbed my hand. "Come on."

She hauled me forward at a pace so brisk that, compared to the ambling throng, we might as well have been sprinting. I elbowed a man in a blue tux out of my way as we sped along the concourse with exactly zero subterfuge.

I glanced back again—and saw two black-suited men striding in our wake, close behind and matching our swift clip.

"We're being followed too," I growled. "Darius, where are you?"

"*Still on the top floor. No sign yet of Aurelia and the others, but I gave my tails the slip.*"

Of course he had. Maybe it was time for Lienna and me to vanish too.

"Walk into that big group there," I told Lienna in an undertone. "I'm going to invisi-warp us."

Nodding, she reached for her cat's eye necklace.

"No, not yet." I gave her a tight-lipped smile. "I can exclude your mind for now. Let's save it for when we really need it."

"Got it."

We made a beeline into the middle of a conversing group of old men. As we wove between them, I launched my halluci-bomb, stretching it to cover the hundreds of minds in the crowded concourse.

I made duplicates of us both that veered off in one direction, while I guided Lienna to the outer wall. I directed our fake versions toward the bathrooms, then dropped the warp once they'd entered.

Lienna and I lurked near the coat check, watching the two suited men who'd been following us pull up short outside the bathrooms. As one of them turned, I saw his lips moving—then noticed the flesh-colored earpiece he wore. Who was he reporting to?

I focused on his mind, trying to sneak a peek at his thoughts without losing my grip on the halluci-bomb that was keeping Lienna and me unseen.

A screech pierced my right eardrum. I swore and yanked my earpiece out, Lienna doing the same. Our eyes met as I cautiously lifted it back to my ear. The deafening screech had gone silent.

"Darius?" I queried.

Nothing.

Lienna and I stared at each other. Our team had disappeared, leaving the two of us on our own. We had no idea what had happened to the others, we hadn't found Kade, and the Consilium could be seconds away from unleashing their weapon.

What the hell were we supposed to do now?

Technology had failed us, and my five human senses weren't a whole lot of good at this point either. Which left only magic.

During our mile-high planning session aboard the private jet, Tim had made it abundantly clear that his telepathy would be less than useful amidst a veritable ocean of brainwaves—and as soon as I closed my eyes in an attempt to tune in to the presence of the minds around me, I experienced what he'd been talking about firsthand.

Instantly, a tidal wave of minds overwhelmed my gray matter. I honed my focus, sheering away the unfamiliar minds, desperately searching for those of my friends.

Darius, Blythe, Vinny, Tim—I had to find one of them. Just one. They had to be nearby. They couldn't all have disappeared. They couldn't all be unconscious … or dead.

My psychic senses stretched, my hold on the invisi-warp getting fuzzier. Lienna let out a sudden gasp as I lost my grip on the little bubble of exclusion I'd created to keep her out of my warp.

But that little bit of freed bandwidth crystalized the minds around me—and I recognized one of them.

Except it didn't belong to any of my teammates.

My eyes flew open, and I spun on my heels. Standing in the shadows, almost hidden beside a rack of posh overcoats, was a heavy-shouldered man in an MPD ball cap, the brim pulled down to hide his face.

The man tilted his head enough to reveal the sinister smirk stretching his mouth. His lips moved, forming two words I didn't need psychic power to interpret.

"Hello, Kit."

22

KEEPING MY EYES ON MY NEMESIS, I refocused my power, once again excluding Lienna from the invisi-warp. The tension in her shoulders released as her self-perception returned. She gave me a questioning look, but I grabbed her arm before she could ask why the hell she'd been unceremoniously dumped into a pseudo sensory deprivation chamber.

"It's Kade," I hissed. "We can't let him get away!"

He was disguised as an MPD agent, and he was hiding in plain sight, just like Tim had said he would be.

Whatever had happened to my teammates, I couldn't search for them now—not with Kade right in front of me. I dashed toward the coat check, Lienna beside me.

Kade tapped the brim of his cap in a mock salute, then ducked into the shadows.

But I had that bastard's number. Or, more specifically, I had a lock on his slippery mind. His anti-Kit bracelet shielded him from incoming Psychica, but it didn't do shit to stop his brainwaves from broadcasting loud and clear.

Invisible, Lienna and I sprinted behind the coat check. Tucked in the back corner next to the rows of outerwear was an unmarked door.

I slammed through it, hiding the noise with my warp. We found ourselves in a plain concrete corridor just wide enough to accommodate a loaded pallet jack. It followed the curve of the concourse, with dozens of doors at regular intervals along the inside wall—access points for event staff.

Kade had already vanished, somewhere ahead of us down the curving hallway. I could sense which way he'd gone, and I took the lead, full-out sprinting with Lienna right behind me. Since there was no one else in sight, I dropped all my warps to save my brain power.

A metal fire door blocked our path. On the other side was an industrial kitchen where all those tasty hors d'oeuvres were being prepared. I skidded to a stop, narrowly missing a young man carrying an armload of dirty dishes. Lienna grabbed my shoulder for balance as she halted beside me.

The busy hubbub of the kitchen staff paused to stare at our intrusion into their workspace.

I concentrated on my target. Darting around the busboy, Lienna and I bolted in Kade's direction. As I rounded the stainless steel prep station in the middle of the kitchen, almost bumping shoulders with a sous chef, I spotted another metal door on the far side of the grill.

We burst into a vestibule lined with staff lockers, finding a continuation of the curving access hall at the other end. Directly on my right was a door marked with a staircase sign.

Lienna looked from the staircase to the hall. "Which way?"

I hesitated, honing my sense of Kade's location. Close. Not moving. He was … waiting.

Waiting to see if I chose the right route.

Turning, I swung the door open, revealing a concrete stairwell with ugly metal railings. As I stepped onto the landing, a door clanged below us, and Kade's mind moved away from us.

"He's this way," I told Lienna, lunging for the stairs.

"Kit," she began breathlessly as we hurtled down half a flight before it doubled back on itself.

"I know." I careened around the U-bend and onto more stairs. "He's luring us somewhere."

Straight into another Kit-napping setup, no doubt.

As we reached the next landing, I slowed to meet Lienna's eyes. "We'll spring his trap, and this time, he won't get the better of us."

She nodded, eyes blazing with determination.

We reached the next landing, and I could practically feel Kade's creep-essence leading me onward, like a trail stomped through the underbrush by a hairless predator. I pushed through the heavy fire door onto the sixty-first floor.

Another hallway greeted us, this one carpeted in a dull brown pattern. A sign on the wall directed visitors toward various meeting and conference rooms.

There was no sign of Kade, but I was fully locked onto his mind, the echo of his brainwaves leaving a clear path for me to follow. As I streaked down the hall, it occurred to me that my burgeoning clairsentient ability was becoming sharper and more singular.

I led the way around a corner, past meeting rooms 6107, 6108, and 6109, and came to a rough stop in front of meeting room 6110. The door was closed, but this was where the trail led. Kade was inside.

"This is it," I told Lienna. "I'll keep him busy since he doesn't want to maim or murder me, and you hit him with everything you've got."

"Exactly what I was planning to do." Her Rubik's cube was in her hands, and she gave it three quick spins. "When I give the signal, dive to the floor."

That sounded ominous, and I was all for it. "Will do."

"Let's go."

I twisted the handle, whipped the door open, and leaped into the room, ready for Kade's attack.

The scene that met my shocked eyes wasn't what I'd expected.

The meeting room was set up for a casual discussion, with leather club chairs arranged in an oval around the room's center point. A sideboard lined one wall, and a projector screen filled the back.

Dead center in the room were two men—neither of whom was Kade. I'd gotten so focused on Kade's psychic trail that I hadn't noticed any other nearby presences—though I only would have detected one of them: Peter Druthers.

I recognized his mug instantly from Tim's incessant drilling, but without it, I still would've seen the unmistakable family resemblance. Druther's broad shoulders filled his suit, and he had the same shiny cranium as his son, though the senior psychopath had added a gray goatee to offset his shaven scalp.

Lying at his feet in a pool of blood was Director Ashbluff.

He'd also been part of Tim's photo lineup. A man even larger than Druthers, with short-cropped brown hair and a silvering beard. Black-framed glasses sat askew on his face, his dead eyes staring sightlessly at the ceiling.

Director Ashbluff was dead. The man we'd come all this way to save was *already dead*.

"*Kit!*"

Lienna's shout snapped me out of my horrified reverie, and I did the only thing that made sense to my frazzled brain—I hit the deck.

It was the right move. A band of blue magic whooshed over me, speeding not at Druthers but straight to my left. It caught Kade in the midriff a split second before he could fire the potion gun he had aimed at me.

The spell threw him back into the wall. He shoved off it, but before he could take aim again, I grabbed the potion gun with my telekinetic fingers and wrenched it out of his hold. The gun soared through the air and into my waiting hand.

Hot damn, I was really starting to get the hang of this.

"*Ori dormias!*" Lienna cried as she flung a stun marble at Kade. Like me, she seemed to have decided that Druthers was a problem for future us. His progeny was the immediate threat.

Kade twisted, the marble whipping past his shoulder and pinging into the wall. I grabbed it too—yep, definitely getting the hang of this—and redirected it into Kade's back. It bounced harmlessly off his armored MPD vest, which was clearly too insulated for the spell to knock him out.

Lips curled in a sneer, Kade came at me with aggressive speed. I raised his potion gun and fired.

He didn't even slow when the purple potion burst over his shoulder. He must've dosed himself with a universal antidote like we had.

I lunged forward to meet him, hoping Lienna was prepping another stun marble. Between the two of us, we could bounce it off that bald-ass head of his and put him down for good.

He tackled me like an NFL veteran, and I focused on breaking my fall instead of struggling. As I thudded hard into the floor with his weight on top of me, I used some extra telekinetic leverage in my grappling throw, flipping our positions so I was on top. Grabbing him by the throat, I cocked my arm back to punch his teeth in, simultaneously glancing up to see if Lienna had another stun marble ready.

I saw Druthers step up behind her.

"Lienna!" I yelled.

She started to turn. Druthers's hand landed on her shoulder as though he were about to offer a patronizing condolence for our failed attack. In his other hand, he lifted a short, shiny dagger, its blade streaked with blood—Ashbluff's blood.

For a horrified instant, I expected him to plunge it into Lienna's body.

Instead, he held it out to her.

She took it in both hands, gripping it tightly, and aimed the point at the soft skin under her chin. She poised it there, otherwise unmoving, her eyes fixed straight ahead.

"Now, Mr. Morris," Druthers said, his voice a touch more gravelly than his son's and just as loathsome, "you will do exactly as I say, or Miss Shen will suffer the consequences."

Lienna didn't move or even blink. Druthers's hand was still holding her shoulder, his fingers digging in.

He was a goddamn mentalist. The senior bastard was a mentalist, and he had control of Lienna.

"Nuh-uh, Kit," Kade rasped through my grip on his throat. "I can sense the moment you gather your focus to attempt something. Do you think you can pull the dagger out of her hands faster than she can put it through her throat?"

My head reeled with a dozen wild ideas on how to get out of this mess, and I couldn't attempt any of them. I couldn't risk it. Lienna was holding that deadly point against her vulnerable skin, and I didn't know if I could act fast enough to save her.

"Now," Kade said with a nasty smile, "stand up and put your hands behind your head."

I clenched my jaw. What choice did I have? With stiff movements, I clambered up and placed my hands as instructed.

Kade got to his feet, nonchalantly straightened the shoulder of his protective vest, then reached out and plucked the earpiece from my ear. He pitched it into a nearby garbage can before turning to Lienna and removing hers as well.

She didn't react, her stare utterly blank.

"In case you were wondering, Kit," Kade said as he faced me again. "My father's mental control doesn't break the moment he releases his victim. She'll still follow his last order after you separate them."

My stomach twisted. Fear pounded through every fiber of my being, and I couldn't come up with a snarky retort.

Kade studied my face with a smile, enjoying my reaction.

"This is what we've been waiting for?" Druthers asked in a musing tone, his hand still gripping Lienna's shoulder while his gaze slid up and down my body in a way that made me want to instantly invisify myself.

"Yes," Kade replied, also scanning me. What was I, a mythic show dog on display for the judges? "I wasn't sure at first if he would fit the bill, but he's rapidly unlocking his abilities."

"How many so far?"

"A portion of the Psychica spectrum." Kade gave me another once-over. "But he doesn't have full control yet, so it's not all clear to me."

"You know, *he* would love to give you a demonstration," I snapped, "if you'd like to see what *he* can do."

Druthers ignored me. "Good. The timing is fortunate. Despite your previous failures, we now have the artifact and the psycho warper."

Kade didn't react to his father's dig about failures and turned a slick smile on me. "Kit was so helpful, sparing me another trip to Vancouver to pick him up."

"Let's get moving. Ashbluff's body needs to be discovered as soon as the voting period concludes, or it may create complications for our candidate."

Their candidate? Nausea roiled through me. We'd gotten it wrong. Kade hadn't come here to set off a weapon of mass magical destruction and kill dozens or hundreds of people. They had planned to kill Ashbluff and install their own puppet director.

Druthers guided Lienna toward the door. Walking without resistance, she lowered the knife to her side. I didn't move, hands behind my head, heart hammering in my throat.

Kade picked up his potion gun, holstered it, then gestured toward Lienna and his father. "Shall we, Kit?"

"Eat shit, asshole."

But I had no choice. I trailed Druthers and Lienna out into the carpeted hall. Kade shut the door and fell into step beside me. We walked together like old pals back the way Lienna and I had come, returning to the stairwell.

Every movement was physically painful. It took all my willpower not to turn and slug Kade in the face or unleash a Blackout warp on him and his father—but even if Druthers hadn't been wearing an anti-Psychica artifact, which I was one hundred percent sure he was, as soon as I tried to warp or use telekinesis, Kade would know it.

So I kept walking, each heavy step like a giant's boot crushing my soul to smithereens under its heel.

"I told you, didn't I?" Kade murmured to me. "That you would cooperate with us one way or another."

"You haven't got what you want yet."

I still didn't know what they wanted with me, but I was fairly confident it wouldn't end at walking Lienna and me through the upper floors of a New York skyscraper.

Kade chuckled low in his throat. "It's almost poetic how well you played into our hands. Considering how long we've waited for someone like you, I'm disappointed that it's over already. I was enjoying our game of cat and mouse."

"You're a sick fuck," I growled.

He gave me a strangely warm smile, as though I'd paid him the world's loveliest compliment.

Ugh.

As Druthers approached the stairwell door, it clattered and swung open. Three black-clad, armor-vested, MPD-cap-wearing agents appeared, their stark expressions shooting straight to our little group.

For one second, one tiny sliver of a moment, I thought Lienna and I might be saved.

"Director Druthers, Agent Kade," the lead one said respectfully. "We're ready for you on the roof."

"Excellent," Druthers responded like a proper department boss and not a mind-controlling murderer.

The lead agent glanced at me and Lienna, not noticing the bloody blade hidden alongside her thigh. "Should we escort your prisoners?"

"Agent Kade can handle them," Druthers replied smoothly. "Report to Commissioner Sparks and send a message to Director Griva. Tell him we've got everything we came for."

"Yes, sir."

The three agents did an about-face and re-entered the stairwell, taking the steps at a jog. I watched them go, my faint hope dying away, leaving nothing but hopeless darkness.

Not only were they taking orders from Druthers, but they also knew who Kade was. He wasn't *disguised* as an agent; he didn't need a disguise. The only proof he was a corrupt killer had come from our little Canadian precinct, and what was that against the power Druthers could wield?

And not just Druthers. Commissioner Sparks of the IA and Director Griva of Special Investigations too. All three of them had combined their power and influence to allow their minions—like Kade—to act with impunity, to engineer Ashbluff's murder, and to take control of the DD by rigging it so their candidate pal got the job.

When we'd rushed to New York, we hadn't been pitting ourselves against the Consilium. We'd been pitting ourselves against the full might of the MPD.

Kade and I followed Druthers and Lienna up one, two, three flights of stairs. We passed the landing for the building's top level before coming to a final door marked with an exit sign.

Druthers pushed it open.

A dusky sky in shades of magenta and purple greeted us as a cold wind gusted in our faces. The skyscraper's rooftop stretched out ahead of us, and at the far end was a broad helipad illuminated by bright lights around its circumference. On top of it, a black helicopter waited, its rotors stationary.

Four more MPD agents stood near the helicopter, dressed exactly like the ones who'd interrupted our stairwell march. Another six were positioned around three figures on their knees with their hands pressed to the back of their heads, just like me.

Blythe, Vinny, and Tim.

As Druthers strode across the rooftop, Lienna walking beside him with robotic steps, I met Blythe's eyes from twenty feet away and saw the flare of hope in them die out.

This had been our last chance to avert disaster, and we'd failed. Now all that was left was to see which of us would live long enough to watch the world burn.

23

ON OUR YVR TO JFK plane ride, while Darius had been telling Blythe the unabridged story about the Consilium and why he'd murdered half the Supreme Judiciary Council in cold blood, one question had dominated my mind: how the hell could he have kept all this from her? If he'd included her from the start, she wouldn't have loathed every fiber of his being for the past twenty years.

But as Druthers paraded Lienna toward the waiting helicopter like a marionette on a string, I understood perfectly. Darius had done what I couldn't. He'd shouldered the burden alone to protect the person he loved most in the world, even though it had stamped out every single burning ember of their relationship.

Unlike him, I'd gone and involved Lienna. Now Kade and Druthers were weaponizing my feelings for her, using her as a hostage to control me. When they no longer needed her, they would kill her.

Striding beside me, Kade glanced at the nearest agent standing guard over Blythe, Vinny, and Tim. "Load those three next."

Did the Consilium want to question them? Was that why they were still alive? Or did Kade and Druthers want a more discreet location than a New York City rooftop to execute and dispose of my teammates?

Hopelessness suffocated me. Once they got us on that helicopter, we were doomed. I couldn't let that happen.

But how could I stop it? At the dullest inkling of telepathy or telekinesis inside my brain, Kade would know—and Lienna would shove that knife straight through her own throat.

As we passed the other three, my gaze skipped across them, their hands behind their heads and anti-magic cuffs glinting around their wrists. Vinny's expression was stark with fear, while Tim had his jaw set, anger and desperation etched into his face, blood streaking one cheek.

My gaze swung back to Druthers and Lienna, then flicked to Kade. He smirked at me, enjoying my obedience. Sadistic confidence oozed from his pores.

I'd bested Tim, an MPD-trained telepath with direct access to my thoughts, to win my agent title. Was I really incapable of outmaneuvering a clairsentient who could only vaguely grasp my intent?

We were nearing the helicopter. The side door was open, revealing a dozen seats with straps. More than enough room for five prisoners and their captors.

I glanced at the four agents guarding the whirlybird, my gaze stopping on the holstered potion gun of the one closest to Druthers.

I looked away again. Kade was waiting for me to "gather my focus," as he'd put it.

But the thing was, I'd been warping since I was a grade-school foster kid. I'd made so many Split Kits that I didn't need to focus. Conscious thought was *not* a requirement.

Right as we were about to step up onto the helipad, I targeted the agent with the potion gun and created a Split Kit that charged at him with a bloodcurdling shout. The agent yanked his weapon from its holster.

At the same time, invisible me slammed my shoulder into Kade's. Halfway through stepping onto the helipad, he staggered heavily.

The agent opened fire at Fake Kit, whom I'd positioned in front of Druthers. The potion balls flew right through the warp and hammered into Druthers's upper chest.

A swift telekinetic pull yanked Lienna backward into my arms. I grabbed her wrist and tore the dagger from her fingers. It tumbled to the concrete as I hauled her away.

Kade pivoted to face me, as did Druthers, who appeared utterly unruffled by the yellow potion liberally splattered across his torso. The four chopper-guarding agents were now aiming potion guns and other fun magical weapons at me and Lienna, while the six guards circling my friends had also drawn their weapons.

Twelve against one, and two of them were warp-proof.

"Lienna," I hissed, arms wrapped around her as I retreated step by step. I shook her gently. "Can you hear me?"

She didn't respond to my words or my touch.

Kade pulled a silver artifact from a pouch on his combat belt. "So you want to do this the hard way after all."

"I figured why not," I said blithely. "Seeing as you were so kind as to not block my magic."

Kade smirked. "Do you think you can warp your way out of this, Kit?"

"Enough!" Druthers barked, directing the word at Kade and the agents. "Incapacitate him *now*."

Magic exploded in a bright flash—but not from the direction I was expecting.

At the other end of the rooftop, a distinguished gentleman had appeared—Girard. Like some kind of mythic Wyatt Earp transported to modern Manhattan, he was firing purplish Arcana darts from two six-shooters, each magical slug bursting into crackling electricity against its target.

Three of the six agents guarding the prisoners went down, and the other three retreated, two aiming artifacts and a hydromage summoning a blob of water.

Kade jerked his attention back to me. "*Ori vinciaris!*"

Lienna's hand flew up. "*Ori repercutio!*"

With a shimmer of distorted air, her new rebound ring sent the blaze of red power from Kade's artifact whooshing back at him, and it barely missed his left shoulder.

Undaunted, he grabbed for another artifact from his pouch o' death—then whipped sideways, arms thrown up to shield his face.

Blood sprayed from his forearm, and a flicker of light momentarily revealed Darius, his dagger slashing past Kade. The anti-telethesian potion was doing its job, making it harder for Kade to sense Darius.

Snarling, Kade produced another artifact and took aim, but not at Darius, me, or Lienna. He pointed it at our handcuffed and helpless allies—at Blythe.

"*Ori caedo!*"

Darius appeared again, ramming Kade's arm down and sideways as the spell went off. A band of magenta magic launched into the concrete six inches from my right leg and shattered it like a giant axe. Debris exploded in every direction.

I recognized the spell as the one that had sliced Söze's head clean off his body five months ago. Kade wasn't screwing around with nonlethal tactics anymore.

With his opponent visible again, Kade grabbed Darius's wrists and shoved him backward—toward Druthers.

If Druthers touched him, if the mentalist took control of Darius, his lumina magic, and his knives, we were royally screwed.

I grabbed Darius with my telekinetic fingers and hauled him sideways. The sudden change of direction broke Kade's hold, and as Darius backpedaled away from both father and son, I shot past Lienna and bodychecked Kade, knocking him into his pop like ricocheting billiard balls.

"Darius, help the others!" I yelled. "I'll handle these two."

His gray eyes snapped to mine. Then he blinked out of sight.

"Kit!" Lienna called. "*Ori dormias!*"

I half turned as she flung a stun marble. The cold wind blew it off course instantly, but that was expected; that's why she'd gotten my attention.

I caught it with my telekinesis and was about to whip it into Kade's fiendish face when I spotted another agent—a pyromage—lighting up a fireball, a split second away from cooking up some Kit flambé.

With a wild gesture, I redirected the marble. It smacked into the pyromage's noggin and his fire snuffed out as he went down.

Kade threw his brawny body into mine, crushing me to the ground. He drew his fist back, and Lienna's foot swung into my field of view. Her leather loafer—which from my prone point of view complemented her pantsuit perfectly—snapped into the side of his head. I heaved his dazed mass off me, then reeled in the opposite direction as yet another agent pointed an artifact at my face.

A flash of sizzling purple shot over me and hit him in the chest—Girard Earp and his six-shooter spells to the rescue. The agent flopped limply to the ground like a nameless Western movie stuntman.

From my peripheral vision, I glimpsed Blythe, sans handcuffs, working to free Vinny while simultaneously deflecting potion ball shots with her telekinesis.

On the other side of the rooftop, the helicopter's twin turboshaft engines started up, its mechanical whine quickly ascending to a deafening decibel level. The rotors spun faster and faster, buffeting the mythic combatants on both sides with a manufactured gale.

Leaping past my partially kneeling form, Lienna launched herself at Kade. My partner was a five-and-a-half-foot lightweight, and he was a six-foot-plus heavyweight. On paper, this was a David vs Goliath showdown.

But that paper didn't account for the fact that, while she was an abjuration prodigy, Agent Shen was also an exceptional fighter. And she was *vicious*.

Her fists flew, connecting in a flurry just below the protection of Kade's vest, and then she spun, leg arcing in a high kick that cracked against his jaw. Now on the receiving end of two Shen-shots to the chrome dome, he stumbled, weaving slightly.

I rolled onto my feet and hit the still-conscious chopper guards with Blackout warps. As they flailed and collapsed, a cracking wall of ice sprang up on my left, blocking the remaining pair of agents who'd been sprinting straight for me.

Kade caught one of Lienna's flying fists. He threw her over his shoulder, dumping her heavily onto the concrete.

"Lienna!" I shouted, my voice whipped into extinction by the helicopter's unnatural wind.

She rolled away before Kade could stomp on her, and I rushed him.

All the agents are down, Tim barked in my brain. *But those two guys in front of the chopper are still conscious. Vinny, can you—*

I lost track of Tim's psychic voice as Kade's lips split into a nasty grin. The clairsentient's eyes met mine, and I knew instantly I'd made a mistake—but I couldn't stop fast enough. He twisted sideways, grabbed my shoulder, and swung me past him using my own momentum.

Straight into Druthers.

The mentalist seized my arm, and his power crashed down over my brain like a dump truck of sand, burying me under it. The tension left my limbs as I was filled with an all-consuming desire to cooperate with Druthers.

"Kill the others!" Druthers shouted at his son as he pulled me with him. "We'll take this one and go."

Kade flashed his bloody teeth in a sick smile. Using me as a shield, Druthers hastened toward the helicopter, and I went with him, drowning in the false eagerness to follow his lead that he was pouring into my neurons.

Pulling another artifact from his belt, Kade aimed it at Lienna, still dazed after he'd thrown her to the ground.

He was going to kill her now that she was no longer a useful hostage. I was under Druthers's control and completely helpless, just like when Xanthe, the last mentalist to get their filthy psychic death grip on my brain, had made me attack Blythe.

Except, it wasn't like that at all.

Xanthe's power had subsumed my whole psyche—I hadn't known I was being controlled—but I knew I was being controlled this time. Part of me was very much aware that I did not want to obey Druthers, and the desire I felt to do exactly that wasn't real.

Either Xanthe had outclassed Druthers by several orders of magnitude, or my own psychic fortitude had grown immeasurably. Hadn't I spent the past five months building my skills as fast as psychically possible so I'd be ready if or when we went up against the Consilium directly? I'd been honing my psycho warper craft, building my stamina, and constantly increasing the precision and complexity of my warps for over a year now. Even my newfound Psychica tricks all combined didn't hold a candle to my OG ability in terms of the sheer mental fortitude required.

Was there really a world in which some two-bit mentalist could best me in psychic strength?

The short answer: not a snowball's chance in hell.

With that realization, the weight of Druthers's power evaporated, and the "obey me" commands he was pumping into my brain flipped from an obsessive need to an annoying intrusive thought I was only too happy to ignore.

I snapped my head back, my skull crunching against Druthers's nose. He staggered, his mentalist fingers slipping uselessly across my psyche, and I added an elbow to his ribs, breaking his hold on me entirely—but I'd taken a few seconds too long. Kade was speaking the incantation for his spell, his mouth moving with words I couldn't hear over the thundering rotors and gusting wind.

As I grabbed for his artifact with my telekinesis, magic flashed off it—the magenta bloom of his decapitation spell.

Ice erupted in the spell's path as Vinny dove for Lienna. The spell hit his barrier, ice shattered, and Vinny and Lienna landed on the pavement with a gory spray of blood.

Panic ripped through me. I leaped off the helipad toward them—and an invisible presence brushed past me.

Darius and Kade clashed at the edge of the helipad as I ran for Lienna and Vinny. Kade roared something, his words obliterated by the chopper's screaming engines.

DUCK!

Tim's telepathically shouted command barreled into my brain, and I threw myself flat onto the concrete.

A wide band of greenish-yellow magic hurtled from another goddamn artifact in Kade's hand. It streaked across the rooftop at chest height, hitting the raised section where the stairwell door hung open, and steel and concrete exploded like a cannonball through a gingerbread house.

I rose into a crouch, my gaze sweeping the rooftop. Girard, Blythe, and Tim clustered together near Vinny's first ice wall. Downed agents sprawled across the ground. Darius was crouched, bloody daggers in his hands, partway between me and Kade.

Lienna and Vinny were still heaped among the remains of the kryomage's hastily constructed ice shield.

Kade's destructive spell had bought him and his dickhead dad enough time to retreat to the helicopter's open doors.

Druthers clambered inside, blood streaking from his busted nose.

As Darius rushed Kade, I sprinted toward Lienna and Vinny. Blythe and Tim had reached the downed pair, blocking my view of who was injured—and who was still alive.

Out of the corner of my eye, I saw Kade pull a knife from a sheath on his thigh and hurl it with deadly force at the oncoming Darius, who deflected it with his own dagger. That slight delay was enough. Kade hopped in beside his father, and the chopper rose off the platform.

Wind blasted across the roof as the helicopter tilted away from the building, flinging grit into my eyes and forcing me to shield my face.

Through the flurry of dust, I watched once again as Kade disappeared into the darkening night.

24

I RACED FOR LIENNA AND VINNY, my legs weirdly numb from the dread swirling through every atom of my being. Blythe and Tim were already crouched beside them, and the expressions on their shadowed faces ratcheted up my fear.

"We have to slow the bleeding!" Blythe barked. "Tim, give me your belt."

As Tim unbuckled his slim leather belt, I slid to a stop beside them, and my heart jumped into my throat.

Lienna was leaning over Vinny, hands pressed to the right half of his chest. Scarlet liquid welled up between her fingers.

"Kit," she said, her voice on the edge of panic. "Take over here."

I dropped to my knees, and as she pulled her hands away, I saw the damage Kade's spell had done. The magenta blast had caught Vinny on the right side as he'd tackled Lienna. It hadn't cut straight through him—but it had cut deep.

As I pressed my hands hard against Vinny's chest wound, Blythe cinched the belt tightly around his upper arm, just below the shoulder. The gash cutting through his bicep was even deeper.

"I have a vasoconstriction potion," Lienna said, pulling a vial from her satchel. "It'll only last a few minutes."

I removed my hands, and Lienna dribbled the potion across the slicing injury, then added some to his arm.

"Tim, carry him," Blythe ordered. "Kit, help Tim pick him up. Lienna, what other first aid potions do you have?"

While Lienna checked her satchel, I helped Tim get Vinny into his arms. Lienna tipped another potion into Vinny's mouth. He was conscious, but his eyes had a glazed, semicomatose sheen.

Through the pounding urgency, a warning pinged in my head. I could sense minds moving closer.

"We're about to have company," I called over my shoulder.

Darius and Girard, who'd been checking that all the downed agents were staying down, hastened toward us.

"We need to get Vinny to a healer," Blythe said. "Kit, clear the way. Darius, hide us."

All of us? I knew from working with Darius that her request was no small feat for a luminamage—not merely to bend light around a single comrade-in-arms who was keeping close to his side, but to make an entire ungainly group invisible.

"I'll take care of Lienna and myself," I told him. "Let's go."

I took point, racing toward the semi-demolished threshold leading back into the stairwell. As I reached the twisted metal that had recently been a functioning door, I caught sight of the troop of fully geared MPD agents ascending the final flight.

With no time to waste on a Creature Feature or Funhouse warp that might not produce the desired results, I targeted the dozen unfamiliar minds and submerged each one of them in the depths of the nastiest Blackout warp I could summon.

They stumbled, cried out, and fell into varying states of panicked writhing. I unceremoniously shoved one out of the way as I skirted around hunks of concrete on the steps.

Of all my warps, the Blackout—erasing all my target's senses simultaneously—was by far the most intense and psyche-draining. The first time I'd spread it into a halluci-bomb, it had literally brought me to my knees. Now, with frantic fear for Vinny pulsing through me, the strain of hitting twelve independent minds with an all-consuming nightmare void while keeping my allies free of that distress barely registered.

Lienna was on my heels as I sped down the stairwell. I descended past the top level, heading for the floor Lienna and I had searched; it was the only one where I knew exactly how to reach the elevator.

We exited the stairwell into the gray concrete staff corridor. I glanced back and saw that Tim was still carrying Vinny, arms soaked in blood, with Blythe right beside him. Judging by the concentration tightening her face, she was using her telekinesis—either to support Vinny's weight or to keep pressure on his wounds.

Darius and Girard brought up the rear. The luminamage's work was about to begin. With a glance at Lienna, I signaled it was time for her cat's eye necklace. She left a red smear on the artifact as she touched it with her bloody fingers. The moment she whispered the incantation, I invisified us, halluci-bombing every mind I could reach. That, coupled with

Darius's light-bending, meant no one batted an eye as our group spilled out of the staff door.

Not that anyone would've noticed anyway. The mood was so shockingly tense in the concourse that I was momentarily worried I'd guided us to the wrong event.

Gone was the carefree, hoity-toity schmoozing, replaced by small groups that whispered in terse conversations with nervous eyes.

Clearly, Ashbluff's body had been discovered.

Leading our group, I cleared a path using a warp of fictitious agents barreling along the concourse. Everyone got the hell out of the way, and we raced for the elevator in the hallucination's wake.

I reached it first and jabbed the call button three times, then retreated as Lienna moved toward Vinny. I adjusted my invisi-bomb to exclude my friends' minds so they could see us as Lienna and Blythe crowded around Tim. Vinny's eyes were closed, his face sickly pale and his breathing frighteningly shallow. I couldn't tell if he was still conscious, but he was alive.

"Kit."

I turned to find Darius a few steps away from the others. Perspiration beaded his face from the effort of hiding the large group.

"Ashbluff is dead," he said quietly.

Had he known that before finding us all on the rooftop, or had he overheard the nervous tittering of the attendees?

"I know. Kade and Druthers killed him." I lowered my voice. "They have their own candidate."

Darius's face tightened, creases deepening between his eyebrows. "We can't let the Consilium take control of the Dissimulation Department."

"I know."

"I need to get the others out of here." His gray eyes burned into mine, as grave and steely as I'd ever seen. He extended his hand to me. "It's up to you, Kit."

I looked down. He was holding out Druthers's blood-smeared dagger, offering it to me.

Ice-cold realization plunged over me. For a paralyzing second, my breath stuck in my chest. Was he asking what I thought he was asking?

No, he wasn't asking. He *needed* me to do this. If I couldn't, he would stay behind instead, and I'd have to get Vinny and the others out of this building with warps and distractions instead of his lumina magic.

It was my choice.

Swallowing back a shiver of dread, I took the dagger. "I'll take care of it."

The elevator chimed, and the doors slid open.

Darius closed his hand over my shoulder, gripping hard—appreciation, understanding, and farewell all in one brief touch. Then he stepped past me, Girard right behind him.

Refocusing on my warp, I shuffled my fake cadre of agents into the elevator as my team loaded themselves in.

"Kit!" Blythe snapped. "Get in."

"Sorry, Cap." I hid the dagger behind my back. "I have one more thing to take care of."

Lienna yanked her anxious stare off Vinny to look back at me. The elevator doors started to close.

My partner jumped forward, her shoulder colliding with a door as she stumbled out. "Go ahead," she told Blythe. "We'll catch up."

The captain nodded, unable to hide her worry as the doors slid closed. I dropped my other warp, keeping only the invisibility.

"Kit," Lienna said, searching my face. "What's going on?"

I let out a breath, guiltily relieved she was with me—even if that meant whatever danger I was about to dive into would drag her down too. Was I a coward, or just stupidly in love with this woman?

"The Consilium has a candidate in the vote for the DD's new director," I said, slipping off my jacket and using it to wipe the blood from my hands. I passed it to Lienna so she could do the same. "We need to find out who it is."

She wiped her palms, tossed my jacket aside, and took hold of my hand, her fingers clamping tight around mine. "Okay."

The contrast between her warmth in my left hand and the cold hilt of Druthers's dagger in my right hand scraped at my resolve.

Invisible to everyone else, we headed for the nearest auditorium entrance. Two suited agents stood guard on either side, looking far more rigid and watchful than they had when we'd arrived.

We stopped just in front of them and peered into the space beyond.

Special Committee members occupied about half the seats encircling the large, raised dais in the center, while the remaining members were grouped in the wide aisle as they conversed. Lights affixed to the circular walls illuminated the stage, leaving the rest of the room in ambient shadows. The ceiling rose for three stories, with the sixty-third and sixty-fourth floors forming viewing balconies around the entire circumference.

As dramatic as those features were, they weren't what stole the breath from my lungs like a jab to the diaphragm. Head tilted back, I couldn't tear my gaze away from the ceiling, as entranced as though I were standing in the Sistine Chapel.

An inconceivably massive Arcana array spanned the entire ceiling. The black lines swirled and intersected, the geometry interwoven with giant runes that stood out in sharp contrast against the white marble. I'd glimpsed the matching array on the floor earlier, but it'd failed to convey the sheer magnitude of magic embedded into this chamber.

On the plane ride here, Darius had grimly informed us that this overwhelming spell held the mythic world record for the largest abjuration array in existence. Its purpose? To block any and all Psychica magic.

Ostensibly, it was to prevent voters from being unduly influenced by all those nefarious telepaths, empaths, and mentalists. Personally, I thought it was unfair discrimination against my class. If they were going to go all out like this, why not block all magic while they were at it?

Regardless, the moment I stepped a single toe within that array, my warps would poof into nothingness.

I dragged my attention down to the stage, where three official-looking folks were discussing something near a podium. A handful of chairs waited off to the side, one occupied by an older woman sitting with the awkward posture of someone who'd like to be anywhere but here, thank you very much.

"Which one of them is the Consilium's candidate?" Lienna whispered, echoing my exact thoughts.

How were we supposed to identify the secretly corrupt asshole owned by the Consilium? It's not like they wandered around with "Hello, I'm a Corrupt Jackwagon" nametags plastered on their ten-thousand-dollar suits. Would I recognize them from the multitudinous lists in the Crow and Hammer's third-floor boardroom?

The official-looking cluster broke apart. Two moved aside, and the third turned to face the podium. A spotlight beamed across his face, illuminating his features in stark detail visible across the auditorium.

My gut took a sixty-two-story nosedive into the skyscraper's basement. "You've got to be fucking joking."

The man at the podium was Jayce Tyrian.

Yes, *that* Jayce Tyrian.

The same Jayce Tyrian who'd recently taken over Trident Ltd. From whom Darius and I had stolen documents about the weapon, whom I'd terrified with a *Matrix* helicopter attack, whom all of Darius's sources had claimed was squeaky clean of the Consilium's slime.

And the same Jayce Tyrian who had scary leverage within the Miami precinct, who intended to bury the two nosy agent-impersonators, and who'd ordered the execution of an employee in his own goddamn office.

Here he was, straightening his black silk tie that probably cost more than an MPD-issued smart car as he prepared to speak. He cleared his throat, leaned closer to the mic, and began by promising justice for the late Director Ashbluff, who'd been tragically murdered by a rogue agent right here in the North American MPD headquarters.

Tyrian had been a corrupt piece of shit all along. The Consilium had passed Trident into the care of another loyal lackey. He'd probably been sitting on the weapon file, waiting for the right moment to "find" a Consilium buyer for Visser's rare artifact.

I couldn't hear Tyrian's oh-so-sincere commitment to taking up Ashbluff's mantle. I could barely hear Lienna saying my name.

"Kit!" She shook my shoulder.

I snapped out of my daze and turned to her. Concern pinched her eyes as she looked up at me. My fingers squeezed the hilt of the hidden dagger.

"What's wrong?" she asked.

I loved her. That's what was wrong. I loved her, and she'd almost died today because I'd brought her into this shitstorm.

This time, I wouldn't make that mistake. I understood why Darius had made the decision he had twenty years ago. And I would make the same one.

Reaching out, I cupped her cheek, drew her face up, and kissed her—a fast, desperate goodbye.

Then I let her go, stepped between the two guards, and entered the auditorium. The world-record array did its job, turning that warm spot in my mind into a cold, dark vacuum.

The agents behind me erupted in surprise as Lienna suddenly appeared practically on their toes. A scuffing sound, followed by a grunt, suggested Lienna had goaded the guards into action—though whether to continue distracting them or in a sincere attempt to get past them, I didn't know.

I couldn't look back to find out. I kept walking, hands at my side, the dagger tucked against my inner forearm. A few heads turned, looking toward the commotion in the threshold, but no one called me out as an intruder.

Tyrian was speaking, his voice amplified by the sound system, but I couldn't process his words through the rapid drumming of my pulse.

Twenty years ago, Darius had planned his every move. I didn't have that luxury. I couldn't warp, couldn't hide, couldn't distract, couldn't deceive. I couldn't wait for an opportunity that didn't involve a few hundred witnesses.

Tyrian was right there in front of me. Alone. I couldn't waste this chance hoping for a better one.

The aisle seemed to stretch on and on as I walked, keeping my pace steady and my face tilted down. Each step vibrated like a thunderclap through my bones. All I wanted to do was turn and run in the other direction.

But I kept going. Then suddenly, there was no more aisle. The dais rose in front of me, accessible by three steps that ran around the entire circumference.

Up the steps, I angled toward the podium. Tyrian paused whatever bullshit "such a tragedy but, hey, worked out well for me" speech he was feeding the crowd.

I was five feet away from him when I finally raised my head. Tyrian's politely questioning expression, as though I were a staff member come to deliver a message, faltered with recognition.

His eyes blazed with fury. He didn't even know he should be afraid.

I lunged for him. My left hand grabbed his shoulder. My right hand thrust the dagger between his ribs.

I'd never killed a man like this before, so close I could feel the final gasp leave his lungs. It was both easier and harder than I'd expected. Hard, because his flesh resisted the sharp blade and I had to shove it in. And easy, because once the knife went in, it was over. Just like that.

One moment alive, the next … dead.

Tyrian collapsed backward, the hilt jutting from his chest, and voices filled the auditorium. I turned numbly toward the cacophony of cries and shouts. A sea of aghast faces swam in my vision.

Then the first flash of magic dazzled my eyes, and I snapped back to my senses. Ducking the oncoming blast, I sprinted off the stage. Mythics swarmed out of their seats and crowded the aisles, the majority trying to flee the cold-blooded murderer.

The minority came straight at me.

I dodged the first few would-be heroes and shoulder-checked another out of my path. But there were too many current, former, and combat-capable MPD agents among the Special Committee. They were closing in on all sides, and I was just one man with no magic and no weapons.

I swerved sideways between rows of seats, then vaulted them, trying to make it back to the exit. Magic lit up on every side—a dozen mages and sorcerers taking aim all at once.

Then the brightest flash yet: a volley of fizzing orange fireworks arcing into the air all across the auditorium. Knowing what was coming, I dropped between the seats and grabbed onto one with every ounce of grip strength I possessed, thankful the construction crew in charge of putting this place together had possessed the wherewithal to bolt the chair legs to the floor.

A nearby man in a smart navy blue suit threw himself at me, ready to subdue me in a likely violent fashion.

Then Lienna's gravity bombs hit their targets, burst with bright flares, and expanded into giant whirling orbs of darkness.

Everything that wasn't nailed to the floor, including my navy-blue-suited attacker, was yanked toward the mini black holes. More screams filled the echoing auditorium as dozens of people hurtled through the air and crashed together.

My entire body was jerked upward with astonishing power, my fingers straining to maintain their grasp on the chair's legs and my joints feeling like they were about to snap apart like Christmas crackers, until the spell faded, dumping me onto the floor.

Leaping up, I sprang over two more rows, cut back to the aisle, and sprinted for the exit. For the briefest second, my gaze caught a face among a group of hysterical committee members: Lienna, her eyes wide and complexion leeched of its usual warm hue as she watched me run past.

I flew out the open doors. Mythics were shouting and running around like the proverbial headless chickens, but the agents among them weren't—and they locked on me instantly.

Except now I was past the anti-Psychica array.

I dropped a widespread invisi-bomb, still running, my escape just ahead: the elevator. I jabbed the call button with a telekinetic finger, and it lit up in response.

But the doors didn't open. The indicator above them showed that the elevator was on the first floor.

"He's there!" someone shouted. "Running for the elevator!"

Either there were other psychics in the crowd, or someone had their phone camera out.

Without slowing, I bent my concentration on the elevator doors. Pressure and burning exertion flared through my arms as the stainless steel doors cracked open, then reluctantly yawned wider, revealing the empty elevator shaft beyond.

Multihued light reflected off the white marble. A blast of pink Arcana whipped past my shoulder and blew a smoking hole in the wall. A fireball grazed my right elbow, singeing my less-than-pristine shirt.

Straight ahead, a cluster of cables hung in the gaping space, seven hundred feet of emptiness below.

I didn't stop. I didn't slow.

I sprinted to the open doors and leaped into the elevator shaft, plunging into the darkness as magic exploded behind me.

25

WITH MY ELBOWS BRACED on a metal railing, I watched the first rays of sunlight hit the Manhattan skyline. Golden hues lit the east-facing windows, turning the dark wall of skyscrapers into a vivid reflection of the emerging dawn. The calm waters of the East River glimmered under the Brooklyn Bridge stretching across to the far bank.

Taking in the view, I let my spinning, planning, plotting mind settle. I felt like a celluloid superhero overlooking the early morning cityscape, finding a moment of peaceful contemplation in the aftermath of a climactic battle.

Come to think of it, I had all the prerequisites for superhero-dom: Orphan? Check. Crazy inhuman abilities? Check. Evil nemesis? A skillful and accomplished love interest? The untenable weight of responsibility burdening my unprepared shoulders? Check, check, and check.

All I was missing was a higher vantage point for my solo moment of self-reflection. I should've been perched on the edge of an urban tower, cape flapping in the breeze, but since I lacked the necessary supersonic flight and/or web-slinging acrobatics to ascend the Empire State Building, I was relegated to sea level with the regular folk.

I hadn't even chosen this spot for its breathtaking view. To my right, in the shadow of the towering bridge supports, was a ferry terminal where I would board a buoyant bus in—I checked my phone's clock—ten minutes.

Assuming the countless number of agents and bounty hunters searching for my fugitive self didn't catch up to me first.

I absently rubbed at the dried blood marring my black slacks—either from Vinny's horrific chest wound or from putting a dagger through Tyrian's ribs. The fate of both men sent a sickening roil through my gut. I had no idea if my favorite frosty frenemy was alive. He'd saved Lienna's life and, for all I knew, sacrificed his own in the process.

As for Tyrian, my strongest feeling about his death was numbness. I'd ended a handful of lives since becoming an MPD agent, but it'd always been in self-defense or in defense of someone else. Logically, I knew killing him had been necessary, and I'd have to deal with the moral fallout later.

My thumb slid across my phone, unlocking it to reveal the MPD notice I'd opened before pulling the SIM card out of my phone and throwing it in a sewer. The text was emblazoned in my brain, but I studied it again anyway, letting my new reality sink in.

Kit Morris was the most wanted criminal in the mythic world.

Yep. *The* most. King of the hill. Top of the heap. The shiny new bounty on my head was a shocking twenty million dollars.

And no, I hadn't accidentally read that number with one or two extra zeros.

My bounty was bigger than the Crystal Druid's, Floris Visser's, and the leaders of the international rogue guild Red Rum combined. If you thought that seemed excessive for murdering a single man, you weren't wrong, because I was actually on the hook for *two* murders. Those Consilium bastards were blaming me for killing Ashbluff too.

The pool of anxiety in my stomach grew deeper and murkier. When I'd taken the dagger from Darius, I'd known it would be bad. The worst kind of bad. I'd expected to be captured or killed beneath that giant anti-Psychica array.

I would have been if not for Lienna. She'd saved my life by setting off her gravity bomb spell. I should've known that leaving her behind wasn't an option; she wouldn't allow it.

I was alone now, though, and all I could think was that I wished she was here at my side, backing me up and keeping me grounded.

Sighing, I scanned the river. A little boxy shape on the water was making its slow, chugging way toward the terminal. It was almost time to say goodbye to New York, New York.

I returned my attention to the bounty listing. Even more surprising than the number of zeros was the big, bold instruction following that juicy dollar figure: Kit Morris was to be captured *alive*.

Any other rogue would have had a dead or alive bounty, but the Consilium needed me still breathing. They had plans for me—plans related to the weapon they'd paid thirty million dollars to acquire. Together, we represented fifty million dollars of Consilium ambition.

My hand went to the pocket of my tailored black slacks. I slid out a piece of paper, unfolded it, and smoothed out the creases.

Filling the page was the levitating man surrounded by magical and elemental symbols. I'd taken it from the Crow and Hammer's boardroom days ago, not realizing I would carry it around the world before I could return it to our collection.

The sun symbol on the man's forehead seemed to blaze against the white paper, drawing my gaze before I dropped my eyes to the figure's feet, which hovered above the ground.

I concentrated on my own feet. Slowly, a feeling of weightlessness filtered through my body. The soles of my shoes parted company with the concrete.

With a thump, I dropped back to the earth and leaned on the railing again, still studying the drawing. Thank Hermes I'd figured *that* one out before merging my atoms with the bottom of an elevator shaft.

Levitation—the rare psychic brother to telekinesis, where instead of moving objects with your mind, you could move your own body.

I couldn't fly like Superman, but falls from any height were less of a concern for me.

Tucking my phone back into my pocket, I considered the symbols surrounding the levitating man. Brief memories flitted through my brain like slides on a projector, flashing past almost too fast to follow.

Reading Lienna's mind by accident. Figuring out telekinesis while Kade's prisoner. My increasing ability to sense psychic energy.

The scorch marks on the train. The sulfur smell on my clothes.

Lienna theorizing that consciously tapping into my reality warping ability had "unlocked" something inside me.

And Druthers's remark about fortunate timing—about now having "the artifact and the psycho warper."

The Consilium had plans for me that somehow involved a Viking queen's ancient artifact. But what did a thousand-year-old weapon have to do with me?

I folded the paper with quick movements. If the Consilium wanted me, they could come and get me. Now that they'd turned me into a fugitive, I could play by my own rules. They'd made my life hell, and I was more than happy to return the favor tenfold.

Nestling the paper inside my pocket again, I turned around.

A dozen men in black combat gear paused their stealthy approach. They weren't marked with MPD badges or guild insignia, so I couldn't tell whether they were bounty hunters or Consilium goons. But they looked competent, split into two groups to block both ends of the wide walking path.

I wasn't sure about the Viking artifact, but I had a pretty good idea why the Consilium wanted to get their greasy paws on me, and I was going to use that knowledge to turn myself into their worst nightmare.

With their ambush spoiled, the combat team drew an array of weapons. The air sizzled with magic about to be unleashed. These guys could taste that twenty-mil payday ripe for the picking.

They were about to get a very rude awakening.

Grinning tightly, I lifted my hands, calling on my magic— magic I was only just beginning to understand.

The Consilium would rue the day they messed with this psycho warper.

ABOUT THE AUTHORS

ANNETTE MARIE is the author of YA urban fantasy series *Steel & Stone*, its prequel trilogy *Spell Weaver*, and romantic fantasy trilogy *Red Winter*.

Her first love is fantasy, but fast-paced adventures, bold heroines, and tantalizing forbidden romances are her guilty pleasures. She proudly admits she has a thing for dragons, and her editor has politely inquired as to whether she intends to include them in every book.

Annette lives in the frozen winter wasteland of Alberta, Canada (okay, it's not quite that bad) and shares her life with her husband and their furry minions of darkness. When not writing, she can be found elbow-deep in one art project or another while blissfully ignoring all adult responsibilities.

www.annettemarie.ca

ROB JACOBSEN is a Canadian writer, actor, and director, who has been in a few TV shows you might watch, had a few films in festivals you might have attended, and authored some stories you might have come across. He's hoping to accomplish plenty more by the time he inevitably dies surrounded by cats while watching reruns of Mr. Robot.

Currently, he is the Creative Director of Cave Puppet Films, as well as the co-author of the Guild Codex: Warped series with Annette Marie.

www.robjacobsen.ca

SPECIAL THANKS

Our thanks to Erich Merkel for sharing your exceptional expertise in Latin and Ancient Greek.

Any errors are the authors'.

THE
GUILD CODEX
WARPED

The MPD has three roles: keep magic hidden, keep mythics under control, and don't screw up the first two.

Kit Morris is the wrong guy for the job on all counts—but for better or worse, this mind-warping psychic is the MPD's newest and most unlikely agent.

DISCOVER MORE BOOKS AT
www.guildcodex.ca

THE GUILD CODEX
SPELLBOUND

Meet Tori. She's feisty. She's broke. She has a bit of an issue with running her mouth off. And she just landed a job at the local magic guild. Problem is, she's also 100% human. Oops.

Welcome to the Crow and Hammer.

DISCOVER MORE BOOKS AT
www.guildcodex.ca

THE GUILD CODEX
DEMONIZED

Robin Page: outcast sorceress, mythic history buff, unapologetic bookworm, and the last person you'd expect to command the rarest demon in the long history of summoning. Though she holds his leash, this demon can't be controlled.

But can he be tamed?

DISCOVER MORE BOOKS AT

www.guildcodex.ca

A vigilante witch with a murder conviction, a switchblade for a best friend, and a dangerous lack of restraint. A notorious druid mired in secrets, shadowed by deadly fae, and haunted by his past.

They might be exactly what the other needs—if they don't destroy each other first.

DISCOVER MORE BOOKS AT
www.guildcodex.ca

STEEL & STONE

When everyone wants you dead, good help is hard to find.

The first rule for an apprentice Consul is *don't trust daemons*. But when Piper is framed for the theft of the deadly Sahar Stone, she ends up with two troublesome daemons as her only allies: Lyre, a hotter-than-hell incubus who isn't as harmless as he seems, and Ash, a draconian mercenary with a seriously bad reputation. Trusting them might be her biggest mistake yet.

GET THE COMPLETE SERIES
www.annettemarie.ca/steelandstone

The only thing more dangerous than the denizens of the
Underworld ... is stealing from them.

As a daemon living in exile among humans, Clio has picked up some unique skills. But pilfering magic from the Underworld's deadliest spell weavers? Not so much. Unfortunately, that's exactly what she has to do to earn a ticket home.

GET THE COMPLETE TRILOGY
www.annettemarie.ca/spellweaver

A destiny written by the gods. A fate forged by lies.

If Emi is sure of anything, it's that *kami*—the gods—are good, and *yokai*—the earth spirits—are evil. But when she saves the life of a fox shapeshifter, the truths of her world start to crumble. And the treachery of the gods runs deep.

This stunning trilogy features 30 full-page illustrations.

GET THE COMPLETE TRILOGY
www.annettemarie.ca/redwinter